MW00958946

ISBN: 9798716706248

He stared at the glass, and several times his heart gave a leap as if it would plunge him into action, but he would be surprised to find himself still crouched in the shadows, motionless. It was the last night the woodmaster would be away from home. Would he do it tonight? Or, like last night, would he return home to the sight of his grey-skinned sister choking on her own throat beneath a layer of rags? And Mother, stretched, red and wet with drink, on the ground of the frozen cellar where they lived.

His heart gave that sudden leap again at those memories, and this time he found himself not still crouched in the dark, but hurtling across the street and smashing the clean pane of the woodmaster's shop with his sharp rock. The shattering glass seemed to scream his name in the crisp winter air, and its gleaming bits seemed to take a very long time to fall across the snow and the sheep skin that lay beneath the woodmaster's treasure.

The drunkard's boy snatched up the figures and stuffed them in his bag, forcing himself not to look up into the dark shop before or the glowing street behind him. His hands trembled in expectation of a shout or a touch. But all remained still, and when he turned to leave, no sound was heard but a faint bumping in a neighboring house and the frightened squeak of his own shoes in the snow as he sped toward the shadowed wood.

Now remained only the long journey to Stockholm. He must reach it by noon tomorrow before word could spread of the

CHAPTER ONE

December, 1852

The drunkard's boy stared through the mist of his breath at the woodshop across the street. His pulse drummed loudly in his ears.

The deed would take no more than a few moments—he had timed it repeatedly, using pine cones and rocks to represent the twelve wooden figures—and surely no one could arrive soon enough to catch him or even to see who he was. The town was tucked up in a blanket of snow, a blanket still falling in fat flakes from a black sky.

He was looking with brooding, dark-rimmed eyes at the woodmaster's treasure, just beyond a window of clear glass. One blow, and it would be his. All he had to do was move quickly.

He licked his chapped lips, wiped his nose with the back of his sleeve, and then slowly flexed his hands back and forth at the wrists, cracking his joints as he stared at the Nativity.

He'd reviewed his plan over and over for three days, and it was certainly flawless. He was quick for a boy of fourteen, and if he ran to the woods just beyond the woodmaster's shop he would find good cover, not only for his fleeing shadow, but also for his tracks among the wet leaves and netted roots.

The plan could not fail, so he told himself again, angry that his hands still shook.

To my kind encouragers

THE NATIVITY THIEF

by Anna Severson

thieving of the woodmaster's treasure.

The evil smelling shopkeeper laughed.

"If your papa could truly sculpt carvings this fine, my little alley cat, you wouldn't be wearing those rags."

"Please," said the drunkard's boy, staring at the ground so the boorish shopkeeper would not see the bitter glint in his eyes. "My sister is sick, and we've had no money because of the doctor's bills. My father has been working a long time on these pieces!"

Standing in the dingy pawn shop where he had spread the Nativity pieces across the top of a grimy glass counter full of corroding watches and pins, Tor could not but think how small and weak he must appear. He was slightly built, and his habitual stoop made him appear even shorter than he was.

The shopkeeper leaned closer until the tip of his dirty blue kerchief brushed the top of the wooden Joseph's head.

"And why come here, my sweet, hmm? Why not go to some wealthy man's shop where you can get much more for such a beautiful work of art?"

"I've tried. Because of my clothes they turn me away."

Again, the man chuckled, and he ruffled Tor's dark hair as if he were a child of five, begging for candy. The drunkard's boy forced himself not to glare up at the man's watery amber eyes. Even more than being likened to vermin because of his rodential features, stooped back, and the foul, oversized rags that hung from his bony shoulders, he hated to be dismissed as a child for his slight size. It was bad to be despised, but it was worse to be ignored.

"Well, my sweet," said the shopkeeper, straightening and scratching his neck with unkempt hands clothed in disraveling fingerless gloves, "you've come to the right place. I will accept your gift."

Tor stiffened, and his hands shot out to gather the wooden pieces together.

"It's not a gift. How much will you pay?"

The man pulled a dusty peppermint stick out of a clay pot and tossed it on the counter.

"There you are, boy. That's more than you deserve, I'll be bound."

Tor snatched up two wisemen and rammed them back into his bag.

"If you won't pay me, I can find someone who will," he said savagely, but with a sickness in his stomach because he knew he appeared to be no more than a cornered weasel.

A strong hand caught his collar from behind and twisted it till it choked Tor's bare neck. The wooden figures in his hands clattered to the floor as he clawed at the fat hands that held him so tightly his vision began to blur.

"Let him go, Peder," said the shopkeeper's nasal voice. "It is Christmas after all. Besides, he'll not tell anyone."

The strong hands released Tor and gave him a thrust. Tor crashed against something hard and stumbled to the floor, gasping and trying to clear away the black clouds that hung about his eyes.

"Do not destroy my shop, Peder," muttered the keeper, his voice sounding thin and distant to Tor's half-conscious mind, yet at the same time quite close, as if he were breathing in Tor's ear.

As the clouds of darkness began to roll back from Tor's vision, he could make out the dirty man kneeling on the floor just in front of him, gathering up the bag with the wooden figures in his filthy hands. Tor flung himself across the floor, grabbing up as many of the scattered pieces as he could. When the shopkeeper pushed him back, Tor turned a vicious attack on him.

Then the unseen Peder intercepted him, lifted him by his belt and collar, elbowed open the door, tossed Tor into the street like dirty dishwater, and slammed the door after him. Tor roared and threw himself at the pawn shop.

"Give it back!" His voice cracked with the strain of the shout, and he heard Peder and the shopkeeper laugh from inside.

"*Ja, ja,* so go fetch the *konstapel.*"

The cold wind and tiny snow crystals cut at Tor's face. He clawed at the latch futilely and finally sagged against the dingy doorpost, digging the nails of one hand into the decaying wood. He clenched his jaw and shut his eyes.

Here he was again, swept out and kicked about like a leaf in the street. He had been humiliated, robbed, and discarded.

Still, this was nothing compared to the knowledge that he had at last lost his sister.

CHAPTER TWO

Tor stared at his mother the following night, his feverish eyes glittering with hatred.

"This is your fault," he said coldly. "Everything is your fault. You drank her life away."

His mother garbled some unintelligible words and shrank against her low cot, feebly raising the bottle to her lips again.

Tor considered attacking her. He knew it would satisfy a part of him, but he couldn't imagine how horrible he would feel when he looked at his mother, bruised and unconscious at his feet. And she was hardly in a state to feel his blows in any case.

He turned away, sliding his fingers through his lank, greasy hair.

Dead, buried, and he'd never even said goodbye. He hadn't been there to hold her hand during the entrance into death. She'd suffered alone in the dark cold. Shivering. Listening to the rats she feared were evil brownies, trying to breath threads of air, trying to wheeze his name, watching the approach of suffocation and blackness.

Kneeling over her empty cot, Tor tightened his grip on his hair and suddenly screamed till his body trembled, in hopes that he could expel the vision of her death from his mind.

Then he slumped down to his elbows on the cot and remained still for a long time, staring at her threadbare blanket.

He did not know how much time passed before a pain in his hip woke him. Running his fingers over the hurt, he realized there was a lump in the pocket of his oversized trousers, and it was pressed between his hip and the floor. Sliding his hand into the pocket, he withdrew the wooden figure of the Christ Child and stared at it dully, remembering he'd had it in his fist when he'd hit the shopkeeper. Apparently neither he nor his minion, Peder, had noticed.

As Tor studied the piece he recalled how, as he'd made his way back home, he'd found it in his hand and had thought to bury it with his sister. If nothing else, it would have been a testimony to her of his love and dedication.

Too late now.

The hammering of a fist sounded on the door, but Tor remained slumped in lethargic oblivion.

"See to th' door," mumbled Tor's mother from across the room.

Tor ignored her.

The hammering continued, accompanied by shouts. Tor lay immovable.

Then—he knew not how they got in—a man was suddenly hauling him up by the coat collar, a man with iron grey eyes and a shaggy mane of light blond hair.

"Where is it?" The woodmaster growled in his face. Tor realized that his feet were no longer touching the ground. The woodmaster held him pressed so high against the wall they were nose to nose. "Where is the Nativity?"

A rich, soothing voice interrupted the woodmaster's snarling.

"Come, no need for violence."

The slender Vicar Arnman stepped through the doorway, peering about the darkness, and edged gingerly closer to the woodmaster. He addressed himself to Tor's mother with averted eyes.

"Woman, the woodcarver seems to be missing his Nativity, which is of great value. Two nights ago it was stolen. Only this morning was this cap found just outside his window where the glass had been shattered."

He gestured towards the woodmaster, who dropped Tor abruptly and pulled a torn brown cap from his coat pocket. He threw it at Tor's feet. The drunkard's boy stared at it, betraying no emotion.

"It is your son's, is it not?" prodded the vicar.

"I don't know," replied the woman, pulling at her dress and pushing her bottle guiltily under the bed.

The vicar turned to Tor. He smiled thinly.

"Have you naught to say in your defense, young man?"

Tor twisted his arm from the woodmaster's hold and walked a few steps away from him, regarding the vicar with narrowed, disdainful eyes.

"I have walked down that street hundreds of times," he said hoarsely. "So have many other people. I could have dropped it just last night when I passed on my way to market for some fish."

The woodmaster broke in.

"The cap was under snow, boy! I saw you wearing it just before I left the village, the day before my pieces were stolen, and there has been no snow since the night of theft. Perhaps you would know that if you had not left the village." He gripped Tor's arms again, painfully, and forced the boy to face him. "You were loitering about my shop all last week, eyeing the Nativity."

"So were many others," snapped Tor. "You do fine work after all," he added with a sneer and an unsuccessful attempt to jerk free.

"How can you distress me like this," interrupted the slurred, weepy voice of Tor's mother, "when my daughter is still fresh in her grave?" She struggled to her feet.

"You have a daughter lately dead?" asked the vicar, glancing about the room and suddenly edging back towards the door.

"Died yesterday." Tor's mother sniffled convincingly.

The vicar snatched a silken handkerchief from his pocket and held it to his nose even as he summoned the woodmaster with a hasty wave.

"Come, my friend, let us leave this house of sorrow. This is no time to bring prosecutions upon them."

"Can you spare aught for the funeral expenses, Vicar?" the woman asked plaintively, holding out a trembling hand to him.

"Vicar, I must have my Nativity," said the woodmaster, ignoring Tor's mother. "The boy took it, I am sure."

"We will find more substantial evidence before we further importune these people," said the vicar, eyeing the red eyes and sickly frame of Tor's mother as he dropped a coin on the table and passed quickly out the door.

Tor watched him go disdainfully.

At least his mother was good for something, he thought sourly, if only for driving away unwelcome visitors.

He looked back at the woodmaster, meeting grey eyes that gleamed like black ice, half hidden in the shadow of his shaggy wheaten hair. The man stared for several long, uncomfortable moments as Tor tried to maintain his expression of contempt.

Suddenly, the woodmaster shifted his hold, grabbing Tor's hands and turning them over to catch the dim daylight from the doorway. He ran a finger over the thin scratch on the knuckles of the boy's right hand. Tor forced himself not to jerk back his hands or even look away from the man's face. When the woodmaster met his gaze again, his expression had hardened still more.

"I know," he said deliberately. "Don't think I will forget about this, boy."

After a long moment, he broke his stare and departed through the doorway.

CHAPTER THREE

February, 1853

Tor stumbled up the street through the snow, his arms wrapped round his helplessly shaking body. Freezing night air seeped under his thin clothes as easily as if it were water, and there was no way to still the click of his jaws.

Ahead, the yellow lights of a large inn looked warm, and he imagined how comfortable it must be inside. He knew he would never feel that warmth, of course. In this large metropolis of Stockholm, not one door had opened to him this bitter night. Furthermore, he could not return to the workhouse. A *konstapel* had tracked him there for the theft of a watch, and he had barely escaped with the clothes on his back. Since then, he had borne the cold for nearly a month, hiding in sheds and cellars. But this was the bitterest night of all, and with a fever that had already sent him into convulsive chills, he had no recourse but to keep knocking until he fell in his tracks. One of two events would occur that night: he would find shelter or he would freeze.

Somehow, despite the rigidity of his body, he was able to shuffle to the door of the inn.

He barely felt his numb hands when he knocked, and when the door opened, he collapsed in a golden pool of light.

❄ ❄ ❄

Sweet spices were his first hint of consciousness: the smell of *pepparkakor* and coffee.

"What's to be done?" clucked a female. "Full of fleas, without doubt, and liable to steal us blind."

"We can't leave him out," said a deeper, matter-of-fact voice.

Tor opened his eyes and struggled to sit up. Someone lifted him, settling his back against a wall, and he saw that a plump couple eyed him anxiously.

"Just for the night, perhaps," said the woman, whose face was rosy and sympathetic. "Bring him to the back quickly before he is seen. He may sleep by the fire."

Strong arms began to pull at Tor.

"Excuse me."

The drunkard's boy jolted as a third voice jarred the air. He looked up, and his chest tightened.

Even in his lethargic state he knew the voice of the woodmaster—the very man who'd hounded him with threats until he'd been forced to run from his village to the streets of Stockholm. Tor's teeth clicked even louder in his head, and he pulled away from the hands that were beginning to lift him off the floor.

"I know this boy," said the woodmaster, his voice as icy as the wind that had seemed to rip Tor's skin to shreds outside. "I'll see to him."

"*Nej*," said Tor weakly. He was ignored by all.

"Who are his people?" asked the woman.

"Of course. Shall I help you carry him to your room?" said her more sensible husband, hinting broadly that the sick ragamuffin was not quite the ornament he wished for the entryway of his inn.

"*Tack*," said the woodmaster, "but he is light enough."

Too weak to resist, Tor could only shrink back as the woodmaster bent close to take him in his arms. The man's body was not as hard and cold as he'd expected. The texture of his shirt fabric and the deep curve of his arm and chest as he cradled Tor were deceptively comforting. The drunkard's boy loathed the warmth of the touch. It was like a reassuring caress from the hand of an executor.

Tor released his deep, hacking coughs, hoping that the threat of disease would persuade the man to leave him to die in peace. It did not. The man only tightened his arms and scarred hands and shifted his hold on Tor, raising his filthy body into a straighter posture.

The ornate, light wood spindles of the staircase blurred softly together in Tor's vision as he was carried up the stairs. He imagined how it would feel to run up this winding stair, dragging his fingers over the smooth spindles, feeling the vibrations and listening to the tiny thumps of his fingers against the wood.

The spindles ran out, and the woodmaster turned to maneuver Tor head first through a narrow doorway. Tor forgot the spindles as his gaze was arrested by a crackling yellow fire in a stone hearth with a rug of red and cream braid just before it.

The woodmaster lowered him to the floor, roughly pulling back the hand Tor reached to the fire. Tor submitted weakly to the touch and sank to his shoulders against the cushion of the red and cream braided rug, hoping that now perhaps the woodmaster would leave him to sleep. This was how he would like to die, the drunkard's boy thought, lying on this soft rug, basking in the fierce heat of the yellow fire and the fragrance of spice cookies. The presence of the woodmaster disturbed his peace, but if the big, blond-haired man would allow him to sleep quietly, Tor could imagine him away.

The woodmaster's touch disappeared, and Tor mentally thanked him for his mercy. The woodmaster was a good man. Every week he went to church and sang hymns in a deep bass which Tor could hear even huddled outside the church. The woodmaster would not torment a dying boy for stealing from him.

A touch below his chin made Tor start and open wide his eyes. The woodmaster was fumbling with the kerchief at his throat.

Tor could smell the cedar fragrance that still lingered on the man's skin and shirt cuffs.

He tried to push the hands away but could feel nothing with his fingers except a distant tingling and soft pressure, like a cat nosing his hand.

The woodmaster pulled Tor's hands away. He raised the drunkard's boy to sitting, one arm supporting his back. Tor watched as his blouse rose up over his head and slid down his arms. He willed his hands to stop the man from undressing him, but they remained motionless at his side.

Never had he felt such an exquisite vulnerability as when the woodmaster lifted him out of his clothes and held him for the few moments it took to lower him into a metal tub filled with warm water.

Tor hardly felt the water itself, but he felt how it took his strength. His limbs were still utterly unresponsive to his bidding, floating before him just under the surface of the water.

The woodmaster began to rub him with a cloth and with his hand.

That rough hand felt very smooth against his skin. It did not feel usual, and Tor slowly realized it was because he was being covered in soap. He had never been covered in soap before.

After the cloth passed over his back he felt himself sliding against the metal tub, sinking deeper into the water and being unable to stop himself. For one dreadful moment, he looked right into the woodmaster's flat grey eyes, horrified that the cruel man would drown him.

The eyes drew close, growing larger, and Tor shrank back, suddenly craving the protection of a liquid grave.

But the smooth hands slipped under his arms and lifted his chin quite above the water's surface again. Tor felt the cold air smite his bare shoulders, and it made him want to cry. He did not want to be cold.

The woodmaster's dark figure moved around the tub to the other side, and Tor could see the fire again. Its brilliance made him want to close his eyes, and he did.

CHAPTER FOUR

When Tor woke the next morning, white winter sun was pouring between the linen curtains onto the braided red and cream rug before the still crackling fire. A solemn pine chair seemed to be conferring in the corner with a well dressed table. Tor could barely see them through the hazy shafts of sunlight.

He himself was tucked under brown woolen sheets and blankets.

Never had he seen any room so beautiful. It made him restful, something which he could not remember feeling except when Nanny, quiet and breathing easily, used to lay her head on his shoulder.

He continued to lie still and realized he smelled coffee. Coffee and . . . oatcake undoubtedly, for there was the comfortable smell of earthy grains and hot grease.

Suddenly ravenous, he tried to sit up, and for a moment he was confused. Then violent, rabid anger leapt in his heart.

He was tied, bound at the hands and, yes, bound at the feet as well. Then the memories of last night returned upon him in a tidal wave, and he swore furiously, kicking off the blankets. He sat up to think and for a moment was dumb-founded, but as the memories settled in, his brain began to work again.

Though he vividly recalled feeling fear and humiliation last night, the sensations had been nothing to those he felt now. He loathed the woodmaster for seeing him helpless and unclothed and afraid, hated the man for washing him like a baby, hated him for his ministrations in Tor's time of need. He could not endure that he had been utterly at the mercy of the person whom he so hated and feared, who had betrayed him, and who was going to punish him.

The woodmaster had seen how he lacked the strength to even move his own arms. The woodmaster had felt Tor's hands pushing him away from his buttons with the strength of an infant. The woodmaster had seen his eyes close and his jaw grow slack and his body sleep, defenseless, in a tub of warm water. Indeed, he would have drowned in the tub if the woodmaster had not lifted him up with his own hands.

The woodmaster had even dressed him. Like a baby.

The drunkard's boy cursed again. This time, the door opened in response to his cry.

"Child, why do you scream so?" asked the innkeeper's wife with her hand to her throat.

Tor knew that nothing he could say would persuade the mistress of the inn to release him. Yet he decided to ask her to help him anyway.

"He tied me up," he said stiffly, too angry to pretend to cry.

The kindly woman set her lips, and her eyes saddened.

21

"Now, lad, if you wouldn't have taken those things which do not belong to you, you wouldn't have to be tied up."

Tor turned and threw himself back down on the bed. He knew better than to try to make this woman believe him. No one ever believed him, no matter what he said. Rage scrambled his mind and twisted a knot in his throat. Now he simply wanted her to leave so he could he execute his own escape in peace.

He heard the door shut, finally, and he began to think, staring at the stitches of the cream colored afghan before his eyes.

He knew he was intelligent, but he did not have high hopes of freeing himself. Nothing in his life had ever turned out well for him. Good luck was a quality he didn't possess, and if he began a race with time he was certain to lose, as always.

As with Nanny, for instance.

He focused on the stitches before him again. Their perfect evenness sickened him. Why was it that everything other people did turned out so perfectly and everything he did turned to disaster? They all lived such perfect, well-ordered lives that looked just like these measured stitches, while his life looked like the back of a cross stiched sampler.

He rolled out of the bed and tried to worm his body backwards through the circle of his bound arms, but he soon found the endeavor hopeless. He then began to examine his bindings and discovered that it was braided cloth, the sort that had been coiled into the beautiful red and cream rug at his feet. He looked at the rug, which he had thought so beautiful a few moments ago, and now saw that it was soiled and stained in parts, worn, no doubt, by the slushy boots of hundreds of guests. He turned his eyes away and clawed at the rope on his wrists, cutting his own skin with his long nails in the process.

Then the door opened again, and the pleasant-faced woman entered with a tray of hot oatcake, salt pork, and coffee. It was good food, such as Tor rarely tasted. But rage gnawed him more sharply than the ache of his stomach, and not an instant after she set the tray down beside Tor he twisted on his hip and kicked it, sending a stream of coffee across the floor and onto the woman's shoes. She gasped and jumped back, and then she looked at him with thunder in her dark blue eyes.

"Some man," she said fiercely, "ought to take you to a woodshed and whip you thoroughly!"

Not bothering to touch the tray or its spilled contents, she left the room, shutting the door firmly behind her.

Tor slithered across the room to the fireplace and began to rub his bonds on the corner of the stone hearth. His eyes flickered in search of some other means of escape, but he saw nothing sharper and stronger than the stone behind him. He could not cut the rope with anything in the room faster than he could tear it on the rock. And there was no other way to get the rope off.

Yet was there?

He stopped moving, for the idea entering his head chilled him like a slow spreading frost.

Rope could burn.

He imagined his skin melting in flame. Certainly, this was not the best way. He could wait for the woodmaster's return, and when the woodmaster untied him he would escape by some less painful method.

Supposing, indeed, that the man would untie him at all. If he wished to see Tor punished for his theft as he had several times threatened, then he would likely return with an officer imminently. In that event, Tor knew his life would be essentially ended, for, even before his father had died in one, he had heard of the horrors of prison. The thought of being committed made him frantic. He rubbed savagely at the stone, but slipped and gashed his forearm so that he could feel blood trickle down to his hand.

Still rubbing, he shut his eyes and mentally shook himself. He must be calm if he were to have any hope of staying free.

Surely, he told himself, taking deep breaths, if he burnt the rope properly, he needn't scorch his skin badly. If he could burn off even a little or simply char the rope, then it would be easier to finish the rest on stone. He felt more and more strongly the necessity of this action. These few moments of pain would seem inconsequential compared to what he would endure in prison. At any moment the woodmaster would return, and Tor's life would be lost, shut up in stone at the mercy of low, hard men who were willing take advantage of anyone and any form of pleasure to distract from their own misery.

He eased himself up to sit on the hearth with his back to the fire and took measured breaths. A very few moments of discomfort, and then he would be free, out on the streets of Stockholm. He wouldn't have to worry about the heat there, he thought to himself, and he smiled dryly, rather to ease his nagging dread than because he saw any humor in the prospect.

He thought of the cold and the way the wind whisked bits of snow around corners into whatever dark alley he had chosen for his nightly lodging. The wind always found him.

Behind him, his forearms felt uncomfortably hot, frighteningly close to the licking flames, but the temperature, he told himself stoically, was still endurable.

He thought of the way the wind seemed to slit the skin of his eyelids to get at his eyes; he thought of how his shoes dampened and froze in the slushy streets and of how the cold took feeling from his fingers, hands, arms . . .

A thrill of pain in his forearms interrupted his focus, thrusting him forward to the floor without leave from his mind. He rolled onto his back and rocked from elbow to elbow, gasping, expecting the flames to burst out from behind his arms and envelope his body at any moment.

The pain in his hands and arms sharper and sharper, frighening him. He rolled into the coffee spill, hoping the liquid would soothe his seared skin, and he heard a slight sizzle.

He was just gathering his wits enough to think again of prison and the need to return to rub the, hopefully, blackened rope on the stone when the door opened, and he looked up to see the woodmaster staring down at him.

From behind the woodmaster stepped Vicar Arnman, dressed in a dark green coat with a cranberry-colored scarf, looking like a thin and garishly clad *Jultomten*, that household spirit which happy children stupidly imagined brought them gifts at Christmas. His walking stick was of well polished mahogany that glinted brightly in the firelight.

"Well," said this man, grimly, "at least you have found the boy."

"A small consolation," the woodmaster replied, stepping over Tor and walking to the fire to warm his hands. His voice was harsh as the sound of a saw on the edge of a wooden plank, and the brief glance he had bestowed upon Tor had revealed eyes that were like a rough sea on a stormy day.

Tor wanted to roll away from the man so that he faced the comforting dark space under the bed, but he stopped himself, unwilling to reveal his injured hands and the evidence of his attempted escape. He closed his eyes instead and listened to the vicar's grave movements as he shut the door and crossed to the corner to seat himself with a great creak in the gloomy pinewood chair.

"I wish you would not have behaved so disrespectfully to the bishop." The vicar sounded peeved. "It reflects very poorly on us both."

The woodmaster said nothing but took off his coat and scarf and hung them on a peg. The ensuing silence seemed to intensify the throb of Tor's wounds. He wished he were not lying on his back with his arms crushed to the floor, painfully, humiliatingly. But then he thought perhaps the pressure on his arms was numbing the burn pain, and he was reconciled.

The fire continued to crackle and rustle among its shifting ashes, sounding as merry as ever and seeming to titter at Tor. He bit his back teeth hard together but did not open his eyes, not wanting to see the blond woodmaster leaning against the mantle of the fireplace, straight, strong, and self-assured in his power over the anemic, stoop-shouldered boy who lay bound, sopping up the coffee on the floor with his sleeves and hair.

That man had been his idol once. He'd seemed so far above the common villagers, who were consumed with their petty affairs of how to finagle an extra wedge of cheese from the dairy farmer at market. Tor had seen the way the woodmaster looked at them sardonically when they gossiped and niggled, and he had known at once from the look of those grey eyes that this man could see their pettiness and hypocrisy as plainly as Tor did.

Now those eyes were looking sardonically at him, and he couldn't bear it. The man was nothing more than an egotist who found everyone foolish and contemptible but himself; Tor saw that now.

Tortured as he was with these thoughts, the drunkard's boy was almost grateful for the sudden painful throbs that surged through his tender flesh like water being pumped through a spout. At least the pain distracted him from the anger he could not release. He swallowed a moan.

Someone knocked on the door. The woodmaster remained silent, so after a moment the vicar called, "Enter!"

Tor peered at the opening door through slitted eyes. Certainly it was an official coming to escort him to prison.

The visitor did not move inside but remained standing in the corridor.

"Sir, I have brought the coffee." It was the pleasant, rosy-cheeked innkeeper's wife who spoke to the vicar.

"Excellent, my good woman," said the vicar, leaning back in his chair and crossing his legs easily. "Just set it here on the table."

"Excuse me, sir," said the lady, stiffly, "but I have a good reason to be wary of that little brownie. He'd surely spill me and the coffee across the floor if I came so close to him." Tor lay in such a way that he blocked the path from the door into any other part of the room.

The woodmaster gave a brusque sigh that made Tor draw his muscles together. The big man crossed to him in a stride and lifted him out of the coffee and crushed oatcake, dragging him by the upper arms over to the foot of the bed where he forced him back to the floor, almost with a shove.

The woodmaster was about to turn back to the mantle, but he paused to look at Tor with narrowed eyes. The drunkard's boy realized then that he had opened his eyes and taken in breath too sharply when his seared arms, having just received a surge of fresh blood circulation, were crushed again to the floor. He pressed his lips and eyes closed, containing his expression of pain and at the same time blocking out the woodmaster's suspicious, demanding gaze.

Tor heard the man straighten, and he might have returned to the mantlepiece had not the innkeeper's wife just then paused in the middle of the room to sniff the air.

"What's been burning in this room?" she asked in the clipped tone of a housewife who has counted only eleven of her one dozen finely embroidered white linen napkins.

The woodmaster stopped to smell the room.

"I thought the smell was from the kitchen," he said.

"It is certainly not," the woman replied, setting her tray down on the table with a sharp clack and turning to look at Tor. "There's naught in my kitchen smells like this. What's the lad done?" Her voice was flat, as if she were steeling herself against the worst possibilities.

Tor could feel all eyes on him, and he cringed within himself. Allowing them to discover his burn at once, he thought, would have been greatly preferable to this small court-martial. Yet he neither moved nor opened his eyes.

The woodmaster suddenly bent down over Tor again and rolled him on his side, exposing his arms to the sight of all.

"He has tried to burn the ropes off his hands and has caught his blouse on fire." Tor bit his lips together as the man began to loosen the ropes about his wrists.

The kindly innkeeper's wife gasped.

"How could he have endured the fire long enough to give him such burns! What has this boy done to make him so desperate?"

"I have told you before that he is a thief," said the woodmaster as he pulled Tor off the ground by his stiff, aching upper arms. He dragged the drunkard's boy over to the wash basin on a side table.

"What did he steal? Surely he has been punished sufficiently?" Tor thought for a moment that the woman would take his part.

"I stole nothing!" he shouted.

The woodmaster made no reply but pulled one of Tor's arms across the basin and began to pour over it a pitcher of cold water.

Tor jerked away. The woodmaster caught his shoulder, but the boy fought the grip, silently. Equally silent, the woodmaster pressed Tor's cheek to the table, pinning him with one hand on the back of his neck; he turned, seized the vicar's wooden cane, and whipped it across Tor's seat with a snap that made the pleasant innkeeper's wife jump and twist her dark blue apron nervously in her hands.

Tor's anger engulfed his sensibility to pain. He clawed the woodmaster arm, cursing. The woodmaster gripped both his wrists, pinned them to the back of his neck, and whipped him again. Tor growled and spit in the direction of the man, who only stepped out of Tor's view and whipped him once more.

Still furious, the drunkard's boy shut his eyes and breathed hard for a few moments. When he looked again he saw the slender vicar staring at him and the woodmaster with curved lips as he chewed a piece of cake. He saw the hands of the round-faced lady twisting her dark blue apron with the white and green embroidery. He could not see the man who was humiliating him, pressing his face to the table, bending Tor's will as he bent his body, but he knew the man was prepared to strike again.

The stings left by the cane seemed to grow wider and deeper; also, his tender forearms were beginning to plead for mercy. Once more, as the rising pain began to eclipse the anger in Tor's heart, he closed his eyes in bitter submission.

"What did he do?" asked the kindly woman again in very

subdued tones.

As the woodmaster made no answer the magnaminous vicar met her inquiry with soothing tones.

"He stole the woodcarver's Nativity set, my good lady. A very valuable work of art which the woodcarver crafted over the course of fully five years." Here the woodmaster pulled Tor up from the table and jerked his arm back over the speckled pottery basin to continue pouring water over it.

"After some inquiries the woodcarver and I discovered that the Nativity had passed through a pawn shop here in Stockholm. We lately visited this shop where the dealer identified this boy out of five of the woodcarver's drawings of boys from our town."

Tor almost shivered at the thought of the grey-eyed woodmaster drawing his face, detailing with his sharp graphite pencil Tor's bent nose and the soft little hairs that always tufted up at the back of his head.

The vicar sighed and met Tor's gaze with sorrowful eyes.

"Unfortunately, the Nativity was sold to a very high church official. We have visited him, but it would seem that His Grace wishes to hear naught of the Nativity being sold to him unlawfully. I am afraid it is lost to the woodcarver."

After a short silence, in which the woodmaster pointedly devoted his brooding attention exclusively to his task of bathing the arms of the drunkard's boy, the pleasant goodwife gathered a larger handful of her apron to twist and nervously cleared her throat.

"Surely," said she to the vicar, speaking quite hesitantly, "the boy deserves punishment, but, Your Honor, might it not be wisest to entrust the choosing of his punishment to one less prejudiced? The boy seems quite afraid of-"

With a curt thump, the woodmaster set down the speckled pitcher on the table.

"I don't intend to see this boy loafing in prison when I could be getting my penny's worth from him. And I won't have him sent to some poor fool who'll set him to shining the silver and wake up to find him run off with spoons, candlesticks, and all. *Nej*, I'll have this boy where I can keep a hawk's eye and an iron grip on him."

As he spoke, the woodmaster pulled off Tor's burnt blouse, tossed it on the puddle of coffee, and pushed Tor to sit on the bed. He then began to pour the water from the basin back into the pitcher. He did not look at Tor's eyes, and no more did Tor look at him.

"Do you have any salve for these burns, *Frü*?" the man asked.

The kindly goodwife looked at the vicar, who shrugged and shook his head with an amused glance, first at the woodmaster, then at the miserable Tor, who sat quite still and pale, staring at his burned arms with hollow eyes.

"I will bring some." She sighed and left them.

The woodmaster pulled Tor's head down over the basin and

doused it, still moiled with soggy oatcake crumbs, with water from the pitcher.

Tor thrashed and shook his head, spraying water on the good vicar where he sat in the corner watching the bath with interest.

"I fail to see," the vicar said, smiling tightly as he dabbed himself dry with a handkerchief, "what recompense you intend to get from that boy. Anyone can see he'll be more a torment to you than a help. You would be better off sending him to the workhouse or, better still, straight to prison."

The woodmaster clenched Tor's hair, wrenching his twisting head down firmly. He finished pouring the water, and then released him with one of his barely constrained shoves.

"Clean up your mess," said he, indicating the spilled breakfast with a nod as he set down the pitcher and began to snatch up toiletries and scattered articles of clothing into his arms.

Steadying himself against the bed, the drunkard's boy stood still, challenging the woodmaster to make him comply.

The woodmaster accepted the challenge most readily, returning almost at once to force Tor to his knees and to rub the boy's nose in the coffee. After a minute or two of this treatment, Tor shouted furiously.

"I didn't take your wretched Nativity, woodcarver, and forcing me to confess will never get you back your kindling scraps!"

The woodcarver's hold became very tight for a moment—

34

almost choking—but then he suddenly released the drunkard's boy and stood up. He walked to the doorway and left the room, slamming the door after him. Tor heard his feet thumping down the wooden stairs.

The drunkard's boy regretted his words. His heart pounded wildly. The woodmaster was going for an officer.

He considered running, but his feet were still tied.

The vicar sat in silence with Tor until the innkeeper's wife returned with a pot of salve. This she began to spread on Tor's arms without looking in his eyes. Meanwhile, Tor contemplated escape, only wishing he knew where the woodmaster was lurking.

All too soon, clumping footsteps were heard on the stairs, and the woodmaster reentered, fat flakes of half melted snow clinging to his hair, beard, and shoulders. He looked like the thunder god, just driven in on the back of his own storm cloud. After one glance at Tor and the round faced innkeeper's wife, he knelt and gathered the spilled food and dishes back onto the tray. He sopped up the coffee with the burnt brown shirt he had taken off Tor, then wrung the blouse out over the water basin, which he then emptied out the window. The draft from the open window caused his shirtless captive to shiver, not simply from cold, but from the fear of cold.

The woodmaster wrapped the brown shirt into a ball and stuffed it into his traveling bag, at the same time pulling a clean blouse from the bag. This, he thrust at Tor.

"Put this on," he said. "And these." He lifted a dark blue coat and grey scarf from the peg next to his own coat and cast them on the bed next to Tor.

Tor did not want to put them on, but, even more, he did not want to feel cold, and he could not be sure that the woodmaster would not take him outside shirtless if he did not obey immediately. He hated that the man had already found ways to manipulate him using his fears.

He put on the clothes and the very sturdy boots which the woodmaster dropped at his feet. At least, he thought, as he untied the ropes binding his legs, if he escaped he would have the consolation of a good coat and boots for his ordeal.

The woodmaster goaded him towards the door, and he obeyed with ill grace. He stiffened his hunched shoulders and put his hands in his pockets. Then he stopped as he suddenly realized that his pockets were empty.

"What have you done with my old clothes?" he said, staring through the doorway into the hall.

"Gave them to the innkeeper's wife to burn," replied the woodmaster, quite callously.

Tor was horrified. He felt another wave of hatred for the injustice of the man who took possession of him and his things merely on the grounds of suspicion.

"They had my sister's things!" he roared at the wooden panel across the hall. "I had a bag with my sister's things, and you burnt them!"

The woodmaster pushed past him and went clumping down the stairs like a great cow jogging sullenly away from the farmer's pricks.

"Perhaps," lectured the vicar, nudging Tor onward from behind, "you will now sympathize with the woodcarver. When you stole the Nativity he lost much more-"

"I never took it," Tor spat, "but he has taken everything from me!"

The woodmaster was emerging from the kitchen when they reached the bottom of the steps. He pushed a small, filthy drawstring bag into Tor's hands and thrust him forward towards the door.

Tor clutched the bag, feeling for the small wooden figure inside with rising dread.

Ja, it was there. He shoved the bag in his pocket with the barest glance up at the woodmaster's face. But the woodmaster had wrapped his blue scarf up to his eyes and appeared not to see him.

CHAPTER FIVE

All afternoon they rode in a carriage, a vehicle which Tor had seen many times but only from the outside. He had always thought he would be pleased to ride in the vicar's carriage, but instead he found himself only humiliated.

When he and Nanny had dreamt of riding in such an equipage, they'd imagined very different circumstances from these. They had imagined themselves well-dressed and rich, and people had bowed or tipped their hats when the carriage passed them. In these daydreams, Tor was always a scholar, a doctor, an official—something great—and he and Nanny lived in a big house full of fresh flowers and windows with white curtains in every room, instead of rats and mold.

How faded that daydream seemed now, with the woodmaster sitting beside Tor—arms crossed, head back, and eyes closed, breathing regularly, but probably far from sleep—and the vicar reading a paper by the light streaming through the glass window of the carriage.

Tor refused to look at that paper, for the tiny letters which the vicar so easily skimmed taunted him. Instead, he stared at the green velvet of the seat beside the vicar's knee, trying not to think about the arms which were still throbbing in his lap, despite the heavy application of cold, fresh smelling salve.

For the rest of the journey the three travelers remained in the same attitude as when they'd started, except for when the vicar folded up his paper, daintily removed his spectacles, and laced his fingers over the front of his coat.

Disliking the man's delicate movements, Tor turned his eyes away. He had discovered over the years that it was best to think about the vicar as little as possible.

They reached the woodmaster's shop just after the dinner hour, and the vicar rolled off in a flurry of confused snowflakes to partake of his cook's good potato soup and meatballs, leaving Tor alone with the woodmaster, staring at the window whose crystal pane he had smashed over a month ago.

The woodmaster unlocked the door and laid a hand between Tor's shoulder blades. Tor moved away from the touch quickly, stumbling inside. As he entered, a chill drifted over him which had not been appointed by the weather. He could not help but cast an eye on the window ledge where the painstakingly crafted Nativity should have rested, peacefully watching snowflakes wander the silent streets.

The woodmaster pulled him through the front shop, then the workshop, and then towards his living quarters in the back room.

Tor wanted to resist. The woodmaster's dwelling had always held for him an air of inspiring mystery. He had been in the front shop with all its intricately carved clocks, cradles, and candlesticks, and he had glanced through the doorway into the workshop and caught the whiff of its brooding wood fragrance.

But he had never seen into the back room, where the woodmaster lived.

Tor had long been fascinated by the brooding creature with his round, clever fingers, ragged blond mane, and attentive grey eyes full of arcane thoughts.

Rumor suggested that the man had abandoned his flourishing occupation as master craftsman in a large city where he had employed numerous apprentices and journeymen and had come to Tor's village to be a humble carpenter in place of the late Gunnar Nilsson.

Ever since the man had come to their village Tor had watched him. And he had often wondered what quiet mysteries steeped in the room just beyond the workshop, mysteries that could inspire such a creature as the woodmaster. If any clue could be had as to the woodmaster's character, any hint as to the thoughts behind his sharp, silent eyes, Tor guessed it would be found in that back room. And that was why, secretly, he had always wanted to explore it.

Now the room held nothing but dread for the drunkard's boy. It was the woodmaster's stronghold. Here, he would keep Tor prisoner and exact revenge at his leisure.

The drunkard's boy balked in the doorway and peered into the room that was just barely outlined with the soft moon glow emanating from a large window.

He did not like how easily the faint light was shed through the crystal pane into the stark room. It enhanced the distinct contrast of the place with his own grungy, windowless cellar, littered with the castoff scraps his mother collected: a soiled picture of a nobleman and his lady on horses, three-quarters of a real china teacup, a spinning wheel without its wheel, scraps of dirty ribbon, a hacked up leather bridle, a bent oyster rake, a moldering fisherman's net. With so much clutter, there had been many shadows and corners in which to disappear.

But here, every wall was bare of decoration, and the sparse furniture was unadorned—not a hint of the swirled engraving and elegant gingerbread that graced the pieces in the front shop. Every surface was cut in sharp, perfect angles and gleamed with polish, reflecting light back at the window pane. Tor felt that when he stepped into this room he would be like an insect stepping before the glass eye of a focused microscope. Here, as on a glass slide, would be no place to hide.

From behind, the woodmaster prodded Tor forward, his hand rough on the tender, burned back. The man pushed past him, moving further into the room, and soon, a flickering light revealed his glowing profile as he bent over a lamp on a table.

"Shut the door. Sit at the table," said the man, carrying the lamp over to the fireplace.

As Tor sat at the table made of swirling light wood that had been smoothed and rubbed down over till it shone, he shivered and tried not to stare at the silhouette of the woodmaster's powerful shoulders against the light of the kindling. The drunkard's boy disliked the muscular grace with which the man lowered himself to a squat and rose again on his strong legs with perfect ease. He also disliked how the fire gleamed on the light hair like the first rays of a golden dawn reflecting off mountain snow.

The woodmaster placed a large earthen jug on the table, then took parcels out of his traveling bag and laid them out also.

He sat on the bench opposite Tor and, without preamble, muttered a terse, rote prayer before reaching to unwrap a portion of brown bread and another portion of goat's milk cheese. He cut both in half with a large knife and lay one half of each before Tor. He laid his own cheese and bread one on top of the other and ate them in four bites.

No sooner had he inhaled this food than he disappeared into a corner of the room. Tor now began to eat his own supper. He would not touch it with the woodmaster sitting across the table; that would be a sign of acquiescence, of submission. But with the woodmaster nearly lost to sight, Tor ate with shaking hands and an uneasy stomach, for he had not eaten in some time.

After several moments occupation with eating, Tor again became aware of the woodmaster's movements. He had dragged out a trundle bed from beneath the larger bed and had prepared it with bedclothes and a pillow.

"You will sleep here," said the man.

Tor eyed the closeness of the two beds with distaste.

"Oh, I wouldn't dare to presume so, my lord," he said, his voice still hoarse from sickness and exposure. "Please let me sleep on the floor with the vermin. I might give you fleas."

"I don't object," said the woodmaster, brusquely gathering the blankets up off the small bed. "I no more wish you breathing down my neck than you wish me breathing down yours." He walked across the room and dropped by the wall near the fire.

"If you try to run away I will leave you tied up all night, each night."

"My mother will come for me, you know," Tor snapped at the man, who was already moving the trundle back under the bed with one foot.

"Your mother is dead, Tor," the woodmaster said. His back was to the drunkard's boy, and he did not turn around. "She was intoxicated and fell asleep outside in the middle of a snowstorm. The body was found after you ran away."

Tor pushed away from the table and moved to his corner. He lay down in his coat and boots with his face to the wall.

After Nanny's death his mother had left and not returned. Now Tor knew why, but he could not decide what he ought to feel at the news of his mother's death.

CHAPTER SIX

Two days later, Tor opened his eyes and looked without recognition at the grey-brown panels of the wall before him. He took a moment to focus on the grain of the wood before rolling slowly to his other side. Above him, he glimpsed ceiling beams hung with strings of crispy *knäckebröd*. Beside him lay a pool of saffron light, cast through the window by a low-hanging sun. He caught the lingering smell of oat porridge, and he heard the rough song of a planer being run across a board again and again just on the other side of the wall in the dusty workshop.

He sat up slowly, half expecting to find himself tied hand and foot—though he knew not why—and tried to remember what had occurred during the last few days. He recalled a burning pain in his arms, recalled being whipped in front of the smirking vicar, and he recalled the woodmaster directing him into this house, where Tor had obeyed orders against his will because he was too exhausted to rebel.

He vaguely remembered moonlight shining through the window as his head was lifted to sip gruel, and he cursed weakly. He'd been sick. Again, the woodmaster had nursed him in his helplessness.

Then Tor remembered wondering how to feel about his mother's death.

Emptiness, he found, was all he had strength to feel. He closed his eyes and turned back to the wall, drained of energy.

He fell into what seemed only a restless doze, but it was hours later by the sign of the absent sun when sounds of activity roused him. He recognized the woodmaster's determined stride across the floor behind him. Cupboards opened and shut; a knife cut through a thick-crusted loaf; a cork was pulled off a jug; one of the benches belonging to the table scraped on the rough plank floor. Then, quiet chewing.

Tor was disgusted by the chewing, but as he tried to block off the sound, it only seemed to grow louder. He gritted his teeth, irrationally furious and fully aware that he could do nothing to vent the feeling.

This was the very reason he had always avoided the man. He'd watched the man like an eagle, yes, but studiously avoided him. He had dreaded discovering that the carpenter had feet of clay.

That discovery was inevitable, of course.

The woodmaster did have feet of clay. He believed the worst of Tor, as everyone did, but, what was much worse, he had decided to take deliberate vengeance on Tor without any right to do so—simply because he disliked him. Tor had seen enough glimpses of the cold anger in the man's eyes to know that he was not forgiven his theft and would not be forgiven till the man had exacted punishment, if even then. The carpenter was as hypocritical and unjust and hateful as everyone else in the town.

And now Tor was galled by the realization that even the woodmaster with his satirical eyes and extraordinary woodcraft was a slave to his appetite and could chew as noisily as a butcher. He was, truly, just like all the others.

Unable to remain still, Tor finally rolled over and stood. He had already recognized his new blue coat hanging by the back door above his new boots—they'd been removed from him, for he remembered falling asleep with them on—and he made his way towards them, ignoring how his legs wobbled and his head ached. He walked through the familiar clouds of dark mist that seemed to drift across his eyes and passed behind the silent woodmaster to the coat rack. He slipped into the coat and wedged his feet into the boots with shaking hands.

As he lifted the bolt of the sturdy oaken door the woodmaster finally spoke, his voice clear and jarring.

"Five minutes, or I will come after you."

Tor pretended not to hear and passed out of the house, slamming the door after him.

He had intended, after visiting the outhouse, to sit outside the back door until he was sure the five minutes were just past spent, but he soon realised the cold was unbearable and quickly returned inside, eager to taste the warmth of the fire and his blankets again.

The woodmaster was sitting on the hearth when he entered, using a spoon to crush sodden chunks of bread into a bowl of warm whey. Tor kicked off his boots with untidy deliberation and passed back to his corner, keeping the coat on.

"Take your supper," said the woodmaster, standing and setting the bowl on the table.

Sending the man a fearless glare, the drunkard's boy lifted the bowl from the table and carried it to his corner, where he sat and ate and waited for the woodmaster to accost him for his churlishness.

But the woodmaster only looked at him for a few moments before turning away and settling into a chair by the fire.

"I see you're well enough recovered from your sickness now," said he, sarcastically, as he leaned back his shaggy head and shut his eyes. "I'm thinking you can start work with me tomorrow."

"I'll be hanged and go to work for the devil first," said Tor. His voice was even weaker and huskier than it had been the night they'd arrived. Just hearing it made him wonder whether he had enough strength now to engage in this battle.

"Yes, I can't but fear you will be hanged one of these days, boy," said the woodmaster dryly, "but, till then, be sensible. It's much more unpleasant than you think to starve to death, which is what will happen if you don't work." He looked at Tor pointedly. "Now finish your supper and come to the fire where I can look to your burns."

In the past, Tor had often wondered what the woodmaster was thinking in the silence, but now he found he did not like knowing the creature's mind so much as he had imagined he would. He set the half-eaten mush on the floor and lay down with his back to the woodmaster.

"I do not want your porridge," he said, "and I do not want your doctoring."

The woodmaster moved too silently to be heard, and he hove Tor up by his blue coat before the drunkard's boy could roll away.

They struggled without speaking while the woodmaster hauled Tor close to the fire, pulled off his coat, and pinned him to the floor. He then took a seat on Tor's stomach and, capturing his bandaged arms, waited for the drunkard's boy to run out of strength and cease struggling.

Tor's recent illness and the heavy weight on his stomach conspired to quench his breath and crush his will very shortly. He closed his eyes, refusing to watch as the woodmaster carefully rolled up one brown sleeve, unwrapped his bandage, and turned his arm in the light of the fire. At last, the woodmaster moved his weight off Tor and knelt beside him on one knee to apply fresh salve. Tor did not stir, though his spirit protested vilely against this position of vulnerability.

"I hate you," he said when the woodmaster had rolled his sleeves back down, raised him to sitting, and walked to the other side of the room. "You're punishing me for something I never did."

The woodmaster turned and looked at him in silent contempt. Grimly pleased to have roused the man's anger, Tor continued.

"You are just like the rest of these stupid villagers: too drunk with your own holiness to see straight. And do you think just because you can trick a fortune out of a few fools for your cheapjack work that you can manage *me*? You can't keep me here. I will get away from you."

"I wish you *could* get away from me," said the woodmaster, jerking down the bed sheets, his voice grating like the grain of rough-hewn wood, "but it seems as though you will not."

"Yes, keep that thought, carpenter," said Tor harshly. "Your pride weakens you." He stood to his feet, trying to repress the trembling of his weak body, and walked to his corner. The wrestle with the woodmaster had utterly drained him.

The woodmaster crossed to the middle of the room and extinguished the winking lamp on the table before easing into bed and turning his back on Tor.

Tor fell asleep and slept well, waking only once when hunger pains forced him to finish the half-eaten dinner in the bowl still sitting by his head.

Tor knew exactly where he was next morning when he woke to the rattle of the woodmaster's pans. But he did not move. He would be sick again that day, and the woodmaster would leave him untied and unguarded as naïvely as he had the day before.

Tor's prediction held true. The woodmaster did go out and presently began to drone his tune of labor with cacophonous instruments.

Tor then rose and assembled provisions for his journey, wrapping up bread and salt fish in the blankets upon which he had slept. He added matches and candles and also any small thing of value which might be possible to sell, such as two brass candlesticks and a china plate on the mantle.

He moved without reflection, feeding upon the anger that had fully revived that morning while the woodmaster had sat at the table behind him, chewing his breakfast with all callousness and self-possession.

The man probably thought Tor wouldn't be idiotic enough to run away right after a blizzard and just as he was recovering from fever. Indeed, common sense warned Tor himself against such foolishness. He hesitated, reflecting on the predatorial confidence that had caused the woodmaster to leave him, unbound and unattended in the back room while he worked with his noisy tools. It was almost as if the man wanted the drunkard's boy to attempt an escape that he might catch him back and bully him more savagely.

But since Nanny's death, Tor had come to regard reflection as his enemy. It had been his coward's overthinking and feeble second-guessing that had cost Nanny her life. To have taken the Nativity on the first night, when he had planned to, would have brought him to Stockholm a day earlier, instead of on late Christmas Eve, and the first two pawn shops he had seen would have been open for customers. At the least he would have returned home in time to do something more for Nanny, if only to have comforted her in her last moments of coherence before she died.

This unbearable thought quickened his movements like the flick of a whip to an unbroken stallion. He slipped on his boots, hands shaking again with fever, and checked his pocket one last time for the tattered bag.

At his first gentle pull the back door would not yield, so he laid his bundle aside and set his left palm half on the door frame and half on the door to prevent the door from wrenching open too loudly. He pulled the latch again with his right hand, timing it to the sound of the pounding mallet in the workshop behind.

The door opened with great resistance.

Tor bent to snatch up his bundle. As he did so a sudden clatter in the workshop made him jump, but he calmed his mind, telling himself the woodmaster had dropped something.

He stepped outside and turned to close the door quietly behind. It would not do to leave the door to bang in the wind.

It was then he noticed the string that was tied to the outer door latch. It ran across the door and along the wall of the house to disappear around the corner. And while Tor stared at this string, wincing from a horrible realization, the woodmaster stepped from behind the corner.

Tor did not move as the woodmaster, breathing deeply from his hurried sprint, stood and stared at him. The man leaned against the house on one upraised arm, making, against the sunrise, a blurry silhouette of shaggy winter hair and chalk-colored blouse billowing out from a leather carpenter's apron.

Then Tor cursed himself for his imbecility. Last night he had accused the woodmaster of arrogance, but he himself had been the arrogant one. How could he have so grossly underestimated the man? Both reason and intuition had warned him of the carpenter's intelligence, but he had been too reckless to consider it.

This was an inexcusable display of stupidity, and Tor could see from the look of the woodmaster's face that he thought the same.

Without stopping to think, Tor swung the bundle from over his shoulder and struck it hard on the side of the sturdy house before dropping it to the ground. The crash and the little tinkling sounds that issued from the bundle revealed the effect of his blow better than words.

The woodmaster surged forward then and kicked open the door with such force that the string, which had permitted the door to open only halfway, snapped, and the woodmaster grabbed the drunkard's boy and shoved him inside.

When he stepped inside the house himself it was to look over at the mantle where the pink china plate had been, then to stare at Tor.

For the first time, as Tor met the man's gaze, he felt nothing towards him but fear, for he saw that the cool composure which had always so circumspectly guarded the man's private thoughts had vanished from his eyes, leaving raw emotions to rampage, and the drunkard's boy suddenly understood that the woodmaster's armor of self-control had not only kept prying eyes out, but also kept violent emotions in.

The woodmaster approached in one fast stride and struck him a hard, precise blow before he walked to the mantle, leaned his head to the wall, placed his empty hands in the spot where the china plate had been, and stood very still.

The moments passed slowly for Tor as he sat on the floor where he had stumbled, clearing his throbbing head and trying not to tremble as he waited for the woodmaster's next act of violence.

"Hello," said a girl-child's voice.

Tor, still alert for movement from the woodmaster, looked up to examine a short person standing in the doorway.

The little girl stood just a step away from the threshold where she could be clearly seen by the growing beams of fresh winter sunlight. Her dress was brown and her shawl, grey. She wore no hat and her cornmeal braids were smooth and glossy. Her age was difficult to suppose, for she stood the height of an eight-year-old child, but her cheeks were ever so round, and she held two fingers in her slack-jawed mouth like a two-year-old.

Her eyes seemed to betray a hint of other-worldliness, so peculiarly shaped were they: narrow, yet wide from side to side. Tor had often seen this girl with her older sister in the marketplace, where she smiled at everyone till her sparkling eyes were almost eclipsed by fat, rosy cheeks.

Her name was Marta, but the village called her "the idiot child," and the good wives clucked their tongues when they spoke of her.

"What are you about, child? Go home to your mother," said the woodmaster, striding between Tor and the little girl.

"I heard a noise. He got hurt."

Seeing the child take a hurried step back from the hulking man when he appeared, the drunkard's boy took grim satisfaction.

"Everyone is fine, girl," the woodmaster said. "Go to Mother."

"He's hurt," said the child, suddenly taking her fingers from her mouth and thrusting one in Tor's direction.

The woodmaster did not turn to look at him.

"*Ja*, he is, but I will take care of him."

These words bore dread in Tor's mind. Perhaps it seemed so to the little girl as well, for she stood still, pulling on her braid while the woodmaster slowly shut the door on her.

Upon the closing of the door the man swung about and leaned his back on it while staring once more at the drunkard's boy. He seemed to deliberate with himself upon Tor's fate, his stance and unhurried movements expressing that he was again fully master of himself.

All the same, Tor raised a protective arm when the woodmaster reached to grip him by the shirt front. He hauled Tor like so much weight of flour out to the workshop where he laid him on his knees before a pile of metal tools scattered over the floor. With them was a log with string tied around booth ends. The strings were joined together and ran up through a crack in the window above.

"Take these up, boy, and lay them out in good order on the table here."

The woodmaster turned and reentered the back room.

Tor, glancing over his shoulder as he began to gather up the tools, watched the man tear open the outside door and reach for the bundle Tor had packed. He then took it to the table, disappearing from Tor's sight.

The tinkling of shattered china mingled with the clatter of the spilled tools. But the sounds of mutual busyness added no air of comradery to the little house; rather it was like the sounds of weaponry being mustered and arranged on either side of the battle lines.

Tor rose to his feet upon completing his task. He was growing more conscious of the effects of the woodmaster's blow; he began to feel heat and tenderness on his left cheekbone and a stinging pain in his nose. Even part of his top lip felt swollen. He looked toward the door that led into the front shop where the outer door stood and thought of running again.

"Sweep the hearth." The woodmaster's voice was abrupt, jarring Tor like a club thudding between his shoulder blades.

The carpenter had not looked up from his work, and Tor shivered a little at his omniscience.

Laying his outspread hand on the work table beside him, he slowly bent his fingers back to crack his knuckles, then he went to the door leading to the back room, behind which he remembered seeing the broom the night he'd arrived. He recalled small details like these—what others did not observe and certainly could not call to mind when needed. Usually his observant mind was a source of pride to him, but he was too disgruntled by pain and his recent foolishness to find any pleasure in this small proof of acuity.

He was afraid to look at the woodmaster from the doorway, but he did so regardless; he needed to observe the man so he could know best how to act.

The woodmaster was seated at the table, laying out the pieces of china with care, and Tor was rather startled to see the six foot, thickly bearded man in his rough, homespun blouse and scarred leather apron hovering over shards of pink china plate, his ready thumb and forefinger suspended and rubbing each other intermittently with unconscious focus.

Anxious to avoid the man's eye, Tor allowed his glance to linger only an instant as he passed back to sweep the hearth.

Again, the fire mocked him with its ruddy cheer. He wished he could toss a pail of icy slush on it so it would be as he: suffocated and smoldering.

After sweeping, he put the broom back behind the door, this time avoiding any glance at the woodmaster.

"Put these things in their place," said the woodmaster gesturing to the plunder Tor had stashed in his bundle, "and put your bedding back on the trundle because you'll be sleeping by me now. You'll get no more leash than you need to keep from choking to death."

Tor's chest constricted, but the memory of the woodmaster's enraged face caused him to acquiesce silently. With angry precision, he replaced everything he had taken.

"Wash your face in the basin and bring in snow to rinse the blood from your shirt," said the woodmaster, still not looking up.

Tor glanced down, touching his face. The blood had run from his nose over his numb lip, and he'd never noticed. This lapse in his sharp powers of observation vexed him; it made him look the fool before his enemy. What did it matter that he remembered the location of a broom from only a hurried glance in the dark when he now wandered the room with blood dribbling down his face like a half-wit?

He snatched the bucket and went outside, once more slamming the door behind him. His alarm from the woodmaster's recent outburst was already beginning to fade on the horizon of his stormy mind.

Even so, for the rest of the day he obeyed his new master's every command to the letter, anxious to demonstrate, even to this hateful man, that his abilities and coolness of mind matched and exceeded the woodmaster's. To demonstrate that, after all, that he was not the simpleton he had appeared when he'd run away earlier.

To be bound to an enemy for a month or two was an ill prospect, but to be bound to an enemy who thought him a contemptible fool was unendurable, and that was the very thing Tor had proved himself to be. Never would the man have let him simply walk out the back door without taking precautions. Tor ought to have known this. And he was determined to redeem his reputation for cunning.

He worked for hours, his pulse thickening in his body and jarring his bruised, throbbing head. The weight of his sickness was returning, and he longed to cease working, knew he should cease working, knew even that the woodmaster would probably allow him to rest if he asked, yet he refused to humiliate himself by showing weakness to or asking favors of the man he despised.

At last the woodmaster tossed down his mallet and began to pull off the leather apron.

"Come," he said, walking to the back room. "Lay out the bread and cheese and herring." He himself took the metal pail sitting just inside the door and began to pour buttermilk into an earthen bowl.

The drunkard's boy obeyed the woodmaster's commands, then sat down and began to tear his bread apart with trembling hands. He sopped a large piece in the bowl of buttermilk the woodmaster placed on the table.

"Blessing," said the woodmaster curtly, standing over him and setting two cups on the table. He sank onto the opposite bench, muttered his short prayer and began to tear his own bread into pieces.

The meal was taken in silence until the drunkard's boy cast a glance at the woodmaster's face and found him looking at his prisoner's shaking hands.

"You will lie on the bed after this," said the woodmaster then, with as much curt authority as if he bade Tor kneel and scrub his boots.

The drunkard's boy did not answer a word, though his heart leapt with relief. Instead, he surreptitiously touched his knuckle to the skin below his nose, as he had done all morning and noon, to see that the bleeding had not returned.

When Tor finally eased himself into bed the woodmaster followed him. He tied Tor's hands, one by one, to the legs of the trundle bed on either side of Tor's head. The lengths of rope were so short that the drunkard's boy could not so much as reach his wrist to his mouth. He endured this ordeal with tight lips, staring at the wooden beams above him and reciting his catechism of hate for the woodmaster. Yet as soon as the woodmaster finished tying him and disappeared into the workshop he was taken by a sweet and heavy sleep.

❄ ❄ ❄

A sturdy knock was followed by the woodmaster's deep "Come in," and Tor's eyes flew open wide.

He was bound to the bed, the woodmaster was still in the workshop at the front of the house, and a visitor had just been invited to enter through the back door. It was an agony of humiliation. The ropes that bound Tor's wrists were in plain sight, and he could not even roll to his side to conceal his bruised face from the prying eyes of this busy-tongued villager.

In unnerving silence, the door opened behind him.

"*Herr* woodcarver!" called a sharp female tongue. "I have brought the salve."

"*Tack*," said the woodmaster, wiping his dusty hands on his apron as he came out of the workshop. He glanced at Tor, and the drunkard's boy knew instantly by his cool expression that he remembered very well that Tor lay bound and exposed to view and that he didn't care a straw's worth.

Shutting his eyes again, Tor promised himself rich retribution. Perhaps he'd take a hatchet to all those clocks in the shop.

The woodmaster took a large basket from the woman as she came up along Tor's bed, and he carried it to the table where he began to empty its contents.

"What is this, *Herr* carpenter?" asked the woman, turning her sallow, bright-eyed face to meet Tor's glare. She was not an old woman, but her skin was creased with wrinkles about the mouth and forehead, making her sharp, cross features look even sharper and crosser.

"Why 'tis the drunkard's boy!" she exclaimed, her thin, keen voice crackling with sudden glee.

Tor would have clipped out a scathing reply if he had not been loath to call further attention to himself when he was in such a pathetic and defenseless position. Instead, he turned his face away and contracted every muscle in his body for as long as he could before relaxing. A trick he had learned as a very small boy to cope with helpless anger.

"What mischief has he been into then? And were you so fortunate as to find the Nativity as well?" probed the woman.

How ironic, Tor thought. A village mother, the wife of the doctor, forsooth, had entered a house to see a boy tied to a bed and with bruises on his face and scars on his arms, and she had immediately supposed *him* to be the one guilty of wickedness. Not a thought given to the safety and well-being of the drunkard's boy. It was always so. Tor was ever the culprit, and the world would never care to hear his explanations.

"*Nej*," said the woodmaster, without looking up. "I found him freezing on the streets of Stockholm; now he has come to help me with my work."

The woman broke into a shrill laugh that caused Tor's startled eyes to fly open.

"And what sort of help," said she, "do you think to get from the drunkard's boy? He who has ne'er done a true day's work in his life but goes about pinching coins off honest men and stoning the chickens and teasing and provoking well-mannered boys to fight instead of going to school? I will tell you that in all my years in this village I have never known a more bullying, swaggering, insolent, slothful boy to walk these streets. It's plain he takes after his mother. Aye, they two be a pair: one wallowing in strong drink and the other skulking and thieving in the streets as their very daughter and sister lays at death's door!"

Tor's fury overcame his discretion then.

"Don't say a word of my sister," he hissed, twisting in his bed to look up at his tormentor with glittering eyes. "I did all I could to-" Here, he abruptly ceased speaking, for he glimpsed the woodmaster's gaze boring into him.

Tor turned his head, retreating from the sardonic grey eyes. The woodmaster would never hear him admit to stealing the Nativity even if it meant Tor could never explain his apparent neglect of Nanny.

Instead, the drunkard's boy whetted his tongue for an attack upon Noomi Hansson.

"And where were you, most pious of doctor's wives, all those long years when my sister was dying from suffocation? I've no memory of *you* ever darkening our door."

"*Tack* for the bread, Noomi Hansson," said the woodmaster suddenly, his voice quite close, interposing between Tor and the woman's second round of raillery. He was untying the bindings on Tor's wrists. "The boy and I have much work to do before the day passes. I look forward to seeing you in church this morrow."

"Don't bow *me* out of the house, *Herr* carpenter. I speak the truth: before the week is out the young devil will have pinched your very cupboards bare and run off. And not that you don't deserve it.

"T'was naught but pride that caused you to display such expensive pieces for all the world to see your wealth and the prized work of your hands. To them that boast of riches and skill, no good ever comes. Moreover, such a costly display was all the temptation this devil needed to discharge his worst vices."

"Good day, Noomi Hansson," the woodmaster said politely, pulling Tor off the bed by his upper arms and thrusting him toward the workshop.

"But stop!" cried the woman. "Where is the pink china plate that sits always on your mantelpiece? It is the last of the belongings of your dear, departed wife, is it not? It is gone! You know the boy must have taken it!"

"I have the plate, Noomi Hansson," said the woodmaster, his frigid tone causing Tor increased discomfort. "It is safely locked away. Good day."

He drove Tor before him into the workshop and shut the door.

The drunkard's boy was unreasonably relieved to be alone with the woodmaster again. His silence and changeless expression offered a measure of security. The man was an egotistical brute, of course, but in his presence Tor had to endure no stifled gasps, no heavenward rollings of the eyes, no dramatic facial contortions. The woodmaster might strike him with a heavy hand, but he would not subject him to eternal lectures upon his wickedness. He was stoic and mostly kept his thoughts to himself.

The drunkard's boy was made uncomfortable, however, by the woodmaster's silence regarding the plate. He couldn't think why the man had concealed his latest outrage from Noomi Hansson, but if the man thought this would make Tor any more compliant, make him despise the woodmaster any less, then he was mistaken. Indeed, the very notion of the man trying to obligate him was offensive. If he'd had a moment to consider it, he would have spat out to Noomi Hansson that he himself had broken the plate, utterly rejecting the man's silent protection.

Instead, here he was, taking up the planer as ordered to smooth the plank before him.

As he thrust the tool across the board a red spot appeared on the wood and he cursed. His nose had begun to bleed again.

CHAPTER SEVEN

Tor awoke to an unwelcome Sunday morning, again tied to his bed. He hated sleeping on his back, his stomach exposed and his arms helpless bedside his head; it had taken hours to drift off last night in this open, motionless position, while in the next bed the woodmaster's broad back faced Tor with what seemed to be mockery.

The drunkard's boy silently railed on him. Then, since the woodmaster had not bothered to tie his feet, he began to kick off his blankets with as much noise as possible. Next to him the woodmaster did not move. After several moments of silence Tor redoubled his efforts, convulsing his entire body backwards and forwards until the legs of his short bed screeched on the floorboards beneath.

The woodmaster's hand suddenly appeared and landed with a slap on Tor's stomach. The drunkard's boy stopped moving, but the hand did not remove itself.

"I need to go out," Tor finally said, sounding stiff as the plank of oak he had polished yesterday.

"That is unfortunate," said the woodmaster, sitting up, shoving off his blankets, and rising from the bed without looking at Tor, "for I would have untied you sooner if you had simply asked."

He went to the hearth and began to mend the fire.

Tor's jaw, still sore where the woodmaster had struck it, clenched.

"If only those good people who praise your lovely, holy singing in choir every week could see the bully you are. You are very clever. Truly, I don't think anyone in the village would ever guess how you act in your own house. What is it they say of your kind? A saint abroad and a devil at home?"

The woodmaster ignored Tor's outburst and continued to stoke the fire. Raging at this unflappability, Tor sharpened his verbal knives and spoke without taking time to think.

"Is that what became of your 'dear, departed wife'? Did you bully her too much for her nerves to bear? Or did you simply beat her to death?"

The woodmaster threw a stick into the fire and snatched a wooden spoon from a stone jar. He approached Tor, lifted him by the feet, and whipped him with the spoon.

More frightened by the intensity of the man's grip than by the sting of the spoon, Tor shut his mouth and forced himself to remain motionless until the woodmaster dropped him and once more moved about the room, making preparations.

It was some time, but sooner than Tor had expected that the woodmaster released him to go outside.

When he faced the house again to re-enter it, he was loath to return, though his eyes already smarted with cold. He turned over the top logs of the wood pile, arranging a dry place for himself to sit well within sight of the door—not wishing the woodmaster to think he was stupidly trying to run away—and sat still for a while, looking at the small tree twigs with their lacy edging of snow.

It was the height of injustice, the way the woodmaster treated him, and he did it from spite, pure spite. He didn't care that Tor had been forced to steal because his sister was dying and no one would help him. What right had he to be angry with Tor? What right had anyone? If they disliked how he behaved, then they should know it was their fault, for they had caused his behavior.

If his sister hadn't been sick and helpless, he wouldn't have stolen for her. If they hadn't made fun of him in school, he wouldn't have picked fights. If people hadn't been suspicious and looked down on him for his drunken mother and his dirty clothes, he wouldn't hate people. If his mother had cared more for him than for cheap liquor, she would have taught him to behave better, and he wouldn't have grown up cursing and shooting dirty looks and mouthing off to adults he didn't like.

It was their fault.

He kicked at a snowy log and watched it tumble down the side of the wood pile and sink into the soft snow.

How long, he wondered, should he wait before attempting another escape? He must wait till the woodmaster felt secure enough to allow him more "leash," as he liked to say. Tor would not then take the first opportunity that presented itself, nor the second, nor the third, nor fourth, nor fifth. He would have patience. He would choose a day when he was least expected to run away.

Yet, how should he behave meanwhile, to get the woodmaster to loosen his grip? Could he pretend humility and submission, pretend that he wished to pacify and even please the woodmaster? And supposing he did, would the woodmaster swallow such false bait?

Nej, not now. But he would in time.

The door of the house opened, and the woodmaster stood just inside, looking at him in silence. Tor muttered a foul word but pushed himself off the log pile and passed by the woodmaster into the house, keeping his eyes down.

"Eat quickly and wash yourself for church," said the man.

Tor started to speak, then stopped. He greatly desired not to go to the church, wished it so much that he was feign to recall the woodmaster's advice to him earlier, about asking for what he wanted rather than demanding. He fought within himself as he ate his breakfast of whey porridge, but it was some time before he mastered his pride.

"Will you let me stay back from church? I won't mind being tied to the bed."

"*Nej*." The woodmaster did not hesitate to answer, and the drunkard's boy threw down his spoon into the bowl with a clatter, cursing again.

"You've huddled outside the windows to hear the singing often enough," said the woodmaster abruptly. "You'll hear better inside."

Tor looked up with surprise.

"I have not," he snapped.

"Boy, if you don't wish people to know you for a liar, then don't tell them what they've seen with their own eyes is false," said the woodmaster sarcastically as he shrugged into his dark blue, embroidered, but rather threadbare vest.

Tor stared stubbornly at the empty trencher before him.

"No one will be wanting me there." He forced the words out.

The woodmaster said nothing but sat on Tor's bed to pull on his good shoes. Tor remained seated at the table, hoping that if he delayed long enough he might avoid the ordeal before him. Carefully, he began to brush up the crumbs of oatcake from the table and sprinkle them onto the trencher.

"Wash." The woodmaster's voice was unquestionably threatening.

A fountainhead of anger burst in Tor's heart. The same anger he felt every time the fat-faced school boys told him he was stupid because he couldn't read and mocked the way his toes slipped through his shoes when he walked; the anger he had felt every time he came home to find his mother, slack-jawed and snoring with a jug in her hand; the anger he had felt every time an honest tradesman told him he was a good-for-nothing no better than the parents he hated; the anger he had felt when his mother let her own daughter sicken because she couldn't lay off the strong drink in order to see her ailing daughter decently clothed and fed, no matter how Tor begged her and railed upon her; and the anger he had felt when he'd learned his sister had finally died, cold and alone, uncared for by the woodmaster and every man, woman, and child who attended that miserable church and looked at him through their self-righteous spectacles.

If Tor had not just then come perilously near to tears he might have thrown the bread knife at the woodmaster, but the knife would not kill the man, would likely not even touch him, and then Tor would rage. Then he would cry. And he would not be seen crying for the world.

Instead, he turned to the wash basin, shutting away all feeling, and scrubbed his stony face clean.

Great indeed would have been the astonishment of the entire village at the sight of the drunkard's boy striding alongside the woodmaster if the good Noomi Hansson had not already spread the news yesterday. Even so, there was much gawking and whispering to be endured by the drunkard's boy as well as the woodmaster, though that man's face betrayed no more expression than that of a great, lumbering ox.

Under almost any other circumstances, Tor would have rejoiced to see the heartless ease with which the woodmaster cut off all inquiry and comment concerning his new charge—even from the good-natured baker, Günter Nyvall, who was a friend of everybody.

But on this day, Tor could take pleasure in nothing. Furthermore, he could not help but be troubled by Günter Nyvall's reaction to seeing him. The baker, who was but a little taller than Tor, despite the boy's habitual stoop, stopped and stared at him with the frozen air of a dog caught in a flowerbed. Then he blinked and said, "Dear me!"

Tor instantly guessed that his nose was bleeding, but when he touched it, he found it dry. He glanced at the woodmaster for a hint at the source of the man's consternation, but the woodmaster was staring straight on with a hard eye.

"My dear friend," said the baker, suddenly cutting between the woodmaster and Tor and taking the carpenter's arm to turn him in the direction opposite the drunkard's boy.

"My dear friend," he repeated in low tones that Tor heard distinctly. "Do you not think it advisable—for both your sakes— that the lad be discharged to some master with whom he shares a less turbulent past?"

Tor saw the back of the woodmaster's head tilt up and heard

him take in a full breath which he expelled loudly.

"*Nej.* Who else do you suppose wants him?"

"It is quite apparent to me that you do not, Wilhelm. Since you were a child I have never known you to beat a person who was not a match for you." Here, Tor touched his still tender cheek bone as he wondered what sort of a bruise he had to cause the baker such anxiety.

His stomach curdled. Only a quarter of an hour since, he had believed no ordeal could be worse than to simply walk to church by the woodmaster's side. But he had not considered how supremely shameful it would be to tread this path with the marks of the man's authority on his face, visible to all.

The woodmaster muttered something to the baker which was too low to hear and then grasped Tor's arm and pulled him forward.

"You'll sit," he said, "up front with the baker's family until I come from the choir." He faced Tor and leaned close to him. "Remember, I can see you from where I stand, and you will answer to me for whatever you do. I'll take you to my pew after we sing."

Tor was too overwhelmed with dread to parley with his pride. To sit in the front pew while the choir sang, and then to turn and face the entire congregation when the woodmaster came to walk him back to his pew sounded very like death by suffocation. Involuntarily, he stopped and gripped the flap of the woodmaster's coat.

"Please, don't make me do that. Let me sit alone in your pew. I promise I won't run, I promise."

The woodmaster looked at him, grey eyes flickering with an expression too brief to be identified. He shook his head.

"You don't deserve it," he said, pulling Tor deeper into the church. The drunkard's boy walked forward, stoically staring at the carved pews glinting in the golden sunlight that phased through the stained-glass windows. Again, he dared not vent his anger for fear of revealing his distress. This spiteful man would force him to endure every possible torment he could devise.

Suddenly, the woodmaster shoved him to the side and pressed him down on a bench.

"Stay there," he said. "I am not above chasing you down in the midst of a hymn, and if I must, I will take you back up into the choir loft with me."

He departed, leaving Tor to discover that he had been seated in an empty pew towards the back on the far right of the church. Weak with unexpected relief, he leaned his forearms to rest on his knees and stared at the floor, avoiding the gaze of those around him.

No one, it was fortunate, disturbed him, yet despite his deep gratitude that he was not seated up front with the baker's family in view of the whole church—especially the mocking eyes of the pretty vicar's daughter—he felt the oppression of the village's curiosity and judgement more heavily in his solitary state. He set his teeth. He could see himself in the eyes of the villagers as a sort of skulking rodent, surly and snarling and ready to attack, but, like a rodent, he knew he was more vulnerable than venomous.

How was it, he asked himself, that he had ever come to be seated here, in the midst of the church of this hated village, the place which, of all other places, he desired least to be? Surely he could have avoided this humiliation. Surely, of all the other places in the world, he might easily have managed to be somewhere, anywhere else this Sunday.

He reviewed every movement and decision of his from the moment he'd seen the woodmaster in the Stockholm inn. How had the man succeeded in forcing him to such an extremity as sitting quietly in the midst of this detestable church? Couldn't Tor have escaped with ease by some clever scheme? He knew he was clever. How many countless times had he escaped from villagers or his mother when in a pinch?

But the woodmaster . . . the woodmaster had been a most brutally thorough jailer. He tied careful knots, created alarms that were treacherously simple, and bullied unscrupulously, allowing no peep-hole for even a street mouse like Tor to escape him.

He was resolved on keeping Tor locked like a block of wood in a vise while he leisurely revenged himself, chipping and carving the drunkard's boy according to his will.

Tor leaned his head on both hands and rubbed his temples as the choir began to sing. He heard the woodmaster's glorious bass sweeping across the church full of stolid villagers, and so insistently did it bear down upon him that he would have put his fingers in his ears had he not feared the man would come rushing down to unplug them.

Again Thy glorious sun doth rise,
I praise Thee, O my Lord;
With courage, strength, and hope renewed,
I touch the joyful chord.

Tor began a small, insignificant rocking backward and forward, moving purposefully out of rhythm with the tune that he might drive its cadence from his head. The song, when heard from outside the church behind the fir trees, was one of Tor's favorites, for the strident words could not be clearly distinguished from that distance, even on a silent winter's day.

On good and evil, Lord, Thy sun
Is rising as on me;
Let me in patience and in love
Seek thus to be like Thee.

Tor thought that the sun was not rising on him, never *had*

risen on him. Nor did God have patience and love. He was a cold, vengeful slave driver, something like the woodmaster. Tor continued rocking.

A hand gripped the back of his neck, and he glanced up to see the glowering face of Herr Lägerlof, the parish clerk, all round red cheeks, mutton chops, and protruding eyebrows.

"You will be still in this church, boy!" the man hissed.

Tor scowled but held still. He did not wish for the woodmaster to accost him next. Oh, how faithfully indeed these good Lutherans "sought thus to be like him in patience and in love." How quickly they all proved their lovely hymns to be meaningless.

The drunkard's boy refused to acknowledge the woodmaster when he sat beside him, except that he pressed closer to the partition in the middle of the pew, as far from the man as he could get. And then, after the vicar's first few words, Tor tried to block out the rest of the message, having no wish to hear the smiling, threadbare clichés that had so often grated his ears before.

"Almsgiving does not decrease your stores; going to church does not waste your time," Vicar Arnman quoted the words with all the infuriating rhythm common to a trite proverb. Tor jogged his knee up and down, deeply vexed.

He had gone to Vicar Arnman once from sheer desperation.

"My sister needs help, Vicar."

"Well, my boy," came the grave reply, *"if you and she had*

come to church regularly perhaps she would not be in such need. As the old saying goes, 'attending church does not ruin you.'"

"She's too sick to come!"

"Well, well, if you will run 'round to the kitchen door and speak to Sara she will find how best to help you."

"Tack, Vicar," Tor had said, trying not to show that he minded being shooed around to the back door like a dog, unfit to tread the vicar's fine rugs and wood floor.

Sara had opened to his knock, disapproval and suspicion already etched irrevocably upon her countenance.

"Vicar Arnman sent me; my sister is sick," muttered Tor to the very person he had hoped to avoid on this visit. Even the vicar's wife would have been better, for her prim and shuddering abhorrence of all things ragged and dirty often caused her to agree with reckless haste to any petition simply so she could escape. She would never visit Nanny, but she might give him money for a doctor to get rid of him.

"Wait there," said the cook after scathing him from head to toe with a squinting glare.

From hope that she had gone to fetch a cloak and bonnet Tor remained silent. Perhaps her hard looks would fall away when she beheld his grey sister shrunken to bones. But when Sara returned it was without bonnet or shawl. She bore only a basket, which she thrust into Tor's hands.

"A day's worth of bread. I never hand out more than that by

orders of Vicar Arnman himself. Those that are truly hungry won't complain of what they get nor mind making a trip every day. And mark you: the basket comes back this very night or I'll send out the konstapel!*"*

"But," said Tor, hugging the basket to his chest without even feeling it, "my sister needs medicine, badly. She will die! Doctor Hansson told me so. I need money for a doctor in Stockholm."

"Money!" sniffed the woman. "I'm sure you do! Money for your alcohol!

"I'll tell you this, boy, you'll get no money from this house to fritter away on the lusts of the flesh! Don't bother to speak to the vicar about it. I know what you'll *do with money."*

She shut the door.

Tor sped back to the front door to drum on the door knocker for five minutes. Ten minutes.

He had received no answer. The parlor curtains had been drawn gently closer together inside with a snow-white hand, shutting the drunkard's boy deeper into the growing darkness of eventide.

"For alms-giving does not decrease your stores," purred the vicar again with the complacent and gently admonishing smile of one who knows first-hand whereof he speaks. He stood very high in the pulpit, beaming upon his flock like a grandfather dispensing Christmas treats. But Tor looked upon the vicar's throne with the knowledge that the man would shudder to draggle his fingertips in the scum of a street urchin's life. He remembered how the man had run away for fear of contamination after Nanny's death.

He might direct tramps and vagabonds to his back door for the prescribed "day's worth of bread and no more," might send them off to *Herr* Lägerlof to stay in the almshouse for the night, might visit the homes of the poor to dispense stale bread and to catechize the children and admonish the parents to attend church more regularly, he might even visit a cold cellar to investigate a crime against one of his more well-to-do parishioners, but to personally waste his time in the sludge of their mucky circumstances was another matter, so it seemed. He built convenient dams and dug careful trenches about himself that the slough of the vulgar herd might seep quietly past and dribble through the proper channels down his set chain of command without contaminating the purity of himself and his good family.

Tor started at the touch of the woodmaster's hand on his jogging knee. Without looking at him the man whispered, "Be *still.*"

The drunkard's boy jerked his knee away and assumed a rigid paralysis, staring at the rounded ledge of the pew in front of him. In this attitude he remained to the last "Amen," refusing even to shut his eyes during the flowery benediction.

The woodmaster stood quickly upon the cessation of that

benediction and stepped from the pew, looking at Tor to indicate that he should follow. The drunkard's boy came to his side with the dourest of expressions, bracing himself for what he thought would be the final great ordeal of the day. Moving shoulder to shoulder with the crowd, he kept his eyes fixed on the smoothly worn floor and advertised hostility in every movement.

"Look, Jan! If it isn't the drunkard's boy back again!"

The voice carried the peculiar resonance of a boy well-accustomed to hurling snowballs and insults across winter fields in the midst of heated battle, and though he spoke only to the boy who stood next to him, he apparently found no reason to modulate his tone for the well-being of the eardrums in his vicinity.

"And with a beautiful new black eye, too! Try to steal the woodmaster's grandfather clock, drunkard's boy?"

Tor turned his bruised cheekbone away from the offensive gaze of the powerfully lunged boy as the rascal's mother scolded him into a more devotional tone. The woodmaster inched forward stiffly in the crowd, paying no attention at all to the insult. There seemed a painful eternity during which the congregation funneled out the rough pine doors of the church to alight into the snowdrifts like red, brown, green, and navy blue ducks spreading out across a placid white pond.

Tor waited silently till the bottleneck of the pine doors drifted him close to the pink-faced cobbler's boy, who had pulled his ears from his mother's pinching fingers and wormed forward through the crowd, all the while casting slurs in a barely moderated tone that was perfectly distinct to Tor's ears. By the time they reached the doors Tor stood two people behind the cobbler's boy, showing no response to the incessant insults other than an increased stiffening of his stooped back and a hardening of his features.

At his side, the woodmaster was well on his guard, casting repeated side glances at his prisoner through waves of thick hair as they exited the doors of the church. Yet despite his vigilance he was not prepared to forestall the lithe twist that propelled the drunkard's boy around the stolid couple before him and full into his enemy's generously proportioned shoulders.

Albin the cobbler's boy dropped like flaccid pork fat and screamed as though he had been seared on a hot griddle. A wide mouthful of soaking snow cut the horrible noise short. Tor was upon him immediately, wrenching his arm behind his back and hissing, "Fourteen years feeding on beefsteak and jam pastries and this is all you have to show for it, Albin?"

However, just as Tor was positioned to give Albin a fine black eye of his own, the woodmaster caught his arm and jerked him up. The drunkard's boy twisted and clawed at the woodmaster with sharp nails, directing his bony knees and elbows to all the most sensitive points. But the woodmaster laid Tor neatly out in the snow, just where Albin had lain only seconds before, secured his flailing, tearing hands, sat on him, and stared at his eyes in frigid silence.

Few boys could boast an eye as sullen as Tor's when he was in temper. He had learned to express all the variegated shades of vice possible to breed in the damp air of a rotting cellar, and when he turned his eye on the woodmaster the devil the villager's claimed lurked in his soul crossed over his hazel eyes and revealed itself in a flash of outrage.

There, laid upon on his back before the entire congregation, Tor met the woodmaster's stare, opened his mouth, and eructed all the profanity he had to command. At the first words, the woodmaster jerked back—though unfortunately without loosening his grip upon the boy's hands—as though struck. He regarded the drunkard's boy with as much horror, it seemed, as he was capable of feeling.

"Silence that boy!" roared a voice from the top of the steps.

Tor turned his curses and ugly glare in the direction of the imperious voice with the intent to scathe the ears of the man, but his voice died on his lips in the midst of a word.

It was the vicar who spoke, and beside him stood his daughter with her softly curling blonde hair and dark blue eyes. She stood at the top of the church stairs in her white fur cape, looking like an angel.

Tor allowed his eyes to close, concealing his despicable soul with the only means left to his disposal, and turned his bruised eye back into the snow. The woodmaster stood and pulled him up, only to be immediately accosted by the vicar.

"How could you allow him to speak such profanity on the very steps of our church?" he choked. "How could you simply sit there and listen to such execrations?"

"Because I was too surprised to move," growled the woodmaster.

The vicar seemed hardly to have patience to hear the woodmaster's simple explanation, so eager was he to get at Tor. He grasped the boy's face in a pale, twiggy hand far more powerful than it appeared to be and stared into his eyes ferociously.

"If you ever," he said, spitting like a savage cat, "speak such words before me again I personally will see to it that the rest of your days are spent in hard labor under the most loathsome conditions to be found.

"And now, Wilhelm, take this fiend back to your shop and whip him soundly so that he will remember it for as long as I shall remember those vile words ringing on the steps of my church!"

The vicar strode off, and his daughter followed him after casting one expressionless glance at Tor.

The woodmaster stared after the vicar's stiff little back with raised eyebrows as the rest of the villagers filed quietly past him. Then, clearing away the astonished expression from his face, he tightened his hold of Tor's coat. "Come, boy," he ordered, moving forward.

The walk home allowed Tor just enough time to develop a vigorous dread of his coming punishment. Usually, he feared physical pain but little because he was used to discomfort and because his great stores of anger distracted him from it, but the smooth-tongued, pious vicar had indeed frightened him with his rabid eyes, and also, the vicar's daughter had glimpsed the depths of Tor's perversion. At that moment, Tor himself saw his behavior in quite a vile light. His silent monologue from this morning about the true cause of his indecent behavior seemed to ring hollow now.

He felt that on this occasion his behavior might really have been inexcusable; he knew at least that a pretty, charming girl like the vicar's daughter was not likely to tolerate an excuse for such vile words as he'd spoken that day.

The woodmaster soon ushered Tor into his workshop and took out a fine, sturdy switch which he applied in good measure to Tor's seat as the boy stood motionless, leaning on the workshop table, wondering if this was truly all the punishment he was to receive. The woodmaster seemed to act without heat, as if he punished Tor merely out of duty and not anger; his attitude, indeed, seemed rather meditative as he struck the required lashes, very different from how it had been yesterday morning.

No sooner had the woodmaster tossed away the switch than a strident rap was heard upon the door.

"Stay," commanded the woodmaster, forestalling Tor's hasty exit into the back room.

It was the cobbler and his boy, Albin, at the door.

"My son," said the cobbler in loud, discordant tones, "is here for an apology! On the very steps of our church he was knocked down by that young devil, and I will not allow such behavior to go unchecked. I demand an apology, and if the drunkard's boy ever does such a thing again I will cane him bloody!"

The woodmaster leaned on the edge of the door with one burly arm stretching across the open doorway and looked over his shoulder at Tor loitering by the back room door.

"Come," he said after a moment, and he turned back to the cobbler.

"I will have you know, carpenter, that the vicar and I will not endure such behavior in our town. The boy is a festering infection that will contaminate our children. His like would ruin the whole community; you of all people should know this!"

The cobbler spoke with such rapidity that his syllables tumbled into each other till almost nothing could be heard but guttural, sputtering consonants. Albin shrank a little at his side.

Meanwhile, the drunkard's boy approached and stood sullenly before the open door. The woodmaster did not take his arm from its resting place on the door frame between Tor and the cobbler as he waited for the man to cease speaking.

"Well, boy? Apologize to my son!" said the man, concluding

his harangue at last in a climax of righteous fury.

The drunkard's boy, seething visibly, shifted his gaze from Albin to his father and said nothing.

"*Herr* carpenter!" cried the man in a threatening appeal to the woodmaster.

"Boy, are you sorry?" asked the woodmaster, turning his head in the general direction of his prisoner but fixing his eyes on some point of apparent interest on the shop wall.

"*Nej*," the drunkard's boy said, after a long, well-considered moment.

"You will apologize," said the cobbler, stepping up onto the threshold, "or I will-"

"Nils," said the woodmaster, moving close to prevent the man's entrance, "I will not force the boy into a lie, and you cannot bully me to do so. *I* apologize for his behavior; it was wrong. This is all the satisfaction I can give you. Tell me now, when does your boy intend to apologize to Tor and to the congregation for his rude and disrespectful outbursts in church?"

"You leave Albin to me," snapped the cobbler.

"Then leave *my* boy to me."

The woodmaster began to close the door.

"One moment, *Herr* carpenter!" shouted the cobbler, pushing against the door.

"Do not try to force your way into this shop, Nils. I do not answer to you," said the woodmaster. He shut the door and firmly bolted it.

Then he turned and saw Tor eyeing him with surly disbelief.

"Go on," he said, pushing the drunkard's boy towards the back room with deliberate roughness, "and let me have no more trouble from you!"

After a meal of herring, rye bread, and cheese the woodmaster lay down on his back beside the fire, rested his head in the crook of one arm, and stared into the flames. Tor shifted and glanced furtively at the door.

"Without my permission you will not leave this room," said the woodmaster, his voice unexpectedly sharp, belying the torpor of his posture.

For some hours the woodmaster dozed, and Tor lay on his bed, giving himself over to meditation as he stared up at greying rafters, trying to make out the detail of the rough-grain wood in the quick, glancing rays of firelight.

The woodmaster was not quite like the villagers, he conceded. The man was superior, just as Tor had always thought. He did not see as commoners saw, did not react dogmatically whenever startled with unconventional, or what others considered to be unacceptable, behavior.

And yet, Tor knew the woodmaster did not like him or desire the best for him. Today, the man had defended—or rather shielded —him from the cobbler, but all the while the woodmaster was clearly bent on taking his own revenge. It was plain that he intended to execute his punishment of Tor in a more painful and effective way than the villagers could.

Unable to help himself, Tor began to imagine what his life would be with the woodmaster if he stayed. Hard work he could be sure of. Dry words and dryer silence. Rigid justice, plenty of oatcake and whey porridge, a bed, good clothes, hard grey stares, an unyielding will, stout as an oak on the peak of a mountain. Church every week. And Albin's insults.

Nej, this was not the place for him, this village where no one would ever see him as anything but the drunkard's boy. He could not bear to be always put down "in his place," to endure constant reminders of and continual sneers for his lowly origins. Foolish, stupid peasants. He would show them his value one day. They would realize their mistake in discounting and belittling him.

But the remembrance of his display of profanity on the church steps gave him pause. That was not the sort of lofty behavior he imagined for himself. Of course, he had been sorely provoked, yet how unfortunate that the vicar's daughter had seen it all.

His mind wandered at the thought of the vicar's daughter. Why did she always make such a point of greeting him every time she saw him, saying his name with that mocking, saucy tone? As if he were some kind of joke that provided her with an endless reservoir of amusement. Tor could not tell whether she wished to humiliate or befriend him.

This question, however, was now irrelevant. She would not look at him again, and even supposing she would he intended to leave this village as soon as he might.

"Up."

Tor rolled his head to the side to see the woodmaster standing to his feet. Surely, he wasn't going to work in his shop on the Sabbath? Not with busy-bodies like Noomi Hansson creeping the streets. The drunkard's boy sat up warily to watch the woodmaster pull on his coat and scarf.

"Get your coat, boy," he ordered.

"Where are you going?"

Tor inquired much against his will, but necessity compelled him; he must be prepared against the horrors the woodmaster held in store.

"*We* are going to dinner."

"Where?"

"Isak Ahlberg's."

Isak Ahlberg's dwelling was not the last place Tor would have chosen. The man lived in near obscurity with his wife in a cabin by the sea. But Tor wished to see no one. For a moment he closed his eyes.

"Why?" he said, the word coming out harshly through his tight throat.

"Because. I said so."

"Can you not simply leave me alone?"

"Yes," the woodmaster said, throwing his blue coat at him, "I can. But I will not. Put it on, Tor." The man used his given name with marked emphasis.

The drunkard's boy struggled within himself, all the while knowing what he would do. The woodmaster had already shown that he was capable of inflicting the deepest humiliations upon him for any disobedience. Not only would Tor be mercilessly punished, but in the end he would be forced to go to the Ahlbergs all the same. Tor knew it was best to do as he was told without incurring further punishment, but he also knew his pride could not take much more strain before it snapped.

His shoulders hunched more stubbornly and sullenly than ever, he jerked on the blue coat, and they sallied out under the cover of darkness and Sabbath evening peace.

"Is it only the Ahlbergs will be there?" Tor demanded as they crunched over frozen slush between rows of candlelit windows. He was brooding suspiciously upon the evil possibilities before him. Heaven forbid the vicar should be in attendance.

But then, why would heaven forbid that?

"I know not," was the clipped reply.

They continued in silence, passing the wharf and moving further along the sweep of the bay. The shore line became more rocky presently, and they had some trouble to navigate the small slippery boulders. Tor was glad for sturdy new boots. There was a reason he scarcely ever came this way in winter: it was difficult to pick his way over the icy shoreline when his toes slipped easily from the holes in his shoes.

They rounded a bend in the mountainous, craggy shoreline and came upon the Ahlberg's secluded hut.

"Boy," said the woodmaster, pausing outside the twiggy fence marking the fisherman's vegetable bed, "if you misbehave in any way to Thea Ahlberg I *will* find an appropriate punishment. Am I understood?"

Tor nodded, gritting his back teeth and fingering the grizzled juniper branches that held together the rickety fence.

"*Ja?*" goaded the woodmaster.

"*Ja!*" Tor snapped, but as the wood-master turned to approach the front door Tor gave the fence a rather violent shove that bent it further than he had intended. The woodmaster rounded on him fiercely.

"I tripped!" shouted Tor, before the man could touch him.

The woodmaster studied his face.

"Then you must have a care in the house," he finally said, reaching over to pull the fence up straight. "Thea Ahlberg has been needing a new fence. That can be a project for your free time as soon as the ground thaws."

Tor had no time to snarl, for the door was wrenched open in that instant by the meaty hand of Isak Ahlberg.

"*Välkommen, Herr* woodcarver," called a bold, merry voice, "and the little fish."

It was sometimes difficult for Tor to recollect his various reasons for disliking one or other of the many villagers, but now he recalled that his motive for avoiding Isak Ahlberg was that he very much hated being called a little fish.

Furthermore, despite all the fisherman's show of friendliness, Tor knew that ever since he had stolen some of the man's herring a few summers ago, Isak Ahlbcrg had regarded him with the same dubious eye with which all the other villagers looked at him. The man was a hypocrite, pretending to be kind but really hating Tor as much as anyone else did.

The woodmaster stepped into the house with a heavy tread.

"Your garden fence grows weak, Isak Ahlberg; it would not take the little fish's stumble." Tor cast a surly glance up at the woodmaster's face, trying to determine if the man knew how much the fisherman's appellation vexed him.

"I will spare him at the first thaw to help you build a new one."

"Ah, you are too generous, Wilhelm, and you, little fish!" rumbled the fisherman. "But I trust I may be excused for taking advantage of your kind offer, for it is not for my own sake that I consent, but my wife's. She will not hear of me adding to my labors by restoring it. She insists upon doing it herself, though it is quite a task.

"You would be a great help, little fish," he added, tapping his pipe on Tor's head.

This pipe-tapping was another reason Tor despised Isak Ahlberg.

By now they had been ushered well into the small room where three other grown people sat by the fire and two boys of ten—twins—played with wooden boats on the hearth rug.

Günter Nyvall, the baker, nodded and smiled at them from his seat, but his wife leaned forward to whisper in her boys' ears. These twins immediately turned a curious eye upon Tor, and though the baker's wife returned to knitting without looking at the drunkard's boy, he knew well enough what the pith of her whispered words had been.

A pretty young woman with a heart-shaped face also sat by the hearth, knitting industriously as she studied the woodmaster through dark lashes. Tor did not know her, but he knew as soon as he looked at her that this girl had set her cap for the woodmaster, and when her eyes flitted to examine Tor he met them with a knowing stare.

The woodmaster had met this new girl before—it seemed she was a sister to the baker's wife—but Tor had to be introduced. When she said his name her mocking eyes informed him that she knew all the village could tell about him already, and he therefore allowed his moody stare to turn hostile.

The woodmaster, who seemed never oblivious to silent communication of this sort, immediately bundled Tor into a chair in a dark corner, placing himself as a buffer between the barbarous drunkard's boy and the civilized villagers.

Seated in his corner, cracking his knuckles, Tor stared at the heart-faced girl as she began to talk to the woodmaster.

"You've taken on quite a project, from all I've been told, *Herr* woodcarver," she said in a lively staccato, nodding at Tor. "Is it true that the scamp stole a very valuable work of art from you last month? Noomi Hansson said as much, but her good husband seems to think the evidence was inconclusive."

"*Ja*, it is quite an undertaking," said the woodmaster, ignoring her last comments, but gracing her with a rare smile.

"And you intend to rehabilitate him?" asked the girl, raising her eyebrows coquettishly.

The woodmaster did not speak for a moment, but looked at the twins playing on the floor.

"I will teach him a trade," he said, at last.

The girl laughed.

"So you don't have high hopes for his sanctification? I'm afraid I must agree with you. If one is to reform a child it needs be much younger than that." She nodded at Tor again. "I regret to say that this one looks set in its ways."

She smiled teasingly, but Tor saw a cattiness in her sparkling eyes, and he glared at her more intensely.

"I do admire your forbearance, *Herr*," she continued, turning back to the woodmaster. "I certainly could not do what you are doing. I'm afraid I am rather impatient, but you are kindness itself."

As she spoke, the girl looked straight into the woodmaster's eyes, but the moment she had finished speaking she glanced down demurely, as if his gaze put her to the blush. Tor saw the woodmaster himself redden just slightly and also look down to examine his coffee mug.

Oh, good Saint Peter, the man is already infatuated, Tor thought, shutting his eyes momentarily. The woodmaster was a stupid man, a stupid, foolish man if he let himself get taken in by that transparent little flirt, and he would see that soon enough if he married her.

And yet, Tor asked himself, why should I be bothered? Tor hated this man. At least if he married, the drunkard's boy would be rid of him, for there was no possibility that the catty girl would let Tor remain in her house.

At this time, the drunkard's boy was startled from his meditations by a sturdy, middle-aged woman in a pine green dress who accosted him with a series of frantic hand gestures.

From across the room, the ruddy, white-bearded fisherman chuckled at Tor around his pipe.

"I guess you are wanted, little fish," he laughed.

"What for?" asked the drunkard's boy, almost plaintively, eyeing the insistent Thea Ahlberg askance.

"Ooooh, who can know?" replied the fisherman with an air of extravagant mystery from his cloud of smoke rings. "Best not to

96

cross her though."

The woodmaster turned from his conversation with the pretty girl and spoke quietly to Tor.

"Go on, boy, and mind what I told you."

Gingerly, Tor stood and followed Thea Ahlberg towards the kitchen, glowering significantly at the watchful baker's wife as he walked an exaggerated circle around her twins.

Thea Ahlberg could not speak. She was a mute.

Yet she had many strong opinions which she seemed bound to communicate by all means possible, and for this reason Tor had never allowed himself within range of her vigorous hands before. He had seen how she silently accosted other villagers at the marketplace, dragging them bodily to her stall and thrusting her displays of fresh and pickled herrings into their hands. Not once had he allowed himself eye contact with her except at a safe distance for fear of suffering public humiliation. Yet now that she had him in her clutches, he knew he could never demean the mute woman by fighting her off with a snarl as he did other people, though he did walk stiffly as she guided him with strong hands on his stooped shoulders.

The prospect of entering Thea Ahlberg's lair was more

discomforting—if possible—than had been the prospect of entering the woodmaster's back room. At the woodmaster's house he could insulate himself with surly glares and bitter insults, but how could one bear to insult a woman who couldn't speak back? He knew instinctively that the forceful but childlike Thea Ahlberg would defraud him of the hostility he used to protect himself.

When at last he had made his way through the gauntlet of villagers and had stepped through the creaky kitchen door, Tor found himself looking into a room that seemed alive. The very air shimmered with activity. Steam rose from boiling kettles on one side of the room, and sprinklings of flour, as if from the gust of a snowstorm, covered a table and drifted lightly over the floor on the other side. Rich smells, both sweet and savory, tingled in the room. Snatches of brilliant color, whether from a blue cabinet, a red bowl, or a yellow stool, were scattered throughout the room.

Thea Ahlberg led him to the floury table where sat a great earthen bowl hosting a fat lump of brown dough. She snatched off a portion of this lump with her usual vigor, slapped it upon the table, and began to roll it out flat. The dough smelled of lush spices that Tor only recognized from times when he had passed the baker's shop or the vicar's house or some other opulent household.

Presently, as he watched Thea Ahlberg's deft hands in timid fascination, she began to nudge him and nod towards the bowl of lump. Tor could feel himself blushing. He touched the brown dough with the barest shy glance at Thea Ahlberg. She nodded more emphatically and motioned him to the other end of the table while she threw out a flurry of light brown flour on the surface before him. Then, without a warning of any kind, she seized his hands one after the other and rubbed them between her own rough, dusty ones till his were equally floury.

She again motioned him towards the lump of dough in the glazed earthen bowl, seemingly intent that he should take some in his hands. He obeyed her unspoken wish, accepting the straight little wooden rolling pin that she thrust at him to flatten the dough.

As he meekly began to roll the dough he could not help thinking he was behaving like a nervous sheep being driven about by the brisk nips of a bright-eyed sheepdog. Meanwhile, he watched surreptitiously as Thea Ahlberg took a round piece of metal like a shallow cup with the bottom cut off and cut the dough into cookies. The cutter was scalloped so that the cookies looked like flowers.

The knowledge then broke upon Tor that he was being inducted into the secrets of *pepparkakor*, and he watched with rising anticipation and dwindling discomfort as the mute woman peeled up the raw cookies and tossed them deftly on a thin metal sheet.

Tor was still finishing his task of rolling the dough when Thea Ahlberg took the metal sheet across the room and placed it into a large, foreign container that Tor, in his nerves, had not yet noticed.

It was a great box, all coal-black metal, with many groves and slits cut in and a long black pipe rising to the roof and apparently reaching right through it like a chimney. There was a large cast-iron pot upon the box, frothing with bubbles and steam.

The black box, Tor could guess, was an oven and stove, something seen only at the bakery and in the houses of the well-off—which did not generally include rough fishermen.

Tor recalled that it was noised about town that Thea Ahlberg was of a very well-to-do family. Her forceful character and embarrassing handicap had made the family willing to marry her off to the only man who asked for her hand: a humble but sturdy young fisherman named Isak Ahlberg who had helped to navigate their family tour of the Baltic isles years ago and who had fallen wildly in love with the pert brunette from the first day he had seen her.

That was a fairy tale Tor had always viewed with suspicion. Yet now, as he cast a swift glance around the room, his eyes lingering on several odd contraptions and his mind burning with curiosity to examine them, he felt he could believe almost any fairy tale of Thea Ahlberg.

The woman rose from bending by the black box, and Tor forced his attention back on the brown dough in his hands.

Thea Ahlberg moved about the kitchen for some time, coming

by occasionally to nod at his work and pat more flour onto his hands or to frantically sweep flour away when he used too much. Inwardly, Tor shrank from her nearness and intrusive touch, but he was unwilling to show his discomfort, not only for reasons of pride, but also because his mind connected her with Nanny. Her handicap made her vulnerable, just as Nanny had been, and he feared hurting the woman inadvertently.

As he worked, gradually becoming accustomed to the strange and busy atmosphere of the kitchen, Tor snatched a moment amid the bustle to wonder why Thea Ahlberg had insisted upon his help, particularly when two able-bodied women sat in the house. Did she not know he was a troublemaker? His thoughts were interrupted by the woman suddenly pouncing upon him—causing a freshly cut cookie to fly from his hand across the table and to the floor, where it in turn was pounced on by a prowling calico—and dragging him away to sit in a corner with a plate of cookies and mug of coffee on his lap.

Having seated him, she stood over and observed him with profound intensity. Tor realized that he was expected to taste the *pepparkakor*. Embarrassed, he conjured a wan smile and picked up the soft, warm treat that he had tasted only three times before in his life.

It was delicious, the flavor spicy and deep, the texture still chewy, but just crisping on the edges. Tor had never tasted warm *pepparkakor*. Cool and crunchy from the Christmas charity baskets they had been delicious, but warm, they were better than anything Tor had imagined.

The drunkard's boy looked up at Thea Ahlberg, and she smiled at him, showing dimples and laughing eyes that looked uncannily wise, as if she knew his thoughts and had known them since the moment she'd ambushed him in the sitting room, as if she had been making merry within over his discomposure and silly fears. She ruffled his shaggy hair with both hands and bent to plant a kiss half on his hair and half on his forehead.

Tor was deeply abashed by the caress, but he also felt warm in his heart when he looked into Thea Ahlberg's eyes—hazel, like his, he noted. It seemed to him they lit up the whole room.

He ate another cookie to hide his embarrassment, and the woman hurried away to see to the pot that was bubbling over.

After finishing the cookies, Tor gathered his courage sufficiently to edge about the room and inspect the food preparations and other objects of interest, and he presently found himself peering over Thea Ahlberg's shoulder as she dropped balls of dough into the bubbling soup. She smiled and lifted the ladle high enough from the soup to reveal fish and dumplings swimming in the broth. Tor breathed in with appreciation and, edging around Thea Ahlberg—rather aghast at his own audacity —took a lump of dough to drop in the pot himself. She smiled and nodded all the more energetically.

It was as he bent over the pot next to Thea Ahlberg, dropping sticky balls of dough into the soup while she stirred, that the door opened far enough to admit the hulking figure of the woodmaster. Shutting the door behind him, the man gave Tor a cursory glance before nodding to Thea Ahlberg.

The warm room, which had seemed alive with merry sounds and scintillating spices grew stuffy and stale.

Tor pulled away from Thea Ahlberg and her soup pot and wiped his sticky hands on his trousers. He departed to lean sullenly against the wall by the back door in silent objection as the woodmaster walked up to take his place next to the woman. Nevertheless, as the drunkard's boy watched their interactions, he was fascinated by the slow, deliberate movements of the woodmaster's hands. The man asked wordless questions of Thea Ahlberg, to which she replied with quick motions indicating a soul of great volubility.

The woodmaster chuckled as she pulled another pan of *pepparkakor* from her black box and, sliding the cookies onto a plate, thrust them at him. Tor tried not to be jealous. It was too ridiculous and quite beneath him. Why should he feel that this woman, whom he had always avoided and mistrusted, was betraying him by her interest in the woodmaster, his mortal enemy?

"Keep a watch on him, *Frü*. Don't let him steal too much *pepparkakor*," said the woodmaster, glancing dryly at Tor as he bit into a cookie.

To any other boy, this might have been an innocent enough remark, but for Tor it shattered the fragile fairyland of the kitchen, making him recall the suspicion and injustice he could not escape.

With a glare at the woodmaster he quickly wrenched open the back door of the kitchen and walked out, slamming it hard behind. He began to stride angrily through the snow, but he could not get far before the door opened and the woodmaster called after him to stop.

The drunkard's boy knew he should stop, knew that he could not get away, but he was too angry to heed reason. Taking a beating would be infinitely preferable to voluntarily submitting to the woodmaster. He began to run.

He barely heard the squeak of the snow beneath the man's boots before he was thrown to the ground and tightly collared.

Pinned on his back, he glared at the woodmaster.

"If you think me such a wicked thief," he yelled, "then why do you let me into your precious Thea Ahlberg's kitchen?"

The woodmaster choked his voice with a deft twist of his hand. Tor longed to scream and fight, but the woodmaster only twisted his collar tighter the more he squirmed. For a time, the woodmaster held him pressed to the ground, looking at him with the impassive eyes that had grown so hateful to the drunkard's boy.

Then the door opened behind them, shedding a pool of faint light across the snow, and Tor shut his eyes.

"Wilhelm," said a clear, twittering voice, "are you well?"

"Careful not to show your temper to the lovely lady," Tor sneered. His words were choked out as the woodmaster pressed his knuckles closer to the boy's throat. Despite the discomfort, the drunkard's boy managed to smirk at him.

"*Ja,*" the woodmaster said, not moving from Tor and not looking at the girl.

"Pray, don't kill the child." The voice held strong hints of teasing laughter.

"No fear," muttered the man, though his hand relaxed a bit.

"I do hope you'll be joining us for supper?"

"Perhaps." The woodmaster gave no indication of moving off Tor's stomach.

"Well," said the voice, its chirp just a touch sharper, "I shall leave you to your very important business, then. Pray, don't spend all night. I do hope to see you before I depart."

The door finally closed.

Thick, mushy snow seeped through Tor's blouse to his bony back.

When they had remained still long enough for the chattering of Tor's teeth to become more than perceptible, the woodmaster spoke.

"If you can redeem yourself by good behavior during supper, I will not punish you when we return home, but if you don't intend to behave tonight we will see to your whipping now."

"You take every chance to bully me, don't you? I've done nothing deserving of a whipping. You will do it simply because you enjoy it."

"You tried to run away again," the woodmaster coolly replied.

"You have no right to call me a thief and make me your slave!" said Tor, spitting like a cat.

The woodmaster sighed and rolled his neck slowly from shoulder to shoulder, allowing the silence and discomfort to grow.

"What is your decision?" he finally asked.

The drunkard's boy considered replying that his decision was to burn down the woodmaster's shop, but when he realised what might be the consequences of that statement he remained silent.

"Well," said the woodmaster, "I suppose we will stay here till you decide. I daresay I am more comfortable than you are."

Tor shut his eyes and breathed. Sodden clumps of snow dropped quietly from the trees about them. Faint laughter bubbled in the cottage. Were they mocking him?

He was soaked with freezing snow now, and the pressure of the woodmaster's weight, which made breathing difficult, was increasing from discomfort to pain, and no matter how hard Tor clenched his teeth he could not stop their chatter. Once more, the woodmaster's silent obstinacy, strong as ever despite the sting of the cold, subdued him.

"I will go home and take the whipping," mumbled Tor, staring at the buttons of the woodmaster's jacket.

"*Nej*," replied the woodmaster, firmly. "If a whipping is your choice we'll have it here before we go inside and take supper."

Tor raged at this injustice; he was being baited like a circus bear. He could not escape going inside. It was either public humiliation or public humiliation preceded by a whipping.

"I hate you," he whispered, finally looking the man in the eye.

The woodmaster said nothing but looked at Tor with that impassive surveillance which Tor used to admire so much.

He remembered the first day he had stopped at the woodmaster's new glass window and looked in at the shop. The woodmaster had bidden him step inside and, watching him with quiet interest, had given ready, succinct explanations in reply to Tor's questions as he handled the carvings.

Then the woodmaster, like everyone else, had come to regard Tor with a darkening brow. He, like the others, had ceased to care about Tor's thoughts and his side of the matter when he got into fights with the pink-faced village boys.

What irony that he who had once been Tor's ideal had now become his chief persecutor. It seemed the definition of Tor's existence, that all his greatest hopes brought his deepest miseries.

His teeth clacking uncontrollably, the drunkard's boy turned his gaze away and shivered for a minute longer. The horrible sweating cold and the weight of the woodmaster on his stomach made him feel sick.

"Please, please, just let me go," he said, succumbing to the very depths of disgrace.

"*Nej.*"

Tears of rage threatened now. His time was short: he must must get out ot this predicament before he shamed himself.

"I will go in to supper." He kept his voice a stiff whisper to keep it from trembling.

The woodmaster grasped Tor's right forearm with his left hand and pulled him up from the ground. He brushed the snow roughly off Tor's head, shoulders, and back while the drunkard's boy stood passively, shivering and loathing his touch. Then they went inside, walking quietly through the kitchen to the room where the guests sat, some seated round the table, others by the fire holding their soup bowls in their hands.

Thea Ahlberg whirled round to look at him from where she stood, tending to the voracious appetites of the saintly twins seated at the table with their guardian angel of a mother, but Tor did not look at anyone. It was all he could endure to imagine how they were all staring at him and his soaked blouse and shivering body. He remembered again his black eye, a mark of profound disgrace, though probably no more dramatic, he thought bitterly, than the trail of melting snow dripping from his soaking hair and back.

The woodmaster made him sit on the hearth beside his own chair. The warm fire provided a brief but welcome distraction to Tor, even though its closeness reminded him of the throbbing pain of his burns from last week.

On the other side of the woodmaster, the pretty girl spoke in her light, staccato twitter.

"I must say, Wilhelm, that though I greatly admire your charity towards the boy I do wonder how on earth you're going to manage him. As I said, I really fear there can be no mending of his wicked ways now." Her tone had fully regained its playful mockery.

"I've told him before if he can manage to get away from me he's full welcome," said the woodmaster, in a manner that seemed somewhat sour for talking to a pretty girl.

"Well, perhaps if God will not make him good and obedient he will make him clever and quick," returned the girl, her banter like the clawed slap of a soft kitten's paw.

Thea Ahlberg, who had just placed a bowl of soup in the woodmaster's hands, straightened up with a sharp movement. She stood still a moment, but Tor did not look to see her expression. What he noticed more was the sudden stiffness of the woodmaster's voice when he replied.

"I suppose the Almighty will do as He likes . . . just as always."

The room paused, as if everyone were trying to find something else to look at or say. Tor wondered what unspoken message they had all heard in the woodmaster's words that caused them such discomfort. The man's tone had been almost bitter.

Thea Ahlberg alone seemed unphased by those words as she returned to press a soup bowl into Tor's hands. His first instinct was to strike the soup away, and perhaps if any other person had handed it to him he would have done, but to do so would offend and humiliate the mute woman, and with a thought of Nanny in his mind Tor accepted the soup without looking at the giver. He immediately laid it down, however, and would not touch it the rest of the evening.

He was surprised that the woodmaster did not order him to eat. Instead, the man seemed intent on forgetting his presence if not his existence and devoted all his energies to sudden lively conversation with the rest of the company, especially the girl with the heart-shaped face.

Tor considered tricking the woodmaster into taking him away by creating an appalling scene. Many times had Tor out-witted his elders, using bad behavior as leverage to hoist obnoxious Christians from his presence or to hoist himself from theirs, but as he watched the woodmaster from the corner of his eye, observing his penetrating gaze and smooth, calculated movements, he realized the plan would fail. The woodmaster knew Tor wanted to be out of the Ahlberg's house, which meant he would keep the boy there as long as possible. Already, he understood Tor too well.

The rest of the evening seemed merry with games and lively

discussion. Firelight played over the semi-circle of round, laughing faces and the gleaming white hair of the twins sprawling once more across the hearth rug. All unpleasantness seemed to vanish as a dark vapor when Thea Ahlberg brought out the *pepparkakor*, and perhaps everyone even managed to give as little heed as they seemed to the black-eyed boy huddling on the hearth in the shadow of the inflexible woodmaster.

Yet behind the door of the kitchen Tor sometimes glimpsed the bright eyes of the mute Thea Ahlberg looking out at him with helpless vexation.

CHAPTER EIGHT

April, 1853

"This board is rough. Did you plane it at all?"

Tor mentally cringed at the woodmaster's voice, though he regarded the man with a belligerent eye.

"I don't suppose a dead man will care for a little thing like a splinter," he sneered, glancing at the coffin board in the man's hand.

"But perhaps you may," said the woodmaster, throwing the board at Tor so that he was forced to catch it before it hit his chest.

Slivers of the rough wood slid into his palms, calloused though they were, and he winced.

"Smooth that," said the woodmaster, "so the next time I throw it to you you'll take no splinters."

Tor picked up the planer and ran it heavily over the board, his heart sickening with the familiar sensation of endless drudgery. Two months he had been with the woodmaster, mercilessly compelled to do the man's will in everything and guarded so resourcefully that he had not even dared to attempt an escape yet.

Each day was much like the last: cutting logs, sweeping the floor, planing boards, cooking porridge, all tedious, repetitive chores. The only variation in his days came with the creative punishments invented by the woodmaster in return for Tor's frequent misdemeanors.

"If you cannot do small tasks well, you will never do anything well," said the woodmaster, tossing back the hair from his eyes and taking up his hammer.

"And if the task isn't worth doing?" muttered Tor.

"You should know whether it's worth doing," replied the woodmaster between hammer blows. "You are the one who caught the splinters."

"Am I to blame if I have a working brain that asks me why I would spend an hour ensuring a dead man doesn't catch splinters?"

The woodmaster reached for nails and looked at him.

"Not a very hardworking brain if that's all you've found to think of for the last hour," he said.

"*Nej*, I've been wondering in general what kind of dull, useless minds some people must have to make them want to waste their time with such a great many useless rules and practices."

"Such as making sure coffin boards are perfectly smooth?"

"Exactly."

The woodmaster bit two nails firmly between his teeth.

"And are you so much better and cleverer than the rest of the world, Tor? To tell all the important rules from the unimportant?"

Tor pressed all his weight against the planer and ground down as hard as he was able on the board.

"*Ja*, I am," he said. "If only because I am not a hypocrite like the rest of you, pretending that going to church and blabbing proverbs make you good Christians. You and your pious Vicar Arnmans and Noomi Hanssons and your 'well-bred' Albin Ovarsson. At least I don't take a boy to church on Sundays and then beat him black and blue during the week."

"*Ja*," snarled the woodmaster suddenly, "holy little creature that you are, you prefer to break windows, steal others' most valued possessions, and then lie about it."

"I never did that," muttered Tor.

The woodmaster made no reply but began to hammer the pinewood coffin furiously, indicating he was finished talking. It had been a mistake, Tor admitted to himself, to deny the theft again. It always put the carpenter in ill-humor and made him refuse to speak.

Tor relished any occasion when he could get a rise from the woodmaster. Not the kind of rise that ended with a black eye, of course—though after their first week together, the woodmaster had seemed doggedly determined not to lay a hand of violence on Tor again—but the kind where the woodmaster lost his patience and began to speak his mind. It was the only diversion the drunkard's boy could expect these days, and even though the man's opinions were all highly unflattering to Tor, the drunkard's boy was fascinated by his way of speech. He enjoyed the man's keen leading questions and subtle irony; they roused him from his monotonous thoughts and gave him energy when he was tired.

"When you've done with the board, go make supper," said the woodmaster coldly.

Tor pretended to ignore the man but was careful to ensure that the board was free of splinters, for he wanted no more in his hand that day. Then he went through the back room and walked outside behind the cottage to collect firewood. As he gathered wood in his arms he noticed the "idiot" child sitting amongst the bushes behind her house and sniffling in the twilight. She wore no coat. Tor slackened his movements, eyeing her ambivalently. He paid her no heed until he was ready to re-enter the house. Then he found himself stopping, turning, and ambling over to the clump of brush where she hid.

She stopped sniffling and looked up as her came near.

"Are you well?" he asked stiffly, staring at the red mark on her cheek.

The child shook her head no, biting her lip and blinking so that several more tears spilled down.

Tor glanced back at the woodmaster's house, wondering how long until his usual five minutes were up.

"Do you wish to help me make potatoes?" he asked, feeling foolish.

She nodded, immediately standing up and grabbing a fistful of his blouse in lieu of his hand, and he walked back gingerly with her to the woodmaster's house, wondering what would come of this strange predicament.

Inside, he sat on the hearth with his load of wood and handed her a log.

"Put it in the fire carefully," he said. "The fire is very hot. It could burn you, see?" He dropped the logs to the ground and rolled up his sleeves to expose the scars from his own burns two months ago.

Her narrow eyes grew big, and she pulled up one of her sleeves to expose a thick red scar of her own. Tor nodded gravely, stroking his finger over the scar.

"*Ja*, very hot," he repeated, "so be careful."

She suspended the log gingerly over the fire with a charming clumsiness and dropped it while it was still a forearm's length away from the dying flames. Sparks flew with the crash of the log, some landing on Tor's bare arms, but he did not notice them as he pulled the child away from the fire. He brushed her skirt and apron somewhat ruefully as his gaze fell on the small burns from the sparks, hopefully, he thought, not too noticeable.

"We must be very, very careful," he said. "The fire likes to trick us. You must be soft as a cat."

He took a log, laid it with exaggerated stealth over the embers, and gave it a pat of approval, shushing it with one finger to his lips at the same time.

"You see we must be smarter than the fire," he said wisely. He felt rather silly, but she had covered her mouth with both hands and begun to giggle at his pantomime, jumping up and doubling over with an encouraging display of mirth.

In the next room, the woodmaster's hammer played steadily, giving no indication that he heard their party. The very tone of the hammer seemed to suggest a tranquil engrossment that Tor rarely sensed in the woodmaster when they were together. He grimaced, aware that the man appreciated the reprieve from Tor's presence quite as much as Tor appreciated release from him.

"Come, help me cut the potatoes," he said to the little girl, casting thoughts of the woodmaster away. This was his hour of freedom when he could be something else besides a brooding, snarling street rat of a drunkard's boy.

This opportunity to act freely in the presence of another human being who would not judge him for his ancestry and anemic appearance and poor education was an unexpected pleasure to him. He guided the child's hands very carefully as they cut the potatoes.

"Why did someone hit your face?" he asked.

"I broke the milk jug and made a mess over the floor."

"Oh. Do you get hit often?" Tor knew little of the Karlssons. They seemed to keep well to themselves.

He had gone to school with Marta's clubfooted sister, Klara, for years, and they'd never once spoken. She and Tor were both reticent outcasts, but the schoolmaster detested Tor as much as he favored Klara, and Tor consequently disliked Klara. He wondered if the clubfoot girl would hit her sister. Klara certainly seemed morose.

"Sometimes," the child replied with simple veracity.

Tor felt his muscles tighten without his bidding. He himself felt a cuff as nothing. He was used to pinches, whippings, even blows, but he recalled now the feeling he had when he saw his mother slap Nanny and he had been too small to intervene.

Nanny. The very word seemed to physically affect him. He thought of how she used to try to stifle her coughs when he came through the door; thought of how intently she used to study his countenance, looking for hints of pleasure, pain, or anger; thought of how she used to nestle against his chest, thin fingers like bird claws curled under her chin.

"They should not hurt you," Tor muttered to Marta, snapping the knife through a thick potato.

The child, who was kneeling on the bench by the table while he stood behind her to help her cut, turned and studied him. He avoided her eye and frowned at his potatoes, but she laid a hand on his cheek and mouth, startling him.

"Be happy," she said, in her strange, slurred way. Tor did not move away from her touch, but he continued to avoid her gaze. He tossed the potato chunks in a bowl and clumsily patted her hair.

"All is well," he said. "Help me cut the potatoes."

They finished the potatoes and put them in a kettle to boil while they laid out cups and a plate and cut cheese and smoked goose.

Tor asked her simple questions about her favorite color and favorite food and favorite story, but when the potato pot began to boil she rushed to the hearth and sat, staring with round-eyes at the boiling water, mesmerized except for when she suddenly clapped and broke into excited giggles that shivered her entire body. She would not heed any more questions. So the drunkard's boy sat and stirred the pot and watched her laugh with a wry, dark smile on his own face.

She laughed more and clasped her little hands together when Tor spooned out the chunks of potato and showed her how to mash them with a large wooden spoon.

He was divided between her gleeful antics and his own quandary of how to send her home without making her cry when the door opened and the woodmaster appeared. He stopped halfway into the room and stared at them for a moment; then he called to someone over his shoulder.

"Never mind, *Frü*, she is in here."

"Oh, thank heaven!" a woman's voice replied, and in a moment the girl's mother bustled through the door. "Marta!" she cried, upon seeing them, "you naughty child, what have you been doing?"

She bore down upon them in the full sail of her long skirt and snatched the girl away from Tor roughly, turning her back on the drunkard's boy to place herself between him and the child.

"I'm cooking potatoes!" laughed the child, clapping her hands again.

Tor looked down and began to mash the potatoes vehemently.

"Perhaps you should keep a better eye on that boy, *Herr* carpenter," said the woman frigidly as she swept out the door. Tor was left in silence with the woodmaster, the wails of the child still quavering in his ears.

"What did you do with that child?" asked the woodmaster, quietly shutting the door to the shop.

Tor remained silent, smashing the potatoes again and again until they began to fall off the plate.

"Why was she here?" the man asked again, his voice growing dangerous.

"Why should I answer you when you will believe what you like of me, never mind what I say?"

"You should answer me because I will punish you if you do not," said the woodmaster, clearly working to prevent his voice from rising.

"I taught her," said Tor acidly, "to cook potatoes, and I listened to her tell me how she gets slapped when she drops things.

"Her favorite color is pink, and she likes to eat cloudberry jam and Christmas cakes better than anything else, and now," said Tor, his voice rising with a fury of insulted pride at the woodmaster's groundless inference that he would mistreat a child, "would you like your supper, *master?*"

He grabbed a great spoonful of smashed potatoes and slung them at the woodmaster. With a miserable splat they fell on the floor, just short of the man's feet.

Tor stood still; he did not try to run this time. He wanted to, but he could not bear the thought of the woodmaster once more wrestling him to the floor. His proximity would be an abhorrence. That he should have such a low and unjust opinion of Tor made him sick to the back teeth.

"We don't waste in this house," said the woodmaster, walking to his bed and sitting down to remove his boots. "That can be your supper."

"I am not hungry," Tor snarled, turning to the fire to take the kettle from its hook.

"Best to eat it now while it's fresh," said the woodmaster, "for you'll not have another bite till that floor's licked clean."

Tor set the kettle on the hearth and took the plate of potatoes from the table.

"Then you may lick it clean yourself," he said, dropping the plate upside-down on the floor. He turned away, leaving the woodmaster to stare in silence at the mess.

Tor had not gotten furious enough to defy the woodmaster so blatantly in weeks, thanks to the man's penchant for publicly humiliating him.

Last month at the church, Tor had called Noomi Hansson a vile name after she said he was not fit to be in the company of well-behaved children—meaning, of course, the pink-faced school boys—and the woodmaster had gagged him for the entire journey back from church, and he had not released the boy till they'd entered his house again. Tor had immediately burst out with a storm of insults, and the woodmaster in turn threatened to make him go, gagged and bound, to supper at the Ahlberg's cottage, where it seemed they two were pledged to appear every Sunday evening.

Since that time, Tor had managed to keep the smoldering embers of anger in abeyance, allowing only his silent eyes to communicate animosity. He wondered sometimes how he had endured the woodmaster for so many weeks and wondered more often how he could possibly go on in this way. Not for more than five weeks, it would seem. Certainly not indefinitely.

His attention returned quickly to the woodmaster, who had stood up from the bed and was now approaching him. The man was like a huge, shaggy, lean lynx; his movements were fluid, and sinew and muscle flexed visibly under the taut shoulders of his blouse. Militant and almost fascinated, the drunkard's boy forced himself to remain still and watch the predatorial approach.

"Tor Neeson," said the woodmaster, grasping him by his shoulders and driving him backwards across the room until he was flush against the wall, "do you want to go to prison? Do you want to be starved on maggoty porridge, beaten and worked to a skeleton by day, and caged with wet mold and vermin and perverted men every cold night?"

Tor stared at him, stunned by the unexpectedly descriptive threat. He thought of asking how the woodmaster would send him to prison when he had never stolen the Nativity, but he dared not, knowing the woodmaster would take his words for the challenge they were.

Suddenly the man shouted, "Answer me!"

"*Nej*," Tor said, looking away. "I mean, *nej*, I don't want to go to prison," he added when the man's grip tightened on him.

"Then pick those potatoes up," whispered the woodmaster, "and do not ever throw such a fit again." He turned from Tor and moved away tensely, running a hand back through his blond mane. As Tor cleaned up the potatoes the woodmaster readied himself and went to bed without taking supper.

For the first time, he did not tie Tor to his bed, and the drunkard's boy lay awake wondering if this was because he was daring Tor to escape or if he had simply made a mistake and forgotten. Or was it because, driven to the end of his wits, he actually wanted to be rid of Tor?

CHAPTER NINE

The woodmaster was up early the next day, seeming so free of ill-humor that Tor suspected the man did after all intend to send him to prison. When they sat to breakfast, each fully devoted to his own bowl of steaming porridge, which had been sweetened with a rare treat of brown sugar and ground cinnamon, the woodmaster observed that the weather had grown warm enough for the ground to thaw. He looked meaningfully at Tor.

The drunkard's boy sought to remember why this should be of significance to him, but he could only think that the snow had melted enough to keep him from being easily tracked or from freezing when he ran away.

"I want you," said the woodmaster, "to go and help Thea Ahlberg to build her new garden fence. I told her you would come this week if the weather kept fair."

Tor's heart started a rapid beat. He studied the woodmaster, who stood and took his bowl from the table.

"Now?" He wanted to add, "and alone?" but he had no desire to appear eager.

"*Ja*," said the woodmaster. "You may stay to supper if asked but be back directly after."

Tor spooned down his porridge and went to don his coat and scarf, calculating quickly whether he might dare smuggle some

124

provisions with him and how he could manage to do so.

There was no possibility, he finally decided as he tied the last knot of his shoe, that he could secure provisions, for the woodmaster was still in the room washing the bowls. Tor chided himself for not thinking to wash the bowls himself, thus providing an excuse to stay in the room till the woodmaster left. Had he been thinking, he might have cleared away the crockery immediately after breakfast with a plausible air of resignation to his chores, but to take charge of it now as a generous afterthought would be too obvious a ploy. Instead, he left the room without a word or glance for the woodmaster and with no provision but the clothes on his back.

All that lay before him then, as he set off in the direction of the Ahlberg's cottage, was to resolve whether he should run or no.

First, did the woodmaster suspect he would run? How could he help but do so?

But why, after two months of guarding Tor like a prison warden, not allowing him from his sight for more than five minutes, would he suddenly send him off by himself for an entire day? Thinking of their conversation last night, Tor could not help but suspect the man finally wanted to be rid of him. But then why would he purposely order Tor to return after supper?

Did he intend this to be a trap? Was he trailing Tor even now, waiting for him to step from the path to the Ahlberg's house so that he might have a reason to administer the punishment he'd so obviously wanted to serve Tor last night?

Tor remembered how his mother, particularly angry at him one morning, had declared he should have nothing to eat for the rest of the day. When they'd gone to the market later she had paid extra for some fresh bread, and when they'd returned home, she'd left it out on the table and went, as she said, to work. After half an hour, Tor had approached the bread, but the moment he'd touched it she'd flown back inside and whipped him furiously.

There was no reason to suppose the woodmaster would not do the same. It would be foolish to play so obviously into the man's hands, as he had done once before.

So Tor made his way towards the Ahlberg's house, studiously avoiding the eyes of the villagers, and he arrived upon the threshold in good time, just as ordered. He knocked politely on the door, shrinking somewhat at the thought of the vigorous Thea Ahlberg appearing in her voluminous wheat-colored apron, spreading her arms wide to enfold him as she had begun to do of late on Sunday evenings.

She remained true to custom, conveying all the energy of her silent but eager tongue through a vehement embrace, and Tor was borne, helpless, to the kitchen, where he was made to sit by the hearth. Here, Thea Ahlberg plied him with soft rye bread and butter as she finished her morning chores.

Every Sunday evening for the last two months, Tor had found Thea Ahlberg's kitchen to be an oasis of unexpected cheer.

Without fail he arrived in a black mood, dreading to find what was the latest selection of guests, and without fail he was carried off to the mute woman's kitchen with the ring of Isak Ahlberg's laugh in his red ears. And yet, also without fail, he was betrayed into some new curiosity about the enchanting kitchen and always fell easy prey to Thea Ahlberg's warm eyes.

This day was no exception.

In due time, Tor and Thea Ahlberg ventured into the forest to gather branches for the garden fence. It was a fine day for the work, the woods coming alive with the twitter of dawn birds and the bright drip of melting snow from the spruce trees. They worked in silence, collecting slender branches for the short roundpole fence.

At first Tor was content to do the work, happy to be in the fresh air accomplishing something other than board planing. He was particularly happy to be free of the woodmaster's terse commands, for Thea Ahlberg was a lenient teacher and let him work without constant correction. Tor felt more inclined to do his work well for her sake.

However, when they sat to their silent lunch after working through a long, wordless morning, Tor began to be eager for conversation. Long bouts of silence made him both weary and restless, weary because of boredom and restless because he was left to the mercy of his darker thoughts.

He began to notice the absence, not just of the woodmaster's commands, but also of his dry wit. And he was even beginning to feel—irritating though the woodmaster's corrections were—that he would rather be simmering under that man's autocratic eye than be plagued by the grief, regret, and self-condemnation that was bred in the unbroken silence surrounding him.

"*Frü* Ahlberg," he finally said, poking timidly at his herring with the knife, "do you know the little girl they call idiot?"

A sharp nod was Thea Ahlberg's reply, together with the sudden look of danger in her eyes.

"Her people hit her," said Tor, smashing his fish into his potato with the back of his spoon as he recalled the events of the previous night.

Thea Ahlberg gave another nod and made a sort of hissing between her teeth and lips which she had been compressing tightly.

"I found her crying outside last night, and I had her come in and cook potatoes with me. She was laughing and clapping the whole time; she loved it. Then her mother came in angrily and took her away, and the woodmaster accused me of having ill-treated her. The little girl had a mark on her face from her own family, and they accuse *me* of mistreating her."

He was uncertain why he spoke these words. The reason he preferred to own was that perhaps Thea Ahlberg could do some good for the child, whether by having her husband speak to the girl's father or by simply showing her sympathy. He had one niggling thought that he also wished to garner sympathy for himself, but he ignored this possibility.

"I wished to know," he said, "if you could do something about that."

Thea Ahlberg suddenly leapt from her chair and retrieved a book and a pencil from a drawer. She wrote down letters on an empty page and showed them to Tor.

Tor was astonished that the woman would know how to write. It must have been difficult for her, learning to read without being able to sound the words out by letter so that, by feeling them on her tongue and hearing them in her ear, she might better remember what they meant.

But now he looked at the letters jumping about the page she put to him and shook his head doggedly, trying to ignore the feeling of shame he had that he should be unable to read what a mute housewife could.

She pressed the book on him insistently, and he was forced to snap out the truth.

"I can't read, Thea Ahlberg."

It was the first time he had shown anger towards the mute woman, and he was instantly regretful of his harsh words. Such a tone would have brought Nanny to tears.

But Thea Ahlberg stroked his hair gently, laid down the book, and sat to take her coffee in both hands, looking out the window with an air of abstraction.

Tor looked at the cooling lumps of potato and salt herring on his plate, wondering, as he did so often these days, how he had come to be in such circumstances, sitting at the table of the overwhelming Thea Ahlberg, still straining at the leash of the woodmaster's will, and now pondering how to comfort and shield the child next door.

They soon returned to their work, stripping down and hauling away saplings and branches for their fence. Thea Ahlberg seemed particularly meditative now. Tor believed she was thinking of how to right the wrongs of her small world, and he knew it was in vain. She could do naught to improve either his lot or the little girl's.

By supper time they had only just begun to dig holes for their posts, and it was clear that the fence would take at least another day to finish. Thea Ahlberg had gone inside to mend the fire and begin cooking, and Tor was arranging the remaining wood for the next day's work when a resonant voice, roughened by songs in the salt sea air rode in to him on the Baltic wind.

"Greetings, little fish!"

Tor turned unwillingly to acknowledge the man who seemed so full of good spirits and noisy intent.

"Fisherman Ahlberg," he said, upbraiding himself for having forgotten the existence of this jaunty sailor, "I was just about to return-" He stopped speaking, catching himself before saying the word "home."

"Oh, *nej*, *nej*, *nej*," thundered the fisherman. "Wilhelm said you might stay to dinner when I asked, did he not tell you? You must not run off without your pay, boy. I'll warrant Thea has some tasties in store for you! She is a great one for sweet things, you know."

During his monologue, the giant man had flown down the path toward the drunkard's boy as if borne on a gale and swept Tor into the house. Now he was seizing off his own wraps and hanging them up on the back of the door, effectively cutting Tor off from all hope of escape. A conspirator with the woodmaster no doubt, thought Tor, somewhat sourly. He would keep Tor there to ensure he didn't run away before the woodmaster expected him back.

Though, if this were the case, it meant the woodmaster was not trying to get rid of him, and that thought gave Tor strange relief.

The recollection of the woodmaster brought a sudden timidity to Tor. In these two months he had been out of the man's sight or hearing hardly more than five minutes at a time, and now, having been away from him the whole day, he felt not merely reluctant to see him again, but shy. He wondered whether the man would be disappointed or smug when he saw him again. Likely, neither. It would be worse: indifference.

Tor and the fisherman entered the kitchen where Thea Ahlberg smiled to see her husband and began immediately to cluck and comb through his disheveled hair with her fingers. The fisherman laughed and settled next to the fire to investigate the soup pot, brimful meanwhile with talk of the sea, how it crested and foamed and tossed his little boat like a nutshell, how the schools of fish wiggled and glimmered beneath its surface and pulled on his net like one great, scaly sea monster.

Tor listened to this talk with pleasure, his mind engaging with the novelty of the fisherman's descriptions. He thought that he should like someday to go out in the fisherman's boat, just to be amidst the foamy waves and feel the fish tugging the net with the small, strong bodies that could propel them through liquid with astonishing speed.

He helped Thea Ahlberg take down the wheels of crispy *knäckebröd* strung along the rafters. He broke the pieces and laid them in a shallow basket, his mind running through pictures of the fisherman's sea, which, as the man said, with a teasing glance at his wife, was like a living woman, sometimes playful and sometimes dangerous, but always beautiful.

Thea Ahlberg made him some violent signs, but the fisherman only laughed. Presently his talk turned to stories of sea adventures, of his own and his father's and his father's father's. He talked all through dinner, his wife sometimes interrupting him with sly gestures which more often than not made him roar with laughter.

"What I should like," he said as he leaned back to polish off his last bit of cheese and *knäckebröd*, "is to read that new book from the Americas, the one about the great whaling ship and the white whale. That *would* be something," he said impressively, "to go harpooning a whale from a tiny boat. T'would be no better than an eggshell to such an animal as that."

Here Thea Ahlberg expressed her obviously disapproving opinion, and again the fisherman laughed.

After supper, Tor wandered from the fisherman's house in deep thought about the book with the white whale. He wished he could know what it felt like to harpoon a white whale from an eggshell boat. He could not help but think, as he had thought many times in his life, that if he could read he would know and, in a way, experience many things that it would be impossible to learn of without an education.

He was so much preoccupied that he forgot about the woodmaster until he was standing before the woodshop, looking again through the twilight at the window where he had broken a pane of glass months before. And he felt that prick of shyness again.

He once more considered his probable reception; perhaps a smirk would be in the woodmaster's heart if not in his eyes when the drunkard's boy appeared at the door, meekly returning to his master's house like an obedient dog. But even a smirk would be better than the blank coolness of a man who would rather not see him at all.

"Tor Neeson." The drunkard's boy started at the hempen voice behind him. "Are you going in? Or still deciding whether to run away today?"

The woodmaster, bearlike with his ragged hair and beard, shaggy coat, and bulky cap, moved around Tor to unlock the shop door and push it open. The drunkard's boy balked a moment before dodging past the woodmaster through the open doorway. He just barely glanced into the man's grey eyes, which glinted, as usual, with unspoken opinions.

As the woodmaster led the way through the front shop, Tor glanced at the display window where the Nativity had been. He had imagined for a moment that the stealing of the Nativity had never happened because he had had a strange wish, after his day at the Ahlbergs, for the woodmaster to feel as kindly towards him as they seemed to.

Yet the Nativity was gone, all but for the one figure of the Christ Child which Tor had hidden in the rafters weeks ago for fear the woodmaster should discover it in his belongings.

In the back room Tor hung up his coat and scarf, aware that the woodmaster was watching him closely from where he crouched mending the fire.

"Is the fence up?" the man asked.

"*Nej.*"

"Did they ask you to come again?"

Tor nodded, certain the woodmaster would think he was lying.

"You'll help me deliver the coffin first thing tomorrow, then you may go."

The drunkard's boy was surprised, but said nothing, only nodded once more. The woodmaster must have guessed the fence would take more than a day's work.

Tor took a package of cloth and string out of the basket he had carried from the Ahlberg's house and brought it to the table. He laid out the bundle of cookies that Thea Ahlberg had made with her intricate cookie mold.

"Thea Ahlberg sent these," he said. Then he crossed back to the door to pull off his boots.

The woodmaster moved to the table with his peculiar clumsy grace and eyed the package with interest. He pulled apart the knot of string which held in place the card Thea Ahlberg had labeled. The drunkard's boy could not read it, but Isak Ahlberg had picked up the package and read it aloud after his wife placed it in the basket: "Wilhelm and Tor." There was another smaller bundle still in the basket which read, "Marta."

Tor planned to keep this in his coat pocket in hopes that he would have an opportunity to present it to the little girl himself. If not, he would give it to the woodmaster to deliver, but he wished that little girl would know the cookies had been carried by his own hand.

The woodmaster bit a cookie with an audible crunch, and Tor looked down at the floor as he stood by the door, stuffing his gloves into the coat pocket hanging before him.

"You're very quiet," the man suddenly remarked, straddling the bench with a cookie in one hand and a mug in the other, showing no readiness for bed.

Tor glanced at him quickly in an attempt to gauge his thoughts, but the man's face was blank.

"I'm always quiet," said the drunkard's boy finally, unwilling to anger the woodmaster and yet also unwilling, when it came to the point, to appear friendly.

"*Nej*, you're not," said the woodmaster, "but I meant your manner is quiet."

Tor said nothing, but dropped to a knee to remove his boots.

"I don't wish to see you in prison, boy. You know that, *ja?*" said the woodmaster abruptly.

Tor did not look up from his boot laces.

"I *don't* know," he answered. "You hate me." His own words startled him.

Not since childhood had he been accustomed to speaking so openly. It had been a great fault when he was seven, but he had learned, after many painful experiences, to repress words that revealed hints of pain or vulnerability.

The woodmaster tossed his head to one side as he was wont to do when in deep contemplation.

"*Ja*, perhaps sometimes," he said, a hint of humor in his tone. "That does not mean I want to see you destroyed."

"You wish only to humiliate me at every opportunity before the entire village," said Tor, struggling, since he could not seem to stem the tide of his impulsive words, to keep his tone neutral or at least sarcastic—and not wounded.

The woodmaster showed no anger. He took a drink from his mug and then stared into it as if there were some curiosity at the bottom.

"That," said he after a moment, "is your own fault. Do as I say, and I'll not punish you."

Tor might have been tempted to snarl back and drive the conversation to a quick, volatile death if the man's tone had not been so innocently practical.

Then too, Tor's labor in the fresh woods had reminded him that there were subjects to consider other than his resentment towards the woodmaster. Living with this man was indeed painful but hardly the end of the world. He had realized, in fact, that there might be much to gain from his present circumstances; for instance, if the woodmaster were willing to teach him to work with wood, he might also be willing to teach him to read. If so, Tor was willing to use his freedom as a bargaining chip for a better future.

All he lacked was the will to acknowledge this to the woodmaster.

He would not ask favors of the man, even if the woodmaster were disposed to grant him favors. Tor decided if he were to get what he wanted, he must depict himself as the one dispensing favors.

"I might behave better," he said, "if I were better occupied."

"You're not busy enough?" asked the woodmaster dryly. "I can remedy that."

"*Nej*. What I am saying is, rather than doing nothing but planing and sweeping and hammering, I ought to do things that exercise my mind. If I were busy reading perhaps I might not have the time or desire to create . . ."—Tor paused, then shrugged —"diversions that are disagreeable to you."

"You're saying you want books."

"*Ja*, that would be fine, but . . ." Tor paused again, realizing that there was no dignified way to tell the woodmaster his secret, so he spoke with as sarcastic an air as he could muster.

"But first I would prefer to learn how to read."

"You can't read?" asked the woodmaster after a moment.

Tor writhed at the blunt words, but, aware that anger would make him ridiculous, sneered his way forward.

"If I could, I would not wish to be taught."

"Education is free."

"I did not wish to attend school."

"Why not?"

"I had other tasks," Tor said.

"What? Stock-piling snowballs to ambush all the children who did attend? If you truly wished to read you would have made the effort."

Tor's facáde slipped. He remembered what he had thought last night when he had thrown the potatoes: that it was impossible it was to live with this man.

In a silent white heat of anger, he jerked back the blankets on his bed and rolled beneath them.

Hateful, tyrannical man. It wasn't enough that he kept Tor bound to him by force, but he had to humiliate him, not merely for his misdeeds—*nej*, that was not painful enough. He also had to humiliate Tor for his ambitions.

The drunkard's boy tightened his jaw to lock back the angry words rampaging in his mind.

Behind him, the woodmaster stood up with a scrape of the bench. As his movements were slow and not threatening, Tor's anger remained undiminished by fear.

"Come, boy, don't soil the bed with your day clothes," said the man, pulling off his coat and hanging it on the door, "and I'll see what can be done about your reading."

Tor's heart leapt unexpectedly, surprising him, and, though he did not look at the woodmaster, he hardly delayed in sitting up to replace his blouse and trousers with a nightshirt.

The next morning, they ate Thea Ahlberg's cookies with their porridge. They did not speak, though Tor would have done so willingly had the woodmaster addressed him.

But the woodmaster was not a cheery man in the mornings, and the drunkard's boy had learned that to challenge him before breakfast was nearly to provoke a sentence of death.

Tor breakfasted silently and quickly, contrary to his habit of cleverly postponing chores by taking each bite with the speed of a turtle. The woodmaster, however, dragged about in sour silence.

After they delivered the coffin to the smithy, they parted, still without speaking, the woodmaster pausing only to slap the sawdust off the front of Tor's coat and then push him away by the shoulder.

Tor walked backwards a few paces, watching the woodmaster disappear in the morning fog and wondering what he was thinking. Reason warned him not to trust the man.

Tor had trusted his mother and been broken by her selfishness and negligence—not just of himself, but, more importantly, of Nanny. He'd also trusted the schoolmaster, the vicar, and a number of other villagers, and all had betrayed him. And now, for the last few years, he had been telling himself that no one else in this village would have the pleasure of hurting his heart.

Still, try as he might, Tor realized, he could not rid himself of his peculiar fascination with the woodmaster. He could not help admiring and even imitating him, no matter how angry the man made him. Tor turned away and shook his head slightly, attempting to clear his mind. That fascination would be the death of him, no doubt.

At the Ahlbergs that day, Tor found that Thea Ahlberg had taken it upon herself to teach him her singular version of dialogue.

He learned "food," "branch," "sea," "house," and many other words which he was made to review repeatedly. The woman seemed intent upon stuffing his memory with as many signs as possible, and he was willing to oblige her, even attempting to form short sentences of his own.

He told her—by tongue—that the woodmaster had agreed to teach him to read, and she smiled and nodded most energetically.

As Tor attempted to learn the mute woman's hand language, he began to feel some of the helplessness of her situation. There was an undercurrent of frustration almost always evident in her abrupt, impatient movements. She could communicate with no one unless they read her signs, none of the other women in the village, none of the shopkeepers, none of the children. Her handicap made her helpless in so many ways.

Tor understood this feeling of powerlessness in a slightly different form. He could speak, but no one would listen because he was the drunkard's boy. They were both outcasts, he and Thea Ahlberg.

Before Tor left that day, he patted Thea Ahlberg's shoulder

when she embraced him and smiled at her as they drew apart again.

CHAPTER TEN

The day following was another Sunday—the first Sunday that Tor concealed his reluctance to attend church. The woodmaster had made no further mention of their agreement, so Tor considered himself on probation; no doubt the clever man wished to see evidence of Tor's reform before committing his precious time to the boy's disposal.

The drunkard's boy determined with almost feverish zeal that the woodmaster would have no cause to revoke his agreement. Tor would overcome any obstacle—even his rebellion toward the woodmaster—to attain his ends.

Still, feeling the eyes of the woodmaster on him as he quickly ate his food and combed his hair and put on his good clothes, he felt a stab of degradation for his compliance. He stomped his heel into its boot and pushed the feeling back.

Literacy would free him from a prison of ignorance. It would help him to organize the thoughts that gamboled chaotically in his mind. A little of his present discomfort, and then he would have freedom.

He did not stare at the ground as they walked to the church, but rather gazed at the tips of the evergreens on the far-off mountain ridges, untouched by the sneering glances of the villagers, thinking instead of how he would escape this stifling village encrusted in its mold of prejudice.

"Hey, drunkard's boy!"

Tor did not move his eyes from the distant line of trees to look upon the insignificant pink-faced village boys that sauntered behind him and the woodmaster. They weren't worth the notice of someone destined to be great.

"Haven't broke your leash yet?" called Albin.

This was a frequent joke among the village boys. It seemed some comments dropped by the woodmaster had been repeated till it was common knowledge that the woodmaster considered Tor a dog on a leash, though he was more than willing for Tor to escape if only he were bright enough to do so.

This gossip was the height of insult. To admit to himself that he could not outwit the woodmaster was quite bad, but to have the fact cast in his teeth by people who were really inferior to him was far worse. Let *them* try life with the woodmaster for a few days and see how they fared.

Still, Tor did not turn to face his tormentors.

The woodmaster did turn, however. He stopped in the middle of the path and smiled at the boys behind them.

"I have more leashes," he said.

There was a wordless shuffling among the boys as the woodmaster looked them over. His eyes settled on the cobbler's boy.

"Albin," said the man, "since your mother and father do not

require your company, perhaps you'd care to walk with Tor and me."

Still facing ahead, the drunkard's boy cast a sideways glance at the woodmaster, wondering with some dread what thoughts were playing in his mind.

Albin shuffled up to Tor's side, but the woodmaster pulled him to his own side, positioning himself between the two boys.

"Walk with *me*," he said invited, his voice tinged with the lilt of a man savoring a rather cruel joke.

"Albin," he continued, "you've not properly greeted Tor."

Albin was plainly cowed. He liked to persecute small things, but he cringed before his superiors.

"Hello," Albin said, not looking at Tor, who was again intent upon the distant pines.

"Tor," said the woodmaster, "say hello and ask Albin how he fares."

Tor struggled a moment to regain the brilliant vision of his imminent scholastic career.

"Hello, Albin. How do you do?" His voice was as rigid and cold as ever the woodmaster's had been to him.

The woodmaster nudged Albin.

"I'm well," answered Albin.

"Now, Albin, I'm sure your mother taught you better. You should ask Tor how he does as well."

"How do you do?" said Albin, mechanically.

"How do you do, *Tor*," prompted the woodmaster, nudging Albin again.

"How do you do, Tor?"

"I'm well."

"And what do you think of the weather, boys?" asked the carpenter, unduly jovial.

Neither boy replied.

"Tor," said the woodmaster, breaking the stubborn silence.

"It is much warmer than last week."

"Ask Albin what he thinks of the weather," the woodmaster said.

"What do you think of the weather?"

"Say his name, boy; you're not strangers are you?"

"What do you think of the weather, Albin," said Tor, sourly grinding out the other's name.

"I think it is much warmer as well," said Albin, after an apparent struggle thinking of what to say.

"Come, Albin, this is not much of a conversation," the woodmaster said with a light laugh that sounded most unusual to Tor's ears. "You must introduce some new idea or there is no good to speaking at all. Come, how is the weather?" And he laid a hand on the back of Albin's neck. Behind them, Albin's companions snickered.

"I suppose," said the cobbler's boy, cringing under the woodmaster's touch and turning a red-faced glare upon his companions, "the days are getting longer."

"They teach you that in school, do they?" asked Tor.

The woodmaster instantly clapped his other hand on Tor's neck, pulling him closer.

"Have you something you'd like to ask Albin, Tor?"

Tor retreated quickly.

"*Nej.*"

"Oh, I'm sure you do. Boys usually have things they like to say to each other. You should be neighborly, Tor."

"How is Lisbet Hansson, Albin?" Tor asked.

Another titter from behind. Albin's penchant for the Hansson girl was common knowledge among the boys. Albin himself admitted the fact "in confidence" to almost every one of his acquaintances.

"How should I know?" snapped the cobbler's boy.

"I rarely speak with her these days," said Tor, airily. "The most I see of her is on market day when she stands across the square, blowing kisses at me from her booth."

Behind them, Lars Pedersson gave an asthmatic wheeze and a snort, and his companions shushed him, snickering.

"Dear me, Tor," said the woodmaster—and Tor's hackles rose at his tone—"what must the vicar's daughter think of that?"

The air was suddenly very still, and Tor found himself unable to catch even a glimpse of his happy vision beneath the blackness of the woodmaster's damper. This was indeed the lowest of blows, worse an insult than the leash. How did the woodmaster know of his fondness for the vicar's daughter? How could he know? For a pinprick of a moment, Tor wondered if this grey-eyed, blond man with the massive shoulders and the hammer-trained hand could read his mind.

And then, angry with himself for letting such a thought come into his head, he felt compelled to demonstrate his defiance of the ridiculous idea.

"She would probably say," said Tor, "that she could not understand how one could spend the time of day on such a simpering, giggling milksop as Lisbet Hansson."

"Is that what she would say?" asked the woodmaster, stopping and turning his back on Albin to look at Tor.

The entire group of boys paused to watch, barely a breath among them, while Tor weighed the cost of his education. How much humiliation was it worth? What were those fine ideals that he was willing to grovel for?

"*Nej*, she probably would not," he said tersely, and he moved on.

The unusual grouping of woodmaster, cobbler's son, and drunkard's boy, with their entourage of snickering school boys arrived at the church in a very few moments, at which time Albin was released to go to his parents, and Tor was released to sit alone in the woodmaster's pew.

Tor devoted the entire service hour to persuading himself to move past the woodmaster's mortal blow. It had been a test, he reminded himself over and over, stoically biting his long nails and staring at the glowing beeswax candles that illumined the silver vessels on the Lord's Table. The woodmaster desired to know if he were truly willing to exchange his rebellion for an education.

Yes, he told himself, of course he was. He'd been willing before, had he not, until the schoolmaster drove him from the schoolhouse? He had already determined, after all, to endure the woodmaster's thrall if he could have again the chance to learn to read. It would be weak to break his resolution at the first test of hardship.

I will do what I must, he told himself, and when I learn to read and write and become a great man I can revenge myself on anyone I choose.

He was still thinking along these lines when the service closed, and all the congregation stood for the benediction. The woodmaster had to jerk Tor's sleeve to gain his attention, and so engrossed in his good resolutions was the drunkard's boy that he nearly snapped back at the man in annoyance.

He spent the benediction warning off his hasty temper and chastening himself for nearly destroying his great opportunity.

The woodmaster moved with unexpected haste when the vicar said "Amen." He dragged Tor quickly out the door where, to Tor's dismay, they accosted the schoolmaster.

"*Herr* schoolmaster, good day," said the woodmaster.

The schoolmaster turned, looked at the woodmaster's hand on his sleeve, and then looked at the woodmaster's forehead. The carpenter moved his hand away, and his tone turned brusque.

"I wished to ask you if, though the boy is over-age, he might attend school this week." He nodded at Tor, and Tor looked back at him in horrified disbelief. This was not the arrangement he had bargained for; how could the man have thought he wished to go back to the school?

Tor felt the schoolmaster's large, vindictive eyes on him, eyes that were lighter than the woodmaster's, but stormier. He was a pale man who might have looked sickly but for his stature, which was taller even than the woodmaster and about as broad-shouldered, though less muscled.

"*Herr* carpenter," said the man with mortifying clarity in the fresh Sunday air, "I have already told that ragamuffin that he is no longer welcome in my school-house. He is a slovenly scholar who brings nothing but insolence and strife into the classroom. I have suffered him in my school for as long as the law requires of me. If he comes again I will beat him. Good day, carpenter."

He turned on the sharp heels of his shining black boots and walked down the path, carefully skirting the mud puddles.

"Oh, did the little pup want to try to learn to read again? I thought reading lessons were for children?" Behind Tor, on the church steps, Albin now taunted fearlessly from the shadow of his mother's skirts.

Tor looked at him, his face red, but his eyes flaming.

Albin, however, stuck out his tongue at Tor even as his mother chastised him for his rudeness on the steps of the house of God. Then Tor swept a rock from the ground and was in the act of hurling it when the woodmaster wrenched his arm behind him.

Tor would not fight again and be beaten by the woodmaster before the vicar's daughter. He turned from the curious congregation to face the wooden buttons of the woodmaster's black coat, his arm still held in an iron clasp.

"May we go back?" he said quietly, his voice never so cold.

They faced the path together and walked from the church, the woodmaster ambling with his usual loose-limbed grace and the drunkard's boy padding rigidly beside him, an arm's length away.

When they had come to the woodmaster's shop and had walked from the front shop to the workshop to the back room Tor removed his boots and coat without a word and went to lie on his bed, his face away from the woodmaster as he prepared their simple meal.

"Come and eat, boy," said the man after he had laid out the food.

"I don't want to eat, please," said the drunkard's boy, his bitter tone a mockery of the politely phrased request.

"Boy," said the woodmaster, speaking more roughly, "if you will make enemies of the people most able and willing to help you, you have no one to blame for your circumstances but yourself."

Tor glared at the woodmaster with feverish eyes and a face white as a potato but for his garishly red nose.

"You never wished to help me. You are all so blind. Can you good Christians not see that you are rotten from the core?

"You think I am so beneath you, but at least I'm not one of you smug villagers living to fatten my belly while the poor starve around me. And I don't mock a little girl for being an 'idiot' or a kind woman for being a mute. I don't pretend to care for the sick by sending them a pious sermon and basket of stale oatcake when they need a physician. I don't run from the house of the dying. I'm not a schoolmaster who humiliates a child for writing with the wrong hand or drives them out of school because they can't understand his teaching, and I'm not a carpenter who enslaves and beats a boy out of vengeance."

The woodmaster stared at him.

"You don't run from the dying?" he asked. "Where were you then when your sister died?"

Surging out of bed, Tor threw the object nearest to hand— which unfortunately was but a pillow—at the woodmaster, incensed that the man would use this moment of vulnerable transparency to try to trap him into a confession. The man cared for naught but his precious Nativity pieces.

The woodmaster caught the pillow in one hand and tightened his jaw as if restricting some choice hard words.

"Why," he said, "if you knew what the schoolmaster would say, did you ask for me to arrange for you to learn to read?"

"I never asked to be sent to school," shouted Tor.

"Why? Because you are too good to sit with the other stupid schoolchildren?"

Ja, thought Tor, but he only said, "I did not ask to be treated like a dumb animal. I did not ask to be publicly shamed because my mind gets confused when I read."

The woodmaster tossed his head to one side to look meditatively at Tor.

"What do you mean by saying your mind gets confused?"

"I mean, while others learn to read and write and spell easily, I cannot understand it."

The woodmaster frowned and continued to stare with his tilted head to one side.

"Perhaps you aren't trying as hard."

"I," said Tor, his teeth clenching, "try harder than any of them, but there is something wrong with my mind. The words-" he paused, searching for what to say. "The words jump all over the page."

"Perhaps you are too easily distracted."

"I am not! None of you ever listen. Don't any of you try to understand?"

"I am trying," said the woodmaster, his voice growing strained and dangerous, "to understand you now."

"*Nej.* You're just like the schoolmaster. You don't believe me. You think I'm making all this up for no reason. Why would I do that? It's not . . . it's not a light matter to me."

"And so when you came of age the schoolmaster ordered you to leave and never come back?"

Tor didn't think the man deserved a reply, but he forced a short nod.

"Fortunately for you, I have little love for the schoolmaster," murmured the woodmaster, as if speaking to himself. "I could easily believe that of him."

He turned to look into the fire, and all Tor could see was the occasional flicker of light over his dark silhouette.

"But," said the woodmaster after a moment, "I cannot judge him based on my private opinions."

"And so instead you judge me based on your private opinions. You never had any proof that I stole your precious treasure."

The whole house seemed to rattle as the woodmaster slammed his fist upon the table. Tor jumped.

"I am tired," said the woodmaster, softly, "of your repeated lies to my face. I have all the proof I need against you, and if you have nothing else to say of the Nativity, then do not *ever* speak of it again.

"Now come here immediately and take your meal unless you wish to be tied and muzzled so you won't be able to eat when we go to the Ahlbergs."

Tor instantly went to the table. The woodmaster said grace in a tone that implied he'd rather not be saying it, and then they ate in silence, Tor choking down his food as quickly as possible before washing his dish and returning to his bed. He did not lie down, however. He took the blanket and the thin pillow and went to the corner where he had spent his first few nights; there, he curled up without a word and pretended to sleep.

After some moments he heard the woodmaster clean his dish and then stretch out before the fire as usual.

Neither of them moved for some hours. Tor did not sleep during all that time, though he had no doubt that the woodmaster slept soundly.

As he listened to the melancholy patter of rain outside he considered how he had fallen from a place of near happiness to a misery worse than that of his first weeks with the woodmaster. Had he not warned himself that the man was no different from anybody else? That he was not to be trusted? How could he have been so deceived?

And how could he have allowed himself to have fabricated such ridiculously rosy hopes about his future? He had become so knit to an irrational fantasy that he had been crushed with its destruction.

His nose began to sting, and he scrubbed at it with his sleeve. He had not cried since the time he'd been too small to defend Nanny from their mother's drunken abuse. He had not cried when the pawn broker took the Nativity from him, nor had he even cried when he'd heard the news that his little sister had passed into death alone.

Now he was crying because the woodmaster wouldn't teach him how to read. His jaw tightened. He wanted to shatter every peice of crockery in the cupboards. Why would he under any circumstances want the woodmaster to teach him to read? It would mean nothing but a perpetual battle between them.

For the next three hours, he tread a cycle of self-pity and self-castigation, unable to think of aught but his helpless, aching disappointment until the woodmaster rose and bade him prepare for supper at the Ahlbergs.

Tor obeyed without looking at the man, although he felt himself watched with uncommon attention.

❄ ❄ ❄

As wretched as the day had become to Tor, he found it could grow still more wretched, for when he arrived at the Ahlbergs, there was the schoolmaster as well as the pretty girl with the heart-shaped face.

When, standing over the fisherman's threshold, he discovered this, he ducked backwards out the door without thinking. But the woodmaster grabbed his wrist to pull him forward and laid an arm over his shoulders, upsetting all plans of escape.

Then there was Thea Ahlberg's violent embrace to endure before the eyes of the company. Tor remembered bitterly how her touch had comforted him last time he had come to the fisherman's cottage. That day he had entertained hopes so sanguine that his whole world had been cast in a very sunny light.

But tonight, for the first time, Thea Ahlberg and her kitchen failed to charm him. He executed her silent orders meekly but listlessly, conscious of her worried glances and intensified efforts to engage his attention with cakes, currants, and cod soup. He could not remember the words she had taught him to sign, and he could take no interest in relearning them, although he played along politely.

When she finally released him to take his supper by the fire in the sitting room he sat by the woodmaster's feet, loathing the man's nearness and yet hoping to hide in the shadow of his strong presence.

The pretty girl's chat, as she sat betwixt the woodmaster and the schoolmaster, aggravated Tor. He saw that she was bent upon cutting a very fascinating figure indeed, flirting with and baiting the two men at the same time, and the drunkard's boy was strangely exasperated that the woodmaster would so easily be led by her hooks without having an inkling of her sly and selfish character. It was clear that even the schoolmaster had a better understanding of her than did the woodmaster.

Still, thought Tor, why should I not be happy that the carpenter makes a fool of himself?

"Now I am surprised at you two," the pretty girl was saying, "for not getting on better. I should have thought you would be the best of friends. The two most intelligent men in the whole town, both successful, well-bred, good-natured. These excellent traits really ought to recommend you to each other, and yet I see how you circle each other like a pair of suspicious wolves, each fearful of the other's genius.

"Upon my word, I have had a thought," she continued, perking up like a dainty doe and tilting her head so the fire-light danced over her gleaming hair. "I shall take you two up as my mission. I shall reveal to each the really sterling qualities of the other, and I shall make the pair of you as thick as David and Jonathon. It will be my contribution to Sweden to unite two such brilliant minds."

And she gave one short nod as if to assert with charming confidence that the thing was as good as done.

The woodmaster tossed his head to one side and fixed his gaze on the girl, partly, as it seemed to Tor, in bewilderment and partly in dry protestation.

The schoolmaster was more biddable.

"I certainly can have no objection to bending to your most persuasive beguilements, but I am sure my lady speaks from some misapprehension. You describe us as suspicious, but for my part, I must protest that I have no unfriendly fear of *Herr* carpenter."

As he spoke, the curve of his lip suggested that perhaps nothing could be found to fear of the woodmaster.

"Ah, just what a suspicious man would say," said the pretty girl. Turning, she said to the woodmaster, "But how do you answer, *Herr* woodcarver? Are you also prepared to bend to my will? Though I warn you it little matters how you answer, for, as my brothers could tell you, I am relentless and cruelly inexorable. I never lose a battle I have set my mind to."

The woodmaster regarded her in silent contemplation for some moments, and Tor, to his own amazement and disgust, felt apprehensive that the woodmaster would be humiliated by this glib pair.

"I'd not refuse to do anything you asked me to do that was right, but I'll not say the schoolmaster and I are on bad terms as you seem to think, and I'm wondering what reasons you have for thinking it."

"Oh, you men!" cried the girl. "Always poking and probing the life out of an idea in your quest for facts. It's a thousand little things: not anything you do or say, but always things you don't do or say; not where you sit, but where you don't sit; not your expression, but your lack of expression whenever you are in each other's company.

"I've often marked it, and I do think it rather craven. If I disliked a person I should have the honesty to say it to her face. I never conceal my feelings for the sake of mere social convention —what a crowd of stilted hypocrites we should be if we all behaved as you two!"

"I bow to your whim, lady," said the schoolmaster gravely. "You command me to become the carpenter's enemy so that you may reunite us in a bond of ardent friendship. I cannot deny you. What do you say, *Herr* carpenter? Shall we take up arms at the behest of this cruel witch?"

Again, the woodmaster was silent. Tor had never talked much with girls, but he instinctively knew the proper part for the woodmaster to act. He ought to flatter and blather any amount of insincerity in competition for his lady's favor. The drunkard's boy could not help but cringe in expectation of seeing it; to play such games was absurdly incongruous with the woodmaster's nature.

Finally the man said, "I suppose if she were a witch I'd have little choice, but she is only a girl who likes to tease."

Tor recognized the tone of gentle chiding in the woodmaster's voice. He was trying to warn the girl that she was being—as he thought—ridiculous.

Here a great laugh rose up from the fisherman, who sat across from them, smoking his pipe and enjoying the repartee.

"You'll get no word of nonsense out of the woodcarver, I'll warrant you!"

The girl's lips, however, tightened in annoyance before she disguised her feelings with a pretty pout.

"There you are, being men again. Never can you admit a woman to be correct; you always persist in pretending our insights are fanciful, and when you are in the wrong you try to change the subject."

"Chastise us according to your pleasure, good mistress," said the schoolmaster, leaning back and speaking with a silver-tongued mixture of submission and arrogance. He was born with social brilliance, Tor thought, in unwilling veneration.

"And so I shall," said the pretty girl, rising, "for I shall leave now and compel at least one of you to forsake this comfortable fireside and accompany me home."

"I'll take you," said the woodmaster, speaking far more quickly than was his wont.

"Dear me, no," said the schoolmaster, still lounging, "*Herr* carpenter never does anything worthy of chastisement, whereas I am an impudent and presumptuous dog ever in need of it. I shall bear this painful punishment."

"Come, come," said the girl in her light staccato, "I'll not be bullied into my decision. I am afraid *Herr* carpenter has indeed merited quite his share of chastisement in this matter, and it falls to me to dispense it—even if I am a mere teasing girl." She laughed, not looking at the woodmaster.

"And yet," she continued, "it occurs to me that he has brought on enough trouble for himself with this young rogue of his. I daresay this child," she added tightly, looking at Tor, "is sufficient to the task of knocking off any man's rough edges." The drunkard's boy gave her an ugly grimace, and she smiled sweetly and offered her coat to the schoolmaster that he might help her.

"Therefore, I do think I should take *you* in hand tonight, *Herr* schoolmaster," she finished lightly, slipping into the coat, which he held for her.

Tor looked at the pretty girl darkly, understanding full well that she intended to punish the woodmaster for refusing to flatter and flirt with her as well as for dragging the drunkard's boy into proper society once more.

"My what a glare!" she laughed, staring back at Tor as she adjusted her coat collar. The woodmaster whirled toward the drunkard's boy and looked him over.

For a moment Tor thought the man would wipe the look of his face with the back of his hand, but instead he said, "Nothing so unusual."

"I wonder," said the schoolmaster, stepping from behind the pretty girl, and jerking the cuffs of his blouse out from beneath his coat sleeves, "why you persist in bringing that devil into women's society. I know what a dirty mind and mouth he has."

Tor took one glance at the man's perfect pale face and icy blue eyes and then dropped his own, wondering why this man cowed him even more than did the woodmaster, who had actually struck Tor, had worked him harder, and had humiliated him quite as excruciatingly. The schoolmaster, by contrast, had done little more than ignore the drunkard's boy.

"Because I think," said the woodmaster, "that a good woman could help to improve his faults."

He glanced at the pretty girl a bit too obviously, as Tor thought with both scorn and discomfort, but she turned toward the door with a slight upward tilt of her chin.

"Goodnight, Isak Ahlberg, Thea Ahlberg," she said, glancing vaguely in the direction of the corner where Thea Ahlberg had been knitting furiously and casting scathing looks at the girl's back. She did not pause in her knitting as the pretty girl and the schoolmaster left, but the fisherman rose to escort them to the door.

Shortly thereafter, the woodmaster rose to speak to Thea Ahlberg, leaving Tor to the mercy of the fisherman. A young courting couple also sat by the fire, but they were too enamored with each other's eyes to notice anyone else, and the fisherman had apparently had his fill of joshing them that evening.

"Well, little fish, a fine fence you've built us—sturdy as I've ever seen."

163

This word of praise, boisterously given though it was, made Tor feel a strange, pitiful gratitude in the wake of the schoolmaster's stinging insult.

"Tack," he said, looking at the fisherman for a moment and meaning the word.

"Ah, lad," said the fisherman, suddenly seeming a bit maudlin himself, "it's a good thing, your coming to the woodcarver. He's a clever man and a decent one and just the sort to see a lad through a rough gale."

Tor looked quickly away at the fire, grated by his own emotions and by the man's well-meaning words. Nothing was good about his living with the woodmaster. If the fisherman expected a happy ending all round with the drunkard's boy installed as the woodmaster's devoted adoptive son, carrying on his tradition of exquisite woodcraft, well, he was mistaken.

The woodmaster soon told Tor to get his coat and boots, and Tor obeyed quietly and without giving effort to display the usual signs of resentment at being ordered about.

They made their way back to the woodmaster's house without speaking. When they arrived, Tor wearily began to prepare for bed.

"Are you sick?" asked the woodmaster as he set his boots by the door.

"Nej," said Tor, pulling off his blouse and turning his back on the man.

"Is this about reading, then?"

"Is what about reading?"

"Your behavior," replied the man.

"Does nothing please you?" Tor asked, throwing his blouse on the floor. "If I protest you beat me, and if I behave quietly and do just as I'm told you rebuke me."

"I am not rebuking you."

"*Ja*, you are," snapped Tor.

"*Nej*," said the woodmaster, "I am not. I want to know why you are so listless. You seem ill."

"I am ill from being here."

Tor slid beneath the blanket on his bed and once again turned to face away from the woodmaster.

There were some moments of silence; then the woodmaster's shadow fell over Tor, and he felt a queasy flutter in his stomach. The woodmaster only ever came this close to chastise him.

Something heavy hit the bed in front of his face, startling him. He raised an arm to shield his head.

"From Thea Ahlberg. She said these would make it easier," said the woodmaster.

A pile of books lay before Tor's nose.

Tor deliberated between curiosity and a sulky desire to ignore the woodmaster.

"Easier for what?" he finally asked, not moving.

"For me to teach you. I can scarcely read myself, so you'll

have to work hard and keep your temper in check."

Tor considered a moment longer, then sat up and opened a book. There were pictures as well as letters.

"Why did she give you these?"

"I asked them of her."

Tor turned a page, running his fingers gently over the words and taking pleasure in the crispness and thinness of the parchment —a bit like birch bark, only smoother and more malleable and less chalky.

"When will we start?" he asked, still staring at the page because he was too uncomfortable to look at the woodmaster.

"Now, if you like."

Tor nodded.

"Come to the table," said the woodmaster, walking to the cupboard and taking out a hunk of cheese. The man always seemed to be eating.

Tor crept out of bed in his nightshirt, laid the precious books on the table, and sat down. He noticed that his heart had suddenly started beating quickly. This annoyed him. He did not want to feel excited. This task would be grueling and probably a failure. He ought to have learned that much by now, but here he was, feeling as nervous as when he was an eight-year-old, sliding into his chair at school for the first time. Little had he known what miserable experiences awaited him in that chair. Imbecile. Probably he faced more of the same kind now.

166

"You know your letters?" asked the woodmaster, straddling the bench opposite and handing him a sliver of cheese, which Tor took between his fingertips and laid beside him, immediately wiping his hands on his shirt to avoid soiling the books.

"*Ja.*"

"Let's hear."

And so Tor spoke his letters, flipping through the pages and pointing to each. It was a lesson he had learned well, for he had repeated it to himself every night for seven years.

"I don't understand why you would have much trouble reading since you know your letters so well," said the woodmaster, layering a sandwich of cheese and *knäckebröd*. "I don't know them so well."

"But I can't put them together," Tor said, already sensing a return of the angst he used to experience at his school desk.

"Be calm. Can you read this word?" the man asked, pointing to the page.

Tor looked and shook his head no.

"Say the letters."

Tor did so, struggling to place the jumpy little symbols in correct order.

"Now make the sounds."

Painfully, Tor made the sounds.

"Now say the sounds together."

Tor made the first sound, then stopped.

167

"Go on," said the woodmaster.

"I can't," said Tor frantically, eyes glued to a word as he struggled to discern the individual letters.

"But this is simple."

"*Nej,* it isn't!" Tor shouted, stomping up from his seat so quickly the bench shrieked on the wooden floor. "I knew this would fail!"

He strode towards his bed, but the woodmaster leaned out and caught the tail of his night-shirt.

"We're not finished here," he said. He swung his leg over the bench so that he fully faced the table and pulled the drunkard's boy to sit next to him, clamping him to his side with a strong arm. He pulled the book across the table and positioned it between them. "Put your finger under each letter and make the sounds once more."

Tor did so belligerently, still attempting to wriggle free of the woodmaster.

"Now read the word," the man said.

Painfully, his finger sliding under each letter, Tor read the word.

"But it is no good," he complained, "if I have to use my finger. It's fine with this book, because the letters are big, but this will never work for small print."

"You will learn," said the woodmaster. "This is only the first lesson. Now it is time for bed."

"Now? We've hardly begun."

"But I thought you wished to go, *ja*?" asked the woodmaster, still clamping Tor to his side with one hand and biting his cheese and *knäckebröd* with the other.

Tor made no reply but took up the open book and gripped it with obstinate hands.

"So, we'll continue," the woodmaster said. "What's this word? Make the sounds."

They did continue for half an hour, and Tor grew increasingly irritated.

"You strain too much," said the woodmaster. "Calm yourself, and you will do better. Tomorrow you will do better." He closed the book. Tor resisted the urge to speak and instead stood to go to bed. Little good, he knew well, ever came of protesting to the woodmaster.

The woodmaster soon followed him to bed. He paused after pulling down his blanket and stood over Tor.

"You will have to do as you're told, boy," he said. "Stay and do your work quietly without complaint."

Tor was silent for a few moments.

"*Ja*," he answered at last.

He thought as he settled under his blanket how quiescent he had become, and he thought he should resent this new trait and resent the woodmaster for creating it, but he found little interest in resentment now. All he could think of, till hours into the night, was the books he would read and the words he would write.

CHAPTER ELEVEN

The woodmaster asked him the next day in the workshop how to spell *bräda*. His back to the woodmaster, Tor stopped sweeping and closed his eyes, rocking back and forth, slightly, on his toes.

"*B*," he said, and paused.

"Say the next sound," said the woodmaster, after a moment.

"I'm trying." Tor pawed at the ground with his broom, only to respread his dust pile across the floor.

"Write them in the dust there." The woodmaster pointed to the sheet of pine dust on his work table.

"*R*," Tor finally said, and he wrote it next to the B. "*Ä*."

"Good. *Brä*. And the rest?"

"*B*—no, *D*. And *A.*"

"Together."

And Tor spent the next quarter of an hour intermittently spelling out or writing words as he worked.

This was grueling, so much so that he had to stop working every time he thought.

Yet Tor found that, though his toils had increased as he focused upon the illusive letters in addition to his other work, he could bear the labor more cheerfully. He also found that he could better bear the presence of the woodmaster despite the increase of his bossy commands.

The woodmaster, however, seemed disquieted; his movements were more abrupt and his words more terse. He was generally in his best humor when silently consumed with intricate woodcraft. He did not like focusing on more than one task. Nor did he like continual interruptions to his work, and because Tor's continual errors and complaints interrupted his peace, he did not love Tor's presence in the room.

Now, the woodmaster's patience waned very thin, and when, after more than an hour of sporadically drilling Tor over four other simple words, he again ordered the boy to spell the word *bräda*, and Tor replied *b-r-ö-d-o*, he drove his chisel into the table and was stonily silent for the rest of the morning.

Yet that night after supper he seemed freshly determined to run Tor into the ground with study. Several times he did lose patience, such as when the drunkard's boy again forgot how to spell *bräda*, but the woodmaster never sneered or insulted, only slammed pots or stared up at the ceiling for several moments. But so long as the man said nothing to belittle him, Tor convinced himself that he could continue to try spelling and writing.

Furthermore, it was so unusual to see the woodmaster annoyed and pettish that his displays were more a source of entertainment to Tor, rather than an offense.

As the days grew longer, Tor was often inclined to stay up out of doors, sitting against the wood pile and practicing his spelling while the woodmaster slept. Sometimes Tor thought the woodmaster trusted him to do this because he was taking Tor at his word of honor not to run away, but in his more rational moments he was sure the man wanted him to disappear so he might be free of a constant nuisance.

Sometimes Marta crept out of her house and joined him at the wood pile. He knew the child's older sister saw them when she limped out on her clubfoot for firewood or laundry. She often met his surreptitious gaze with pale, yellow-brown eyes so deep-set that they lent her angular face a perpetually eerie glare. However, it seemed she never mentioned Tor and Marta's meetings to anyone else. Tor thought that probably she, like the woodmaster, was glad for an excuse to be rid of her burden for a while.

Marta showed little interest in letters, but she liked to watch Tor make people and villages of weeds and could entertain herself with them for hours.

She would dance her grass dolls in and out of twig huts and, as Tor sounded out his words, repeat his "oo"s and "ah"s and hisses with delighted giggles.

These things made Tor cheerful, and he brought new energy—if not more care—to the workshop. When the woodmaster scolded his inattentiveness he merely smirked, muttered something about pickiness, cracked his wrists (which he knew would annoy the woodmaster), and immediately repaired his shoddy work.

The woodmaster would glare at him and bark out words for

him to spell, eager to quench this obnoxious cheer.

But even the presence of Noomi Hansson delivering cheese could not abate Tor's good spirits.

"And so, the boy is still here," she would say, grimly.

"*Ja*," the woodmaster would reply—tersely, for he was wearied by this frequent observation.

"I only hope," Noomi Hansson would say, "that you will see his cunning nature before it is too late."

And then Tor would say with an evil smile, "It's of no use, Noomi Hansson, to try to save the woodcarver's soul now. He is entirely under my influence; we lay spells over all the furniture with a potion of wolf's blood and witch's hair, and at midnight this midsummer, all who have his pieces will break into lunacy and begin to tear at each other-"

"That will do!" the woodmaster would growl, smacking Tor on the back of his head.

"You see how he dodges the truth!" Tor would cry, himself dodging to avoid a second blow.

Noomi Hansson would exclaim as she scurried out the door, "You will come to no good, *Herr* carpenter!" and Tor would smile at the woodmaster from the other side of the work table.

CHAPTER TWELVE

June, 1853

It was Midsummer's Eve, and the woodmaster was in the back room preparing potatoes to take to the celebration. He did not trust Tor to do it, he said, because the boy would likely poison the village. Tor had looked up from the nail he was driving and smiled unpleasantly. Such dry jokes from the woodmaster were growing commoner every week, but the drunkard's boy no longer took offense.

He drove his nails steadily as he thought about the celebration. He'd been to them before, but he went only for the food. Now that his belly was regularly filled he could have easily foregone the festivity, especially because it reminded him so strongly of Nanny.

All year long they'd dreamed of the midsummer's feast, huddling close together in the icy cellar, whispering about *smörgåsbords* loaded down with tasty herrings and soft potatoes and berries and cheeses and cakes. They could almost see the feast before them, glimmering in the dark, spread with colorful tablecloths and lavishly decorated with every flower Nanny could name.

It seemed midsummer had been the only time of the year when Nanny had been strong and healthy enough to do anything like celebrating. She had stayed at the Midsummer's Eve festivities well into the night, which always pleased Tor, because everyone liked gentle Nanny's shy smile, despite her sallow skin and the dark rings about her eyes. And Tor liked to see the villagers smile at her. When he was with Nanny, they spoke civilly even to him. Sometimes he wondered if he had been more protected by her than able to protect her.

And yet how often he had promised to give her all the good things she'd been denied: all the sweetness and light she had always craved. He'd promised her a house with an abundance of thick blankets, cupboards and cupboards of jam and white bread, fresh flowers in glass vases, embroidered tea towels, and filmy white curtains to let streams and rivers of light into her own little sitting room.

Nanny. He could no longer recall clearly what she looked like. He missed her far more than he had even imagined he would.

He laid down his hammer.

"'Nnn,'" he murmured, drawing in the ever-present dust layer. "Then, 'ah.' 'Nn.' And a Y." He drew a line beneath the name and stared at it. It was like her, he thought, with kind, comfortable sounds.

A hand suddenly appeared and squeezed in another 'n' with a thick finger.

"Three," said the woodmaster, walking around him to the other end of the table.

"How would you know?" asked Tor, sweeping away the letters, offended by the intrusion and also frightened that the woodmaster should know the grief that silently tormented him at night or in the stillness of a long, tedious day.

"Because my daughter's name was Nanny," said the man, suddenly absorbed in lining up his measuring stick.

Tor looked at him. Without thinking, he began to crack his knuckles one by one.

"You had a daughter?"

"A daughter and a son," replied the woodmaster as he marked his board with tiny knife cuts, "and would you cease doing that."

Tor stopped twisting his fingers and picked up the hammer.

For the barest moment he thought to ask sneeringly whether the woodmaster had chased his family off with his tyrannical behavior.

He had once before taunted the woodmaster with the absence of his wife, but today he felt the instinct quenched almost as soon as it rose. It was stupid and childish to mock at such a heavy trial. Suppose the woodmaster would begin to sneer at him for his loss of Nanny?

But he did wonder what had become of the woodmaster's people.

"You've nailed the board wrong side up," the woodmaster suddenly snarled, coming over to seize the hammer from Tor's hand and jerk out the nails.

Tor stepped back, rolling his eyes upward.

"Good Saint John, not again. It will be the third time I've nailed this board."

"Pray heaven it's the last," snapped the woodcarver, "or you will be back to cleaning tools and planing wood all day."

He turned the board to lay it in place properly, tossed the hammer down, and returned to his own work.

"I know you've a brain," he said. "I only wonder what it is doing half the day."

"Thinking of more important things than nailing boards."

"Nailing boards," said the woodmaster, picking up his measuring stick, "means sweet sleep and food for your belly."

"Vicar Arnman doesn't nail boards, and he has plenty of food for his belly and no doubt very sweet and holy dreams," Tor said. He took up a nail and set it carefully in place. "I think I would like to be a vicar. All that is required of them is to sit about reading all day and then spout their opinions to the town each week, and they are well fed."

The woodmaster snorted, but Tor noted from the corner of his eye that he half smiled.

"I would faint on the threshold if I ever saw you filling a pulpit, boy."

"And I in the pulpit if you ever appeared on my threshold. I would shepherd only the most devout of men. There would be no place in my flock for ill-natured carpenters who can't say a civil word before breakfast," said Tor piously.

The woodmaster snorted again, and turned from Tor to hide his deepening smirk.

"Come. See to your work," he said. "I want that bench finished before we leave for the festival."

Noomi Hansson looked at Tor suspiciously as he walked beside the woodmaster up to the colorful *smörgåsbord*, and the drunkard's boy smiled at her maliciously, hoping she was envisioning his threat about the cursed furniture. Beside her, Lisbet Hansson smiled back at Tor, causing him to instantly look away.

In the past he had encouraged Lisbet's infatuation for the sake of vexing Albin, but her attentions had become far too uncomfortable of late, and he was afraid to go near her.

Instead, therefore, he turned his attention to the *smörgåsbord* and began to count the several varieties of pickled herring, pondering which to taste first. There were also platters of brown bread and bowls of fruit nestled among decorations of scarlet poppies, golden buttercups, and oak branches.

The pretty girl with the heart-shaped face sauntered up just then, leaning on the schoolmaster's arm, her fair tresses wreathed with chicory blossoms and yellow *smörboll*.

"You are to compete with the schoolmaster in *kubb* this evening, *Herr* Andersson," she said, without preamble. "He assures me that he was always counted the best in the town as a lad, and, I have heard you mention the acclaim you won in your boyhood village as a *kubb* player."

"Is this to help us become friends?" asked the woodmaster, with a small, rare smile that made Tor a bit angry. His impudent speeches had made the woodmaster smile sometimes over the past few weeks, and Tor rather liked that. But he did not like that this conceited flirt should have that same power.

"Yes," answered the pretty girl. "In my house, when my brothers didn't get along, my mother tied their hands together for a whole day, and by nightfall they were laughing."

"And you intend to tie us together today, lady?" asked the schoolmaster with a sardonic lift of his eyebrow as he leaned forward to graze among the berry bowls.

"I myself shall be the link between you. Come, Wilhelm," she said, motioning for the woodmaster to offer her his arm.

"If you'll promise me a *polska*," said he, obeying her.

"I never make promises. It's unscriptural, you know. One never knows if one can keep them."

These days, Tor no longer felt ashamed for pitying the woodmaster's foolishness. It was really too bad that the man couldn't see through that girl.

He took a ginger cake and bit it, watching them go. Soon they were lost to sight in a throng of merry villagers, women in embroidered skirts with wreaths of white, pink, yellow, and blue blossoms on their heads, and red-vested men with jovial smiles and booming laughs.

Tor's thoughts instantly flitted to running away, as they always did the moment he was out of sight of the woodmaster. The thought passed away swiftly, much more swiftly than it had four months or even one month ago.

"Hello, Tor."

The voice of the vicar's daughter startled him halfway into his third bite of cake.

"Hello," he managed to reply after choking down the cake.

"Someone has stolen your companion," she said, smiling that peculiar smile that bespoke secret mirth. "Perhaps you'll join me watching the races?"

Her intensely dark blue eyes made Tor's heart falter.

"Of course," he said, trying to convey nothing but politeness in his tone. She turned, and he followed her, noting how fresh and pretty she looked with peachy rosebuds in her hair.

They joined a group of young people cheering on the sack racers, and Tor tried to ignore the disapproving or jeering glances sent his way.

"I hear," said the vicar's daughter as they sat to watch the races, "that you have built a fence for the Ahlbergs."

"I helped Thea Ahlberg," he said.

"Such a strange woman," said the girl. "She does make me laugh—all her wild attempts to sell fish at the market. Last week she all but tackled the schoolmaster." The vicar's daughter giggled.

Her mockery made Tor uneasy. He didn't want to laugh at Thea Ahlberg, but he did want the vicar's daughter to like him. He didn't know how to reply.

However, he was spared the embarrassment of offending her by the distraction of a different embarrassment.

"How are the reading lessons, drunkard's boy?" called Albin from where he sat nearby with his comrades, "Are you being a good student? Have you learnt your alphabet yet?"

"*Ja*, I have," said Tor, sneering in Albin's direction without looking at him, "and I'll be happy to teach it to you anytime."

"Ask him if he can spell *dum*, Albin," Jan Borgmann called loudly for all to hear.

"Simple, Jan," Tor smirked at the other boy, "It's spelled 'J-a-m.'"

There was a long moment of silence, and then everyone exploded into a horrible laugh that seemed to shake Tor to his bones. He knew not what kind of mistake he had made, but he suddenly wished the grass were a blanket underneath which he could crawl.

Only the vicar's daughter remained silent, staring at Jan, her expression hidden from Tor.

"'J-a-*m*,' drunkard's boy?" asked Albin, bent almost to the ground with laughing. "Are you trying to spell Jan? How strange, because I have heard it usually spelt with an '*n*.'"

Tor did not move visibly, but his every muscle stiffened. He was staring at Albin, his thoughts a battleground between humiliated pride and common sense. He knew that to set upon the cobbler's boy would mean ultimate humiliation at the hands of all Albin's friends, but he was almost past caring.

Then he realized that the vicar's daughter was speaking.

"I believe you are mistaken, Albin. Tor said 'n.' I heard him distinctly." She was now watching the racers, her cheeks flushed, and she did not move her eyes from them as she spoke.

"I heard him say 'm,'" taunted Jan.

"I did too!" six-year-old Lars piped up. He had just learned his letters and was pleased to have an opinion to contribute.

"And I," said the vicar's daughter, still cool and imperturbable, but turning to look pointedly at Jan, "heard Tor say 'n.'

"Though I believe," she continued after a moment, looking back at the field, "that the correct spelling is *d-u-m*, is it not?"

Her question was addressed to no one in particular and was answered by no one, but all fell silent.

Still, Tor's mind was a clamor of offended pride at the words of his enemies and of excitement at the quiet defense of the vicar's daughter.

Soon, Albin, Jan, and their company rose to participate in the races. Lars and two other small boys loped after them.

The vicar's daughter, however, kept at Tor's side, continuing to watch the races with neither discomfort nor particular interest.

"You dislike society, Tor?" she asked suddenly, tossing her curls over her shoulder and pulling apart a tall weed with her slim fingers.

He looked at her and then at his hands, unsure of what to say.

"You seem not to enjoy the company of the other boys."

"Should I?" Tor asked, trying to smile to offset the bitterness he knew would creep into his tone.

"Why not?" She turned and stared at him relentlessly.

Surely she knew the reason was that he was a drunkard's boy and they would not associate with him. But he refused to humiliate himself by admitting it.

"I don't like them."

"Why not?"

"They are loud-mouthed, fat-headed idiots," Tor said bluntly, fearing he gave offense but driven to answer by the uncomfortable pressure of her steady blue eyes.

"You think they are hypocrites, don't you?"

Tor was surprised. It hadn't been the reason he'd given, but it was certainly one of his main considerations.

"*Ja*," he said.

"And cowards," she continued. "They'll talk big enough behind their elder's backs, but they don't dare make a contrary peep to their faces."

Tor snorted.

"*Ja*, they are certainly cowards," he muttered.

"Do you know, I can't bear people who do things and keep meaningless traditions just because their elders tell them to," said the girl, suddenly turning away and snapping a grass stalk vehemently. "So many rules: what to wear, how to sit, how to stand, where to go, when to speak, what to read. Who's to say that merely because someone is older they are right? Why should we have to obey what they tell us? We are intelligent. We have brains. In fact, our brains are sharper than old ones."

She tossed the weed in her hands to the ground and pulled up another.

"You aren't like them at least," she said, once more turning her gaze towards him as she wound the plant around her fingers. "You never do things just because someone tells you to. You stand up to them. While everyone else does and says things simply because their ancestors did so, you, at least, are capable of thinking for yourself."

Tor stared at her in silence.

"You know what I'm speaking of," she pressed. "You refused to go to church until the carpenter absolutely forced you. You know it's worthless and full of hypocrites and that the sermons are nothing more than one man's opinions about an ancient book. You thought for yourself."

Tor was astounded by her words. He had never guessed that the perfect vicar's daughter harbored such thoughts.

She continued.

"Don't you sometimes wish you could simply throw off all the rules and do as you please? That's what I intend to do. As soon as possible, I'm going to live with my cousin in the city. She knows many progressive thinkers, and they have such fine times."

The girl's eyes sparkled as she tilted her head and looked at him. "You would fit well there, I think," she said.

Suddenly, Tor felt lost in the depths of her brilliant blue eyes. No one had ever made him feel this way: nervous and uncertain, yet at the same time bold and wise.

"Daughter!" came a shout from a group of women. It was the vicar's wife. "Come away!" she called, gesturing wildly. The vicar's daughter looked at Tor and grimaced.

"Just let them wait till I come of age," she whispered.

Then she stood up and walked away, and Tor was left with a swiftly beating heart to contemplate the stumbling sack racers.

He stood, not wanting to sit by himself where all the party of young people had been as if he had been deserted, and wandered back to the *smörgåsbord* for some cheese and *knäckebröd*. For some time, he sat beside a thick tree trunk near the table, sampling various foods and thinking complacent thoughts of himself and of the vicar's daughter, the only person in the town, it seemed, who was clear-headed enough to see his true worth.

He entertained himself with these thoughts for some time; then the dancing started, and he repositioned himself to watch the vicar's daughter dance, wishing he could dance himself.

The woodmaster, it seemed, had won his suit for the pretty girl's hand in a dance, and furthermore, she was smiling sweetly into his eyes and looking nowhere else as he twirled her about. She even said something, Tor noticed, to make the man blush, but the drunkard's boy was not as peeved about this as he would have been earlier. He was filled with greater thoughts than the woodmaster's future.

He heard a step near him and looked over to see the schoolmaster, who was again picking berries off the *smörgåsbord*.

"Your master is wasting his time, boy," said the man, not bothering even to glance at Tor. "If he weren't so foolish, he'd see the little flirt is using him to get to me."

Tor snorted. He was inclined to agree with the schoolmaster, but he thought the man had no right to insult the woodmaster, who was far superior to him.

"If that's her plan, then I hope she succeeds, for you deserve her."

Two hours before, Tor would not have dared make this speech to the schoolmaster, for he feared him more than the woodmaster. The woodmaster had a bad temper hidden in him, but in the schoolmaster was a vein of cruelty. How many times had Tor sat in silent mortification while the schoolmaster ignored his questions, his struggles, and finally, his very presence in the schoolroom?

For most of those years, the man had looked straight through Tor as if he were not a person. It seemed to everyone in the classroom that the drunkard's boy remained as loud and belligerent as possible, but Tor alone knew how his spirit had shriveled in the presence of the schoolmaster. The world saw that the man was extremely forbearing towards the young devil, but Tor had felt a hundred lacerations in his heart worse than the few bruises he'd gotten from the woodmaster.

Today, however, the vicar's daughter had made Tor bold. Her eyes and her words had intoxicated him to the point of audacity. It was as if her attentions had raised him to a level worthy of the schoolmaster's notice. The man would be forced to acknowledge him; today he would not turn and walk placidly away as if Tor's insult had been no more than the yap of a puppy.

But he did just that. After standing by the *smörgåsbord* just long enough to finish his bread and cheese and assure Tor by his unchanged expression that the boy's words had been spoken to empty air, he walked away.

Watching him depart, Tor felt a twinge of the worthlessness he had experienced whenever he raised his hand to ask a question and the schoolmaster approached the person behind him to ask if he needed assistance.

Tor tried to ignore the debilitating feeling, but as he watched the schoolmaster, his pain grew to rage, for the man approached the vicar's daughter and seemed to ask if she wished to dance. The girl replied in her usual bright, saucy manner and turned to watch the dancers again.

Tor waited anxiously for the schoolmaster to leave her side, but he did not; instead he turned to watch the dancers as well, still standing amicably by her side.

She of all people, thought Tor, should know how he has treated me. Why doesn't she send him away?

But she did not send him away, and presently, when the previous dance had finished, she allowed herself to be led by him among the dancers and took her place with the composure of a princess. Tor stared at her, almost as if greedy for the pain her betrayal caused.

But then, he asked himself, how had she betrayed him? She was merely dancing with her former schoolmaster who, as Tor recalled with disgust, had always treated her courteously and favored her almost as much as he had the clubfoot girl.

Brooding, he watched the two finish the dance and part. The next dance began, and the vicar's daughter was claimed by the grocer's eldest son. So absorbed was Tor by the girl's movements that he was not aware of the three boys approaching on his left.

"Did the schoolmaster steal your sweetheart?" Jan's voice

jarred the drunkard's boy. His tone was sweet as dripping honey and his words poignant as the sting of the bee.

"No, Lisbet is just waiting for me over by the dancers," Tor answered, nodding towards the group who stood watching the dancing and clapping in time.

"Hah!" said Albin, trying to appear scornful instead of furious, "No girl in this town would ever have a guttersnipe like you."

"I'd be doing any girl in this town a favor to marry her," said Tor. "When I'm a man, I will be able to take my pick of any girl I wish, because I will not be a toothless peasant as you all will become."

Tor spoke his words without haste and without heat, not standing, not looking at any of the boys around him, but keeping his eyes fixed upon the dancers as he unwound the long stem of feathery grass he had twisted between his fingers. He imitated the schoolmaster, expecting that this would make him feel as superior as that man appeared.

But it did not. He still felt like the guttersnipe they said he was, making a fool of himself.

Olaf, the meatiest boy of the three, knelt beside Tor and grabbed his collar.

"If you do not want to be toothless now, drunkard's boy, apologize to your betters for these insults."

Tor looked at him unflinchingly, his blood still high, both with elation and offended pride.

"Show me my betters," he said, and as Olaf drew back for a powerful but sluggish punch, the drunkard's boy boxed his ear mightily, throwing him off balance.

Immediately, Jan advanced upon him, and Tor, like a wiry wildcat, sprang at him and threw him against Olaf. The two boys tumbled to the ground but quickly gathered themselves and advanced again on Tor, who, against his better judgment, refused to turn his back and run, even at the expense of his teeth.

When they rushed at him together, it was with such force that they all were thrown against the table, and then the groaning *smörgåsbord* crashed to the ground, and the fiddlers and pipers ceased playing by the dancers.

Olaf and Jan pulled back from Tor, aghast, and perhaps thinking of their father's belts, but Tor, enraged, flew upon the boys till he had Jan pinned and at the mercy of his fists.

There were only a few moments of glory before Tor felt himself forcibly pulled off Jan, and, without thinking, he began to curse. The man holding him beat him about the head and shoulders, but Tor didn't care and did not cease cursing till the man gave up beating and clamped a hand over his mouth instead.

Then Tor began to bite, savagely, and the man withdrew his hand in haste. Yet before Tor had a moment to triumph in this small victory the woodmaster appeared before him and seized him from the other man's hands.

"Quiet," he roared at Tor, grabbing the boy's face and squeezing until his cheeks met inside his open mouth. The man's rough nails pressed into his skin, causing Tor's eyes and nose to smart, but he shut his eyes and continued to thrash.

The vicar's voice now sounded distantly beyond the pounding in Tor's head.

"If you do not send that boy away, *Herr* carpenter, I will do it myself!"

Then the woodmaster lifted Tor and propelled him through the crowd.

"Why do you continually bring this boy into public if you cannot restrain him, Andersson," shouted the vicar. His cry was followed up by Noomi Hansson's, the cobbler's, and several others. The woodmaster continued walking and said nothing to anyone, but Tor could feel tremors of anger in the hands that gripped his arms.

❄ ❄ ❄

Once well into the forest, out of sight of the others, the woodmaster let Tor go, but continued to drive him before, shoving him periodically with a force that almost threw the boy to the ground.

"Stop!" Tor finally screamed, turning on the woodmaster. "If you wish to whip me, then do it now!"

"I'll whip you when I please," said the man.

"Do you not even care who started that fight? I was sitting under a tree doing nothing when they came to me!"

"*Nej*," said the woodmaster harshly, "I don't care. Now move on."

But the drunkard's boy stood his ground, staring at the woodmaster, realizing how much he'd trusted this man only after he'd been betrayed by him. To be spurned and misjudged by someone who knew hardly anything of him was one thing, but to be condemned without trial by the one man who did know something of his hardships and especially his vulnerability was another.

"It would have been better to freeze to the street than to come live with you," Tor said, almost choking out the words.

The man's face grew white with severity, and by his unconstrained movements Tor could see he'd lost control of himself for the second time in their acquaintance.

"I said, 'Move on!'"

The man's voice was a growl. He grasped Tor and pushed him forward violently. This time Tor allowed himself to fall and did not rise. He cared little if the man beat him; he'd already done his worst by betraying him.

But the woodmaster refused to be manipulated contrary to his will. He'd said he'd whip Tor when he pleased, and Tor knew that, even in his anger, the man remembered his words. Instead of cutting a switch from one of the many birch trees, the woodmaster stood over the drunkard's boy and waited for him to rise. When Tor did not move, the woodmaster pulled him up by the front collar of his shirt and dragged him along some paces. The drunkard's boy remained stubbornly limp, too exhausted to struggle against and too angry to comply with the woodmaster's iron will.

As they dragged onward, Tor sensed mounting exasperation in the woodmaster's jolting movements, and he waited for the inevitable explosion, but the worst that occurred was the woodmaster suddenly bending towards him and throwing him over his shoulder with no more care than if he had been a sack of grain. They walked all the way into the town in this unseemly manner, Tor only able to stomach the indignity because there was no one to watch.

But just as they were coming upon the woodshop a small, slightly slurred voice cried, "Tor! Are you hurt?"

Tor struggled for freedom, but the woodmaster welcomed the opportunity to humiliate him.

"*Nej*," the man answered Marta, gripping Tor tighter, "he is not."

Tor attempted to kick the man with his knee, but the woodmaster tightened the vise of his arm.

"Don't hurt him!" Marta suddenly cried. "Don't hurt him!"

And Tor heard her come trundling off the small porch of their house toward him. Immediately, another voice cried for Marta to stop.

Tor shut his eyes and struck the woodmaster's back with all the strength of his bony elbow. Why had not Marta and her sister gone to the celebration?

Marta came pattering up and flung her arms around the woodmaster's leg, who instantly stopped moving.

"Well," said yet another voice. "What an interesting scene."

It was the schoolmaster. Tor almost gave a roar of frustration. Only half an hour before, he'd seen the man dancing smugly with the vicar's daughter. Before that, he had been flirting with the woodmaster's pretty girl. Now, he was in the village keeping company with Marta and her older sister. Was the man everywhere?

"I must say, *Herr* carpenter, that you and the boy certainly provide rich entertainment for this community if nothing else."

Tor was about to deliver a scathing reply when the woodmaster interrupted his thoughts. The man's tone was dry, as usual, and also harsh—much harsher than Tor had ever heard the man use on anyone but himself.

"Of course, *Herr* Askenberg, I came to this town for no other purpose than to amuse you, as I know you must have some diversion to fill your idle hours."

Tor had no opportunity to observe the schoolmaster's reaction to this startling attack, for Marta's sister suddenly stepped forward to take the little girl by the shoulders.

"Come, Marta!" She jerked the child away roughly. "I'm sorry, *Herr* Andersson," she said, dragging Marta away, her eyes on the ground. "Marta, if you don't behave I'll slap you!"

Tor forgot *Herr* Askenberg and the woodmaster and even his own humiliation for the moment.

"If you hurt Marta," he hissed, "I'll tear your laundry to pieces next time you lay it out!"

The girl looked up at Tor suddenly, as if startled. Tor glimpsed a crescent of green and purple beside one eye before she quickly looked away again. She picked up the crying Marta and limped to her house.

For a moment, Tor was distracted by the bruise the girl so evidently wished to hide, and he scarcely noticed when the woodmaster carried him into the house. But when the man set him on the floor, and Tor once again saw his face, every thought but fear fled him.

Only once before had he seen the woodmaster so incensed. The man forced him down on a heavy bench and took a length of rope from its hanger on the wall. With this he bound Tor's hands together tightly behind his back and bound his legs to the bench.

"Why is everything that happens my fault?" Tor suddenly demanded. In his mind the words were a frantic appeal, but in the air they were only an angry shout.

The woodmaster ignored him, opened the front door, and was gone.

Tor stared at the door, dazed by the change from the woodmaster's maelstrom of wrath to the sudden creaking quiet of the workshop. He wondered how long the man intended to leave him here.

Of a sudden, the door crashed open again and the woodmaster strode in at the drunkard's boy, who could not help but cringe at his approach. The woodmaster, however, did not look at him but knelt behind him and began to untie the rope binding him.

Tor became aquiver with sick expectation. If the woodmaster was untying him, undoubtedly it was because he had something worse in mind for him.

But no. He was retying him. He'd only loosened the ropes that bit into Tor's wrists.

Then he was gone again, leaving Tor to sit listening to the dissonant tick of the woodmaster's little clocks in the front room.

For hours Tor remained there, watching the sun shadows creep very slowly across the floor until it was night. His familiar, silent rage—all the more turbulent because he could not move—returned to drive out the fear.

Why did these people invariably assume he was at fault? Always the instigator. Always the insulter and never the insulted. Always the attacker and never the victim. Always the one who knocked down tables and never the one knocked into them. Why was he always the villain because his mother had been unmarried and a drunkard?

Idiot woodmaster. Could he not even see?

Nej. The woodmaster was the worst of them all. He had at first accused Tor of stealing his Nativity with no proof but his own suspicions. That had been disagreeable, but now Tor was even more furious that the woodmaster, having seemed so reasonable and tolerant of late, should have turned upon him with the rest of those simpletons, as if he thought no better of Tor than they did. As if he had not seen Tor's diligence and feverish struggles late every night, early every morning, and all throughout the day to learn to read. As if he had not noticed Tor's effort to behave and execute his work well; as if he had not noticed that Tor had upheld his bargain not to run away.

At last, fury was exhausted, and Tor slumped with fatigue. He was bound to the bench with nothing to lean upon. The woodmaster's punishments were often just so shrewdly contrived that Tor scarcely realized they were bad enough to be punishments until well after they had begun.

Tor yearned to lie down or at least rest his back against some surface, but the bench was too heavy and bulky to navigate through the crowded workshop, even if there had been space enough against the walls to accommodate its length. And of course, the woodmaster had taken care, even when loosening the ropes, that they should be impossible to escape.

Tor managed to inch the bench backwards far enough to rest his back on the edge of a table, but that was all. So he sat slumped on the bench till the last rays of the sun gave way to a vague twilight.

The woodmaster did not come, and the hours passed in painful lethargy.

Occasionally, Tor stretched his aching muscles and tried to sit up straight, but to remain straight was too great an exertion, and before long he would find himself in another nodding but sleepless slump.

To distract himself from his exhaustion, he tried to think of the vicar's daughter, but this only led him to the memory of her dancing, sylph-like, with the detestable schoolmaster. Then he would grow angry as he continued to think about the schoolmaster and the school boys and the woodmaster. Then he would brood helplessly until he lapsed again into exhaustion.

At last he heard the back room open. Someone entered, removed his boots and went straight to lie down on the woodmaster's bed. Then all was still once more. Tor fumed silently, knowing that screaming a demand to be released would only prolong his imprisonment.

He would not ask to be released, though he considered it many times that long, light midsummer night.

At last, when the sunshine had infused the dusty room till it shone full in Tor's face, creaks and footfalls announced the rising of the woodmaster.

Tor felt little else besides the anticipation of being free from his bonds, but as the woodmaster continued to delay, clattering dishes and pots, his anger once again mounted. He must not shout, he told himself, now that he was so close to release.

The woodmaster made breakfast, ate breakfast, washed, and dressed before finally opening the back room door and coming to untie Tor.

The drunkard's boy kept his now alert eyes fixed on the knees of his trousers and said nothing. The woodmaster slapped a wedge of cheese and three portions of *knäckebröd* on the table before him before releasing him and rubbing his tense arms and hands up and down to revive full circulation.

"Eat," the man said at last, backing away, "and then plane those boards in the corner and see that you plane them well."

Tor ate the food slowly, curbing the surges of emotion that alternately tempted him to throw the woodmaster's food in his face or to lie down on the floor and never get up.

The woodmaster did not rebuke him for his slowness but began his work without giving further attention to him. All day he did not speak to Tor or notice him unless to tell him his next task. He did not even approach to inspect the boy's work for shoddiness, but simply left him to his own devices.

Tor dragged his heavy feet and fumbling hands through the dry dust, counting down the hours to the quarter mark of the work day, then the half, then the three-quarter, until he should be sent to prepare supper. He drew several splinters from the rough boards and skinned his knuckles more than once in bleary-eyed clumsiness. He thought several times that he would insult and rail on the woodmaster until the man was forced to speak, but then he would consider that he'd only be tied up again for his pains.

Finally, he was sent to prepare supper. As soon as he had done so he lay down on his bed and slept, thinking that he preferred to die of starvation rather than exhaustion. He did not wake until late the next morning.

❄   ❄   ❄

The woodmaster was not in the house when Tor arose, neither in the back room, nor the workroom, nor the front shop, and Tor remembered that the man had a load of wood to pick up at the wharf that morning.

Quickly, the drunkard's boy knotted a few provisions into his blanket, taking only what he thought necessary for a lengthy journey. He shoved on his shoes and took the blue winter coat the woodmaster had given him so many months ago, and he walked out the back door and into the woods.

Deciding to take his chances in another small village rather than go again to Stockholm, he began to plod through the leaves and tree roots, feeling not angry, but miserable as he thought of his reading lessons and Thea Ahlberg's warm kitchen and the summer evenings with giggling Marta and her straw villages.

He kicked a dead branch and told himself it was the woodmaster's fault. Tor might expect bad treatment from the villagers, but not from the woodmaster. He was shrewd and just.

And yet the man had imprisoned and tyrannized over him for months. He had struck Tor once, and several times he had starved him to make him obey. Indeed, he'd really been tortured by the woodmaster, absolutely tortured.

The man had never tried to understand but had ever supposed the worst of Tor and punished him according to those assumptions. He kept Tor as a convicted criminal on a chain gang. It had always been inevitable that Tor would run, always. The man was unjust and mean: a bully, absolutely a bully.

His head filled with these accusations, Tor walked all day to reach the next town, dodging off the road at the approach of any traveler. He spent the night in a deserted fisherman's shack. He passed quickly through the town once he'd reached it, for though the woodmaster did not often venture from their town, others did, and they would be only too eager to spread the news of Tor's whereabouts.

Not, Tor told himself as he nibbled the edges of his *knäckebröd*, that the woodmaster would follow him. He'd said plenty of times that the drunkard's boy was welcome to escape if he were able. Hateful man. His taunt had been a constant mortification to Tor.

Still, sometimes, as he wandered along the road, he would become lost in troubled thought, and when he looked up, startled by a bird call or a scamper in the forest, he would expect to see the woodmaster beside him, asking him how to spell "broom," or "hammer," or "work." And when the drunkard's boy recalled that the woodmaster was not to be seen, he experienced something like the emptiness he'd felt when Nanny died.

The next morning Tor rose and went on his way, nagged by the thought that he ought to find some job or other to gain a few more provisions, but he hated begging, even for work. People always looked at him as if he were a mutt nosing a hen house. Therefore, he walked on, spending the next night in the forest.

He woke in the night to horrible foot cramps and a back that was sore from his weary night on the bench.

Staring at the stars, wakeful from pain but half asleep from exhaustion, he questioned his decision to leave the woodmaster. He could starve. He could freeze. What made him think he could escape the same fate he had met with last winter? His ragged clothes and haggard looks would prevent him from finding good work.

Yesterday, his greatest annoyance was that the people of his village looked down on him. Today, he already feared starvation.

CHAPTER THIRTEEN

On the fourth day, Tor's provisions were depleted, and he was then forced to ask for work. He wandered down the street of a village from the butchery to the smithy to the grocery, and no man would take him. He went to the mill and to the docks, but could find no work.

He came at last to the carpenter's shop, and he balked a moment before entering. Had it been only that week that he felt he would do anything rather than work as a carpenter? Now he was begging for that position.

At last, he moved toward the door. Doffing his cap and bowing his head, he spoke humbly.

"*Herr* woodcarver," he said, "Do you have some work you would like me to do?"

The man, who had brown, curly hair very unlike the woodmaster's, shook his head without looking up.

"*Nej,* boy. Sorry."

"I've worked in a carpenter's shop before. I know I could be of use to you," Tor persisted, crushing his pride with a great effort and forcing the words out.

"*Nej*, I have nothing for you."

"*Herr* carpenter, I have asked everyone. I need food."

The words now flowed from sheer desperation.

The carpenter hammered a moment longer, then laid down his hammer and took up a board.

"I cannot give you work," he finally sighed when Tor had despaired of a reply. "No one here can afford to take you as a liability, boy. No one has the means to pay you, and if you get into mischief, the expense will fall upon your employer's head. How is anyone to know what you are, who you're running from? If it's food and a bed you want you can go to the almshouse, lad."

Tor walked outside, feeling like a cuffed dog with his tail twixt his legs. Certainly the entire village was watching him and whispering of him as he skulked through the streets. He looked up angrily, pulling back his shoulders and trying to blink off the redness he knew was about his eyes as he walked to the almshouse by the church. There, he presented himself brusquely, accepted his meal of bread and porridge, and departed for the next village.

He slept again in the forest and bathed in the sea next morning. He trembled with hunger and the chill of his sea bath as he proceeded on his way. Recalling several occasions when the woodmaster had drawn him a warm bath, he shook the more. He wondered if he had a fever, but he told himself the thought was ridiculous. It was summer, and it was not reasonable that he should have such bad luck—especially after he had endured so much of it already.

In the next town, a kind woman agreed to feed him a hot supper if he would chop some wood, but when her husband came home he was not pleased to see the disheveled drunkard's boy seated at his table with his three children. Tor immediately relinquished all hope of a comfortable bed that night and departed as soon as possible.

The next morning he continued his quest for work and found another odd job scouring the stone floor of the church. This task provided two more hot meals, and Tor, faintly pleased, continued in that town the next day in hopes of a more permanent job. But that day's hunting proved fruitless. He wandered till mid-afternoon asking for work, but there was none to be had.

He begged lunch at the almshouse and then returned to the streets, feverish and somewhat frantic. He was certain he was sick now. If this was how he fared in June, what would he do upon the arrival of inevitable winter snows?

He at last approached a portly, well-dressed gentleman standing outside the post office with a paper in hand.

"*Ja*," said the man, abruptly, in answer to Tor's request for work. "Come with me."

Tor obeyed with a beating heart. He'd never supposed that such a well-to-do man would give him work. It was inconceivable. Tor resolved as he followed the man that nothing would cause him to lose his temper. He would accept any sneer or taunt humbly. He would not curse. He would not ridicule or satirize anyone. He would be a model worker no matter how low the position.

The drunkard's boy was so far taken with his resolutions that he did not notice where they were going until he suddenly realized that the well-to-do gentleman had brought him to another man. He looked up at the stranger . . . and flinched.

"Come, boy, have you something to be afraid of?" asked the portly man who escorted him.

"*Nej*," Tor answered slowly, eyeing the *konstapel*, who returned his scrutiny with tired eyes. If this was some kind of trap, then there was no hope of escape now. He might outrun the portly man, but not the wiry *konstapel*. Best to bluff.

"What is your name?" asked the *konstapel*, not unkindly.

"Tor Neeson."

The *konstapel* looked at the portly man.

"And why have you brought him here, *Herr* Lund?"

"He is a vagrant," replied the portly man. "He has been wandering the town for days, unable to procure work, and now he is disturbing the residents. The king frowns upon vagrants moving about the country without work. He must be sent to the workhouse."

The *konstapel* sighed. He looked past Tor down the street and massaged the side of his neck deeply with strong fingers.

"Have you any people, lad?" he asked.

"*Nej*," said the drunkard's boy. He had already drawn up his hard belligerent shell about him, and now he fixed his sullen glare on the ground, demanding of himself how he could have let his guard down yet again, how he could have believed that some person other than himself would like to help him.

The *konstapel* shook his head, sighed again, and laid one hand on Tor's shoulder.

"A coach leaves for Norrköping this afternoon," he said to the portly man. "I will send him on that," "For now," he continued, looking at Tor, "you may sleep on one of the prison cots, if you like."

And so Tor walked with the man to prison. He slumped down on his prison cot almost gratefully, for it was more comfortable than anywhere he had slept in the last week.

❄ ❄ ❄

The coach took him with all haste to the workhouse, traveling well into the lengthening night. At two 'o' clock in the morning, they arrived at a huge grey structure which loomed, stark and rigid, against the black sky. Tor felt, when he stepped over the threshold, that it was like a hungry monster, accepting the human sacrifices that the guilty city shoved its way and regurgitating them only when it had drained out the life. That was the workhouse.

Tor was given a cot assignment and a work assignment. Breakfast would be at six 'o' clock, but since he was to help in the kitchen he must be ready at four 'o' clock, in two hours.

He slept his two hours away heavily and then was driven from his bed to peel potatoes for another two hours. He felt horribly sick, and his bleary eyes played him false; he cut his fingers three times. The cook grew angry at him for bloodying the food.

He washed dishes after that, hundreds of dishes. Then he was set before the hot fire for an hour or two to stir vats of porridge. Grease, sweat, and dirt from his travels stung his eyes. There would be no bath, he knew. He would be fortunate to have a basin of water and a chip of soap to wash with sometime before the month was out.

After lunch he cleaned more dishes—there were hundreds of poor in this workhouse, though not as many as in the Stockholm workhouse where he had stayed one week last winter.

That night, serving supper, he looked at the faces of the long trail of people who came through to receive their portion of oat porridge. Hardly any of them lifted their eyes to his. They had not the energy to look past their own exhaustion or the needs of the little ones in their care.

Tor knew very well that soon he too would no longer have the energy to look up from his feet.

When he at last tumbled to his cot, the black-toothed man

who slept in the next bed was very eager to share his woeful stories and his tales of the good days he had spent drinking liquor with his fellow fishermen, but Tor rolled over to face the other direction.

Instead of listening to the wretched blatherer, he chose to spend his few moments of freedom thinking about the woodmaster's house and how much better he had lived when there, and then trying to rekindle all the justifiable bitterness which had persuaded him that running away from Wilhelm Andersson had been the reasonable thing to do.

CHAPTER FOURTEEN

He was miserable. More miserable than he had ever dreamed of being at the woodmaster's house. More miserable even than he had been at the Stockholm workhouse or in the dank, rat-infested cellar where he had spent most of his life. He had been raised in muck and moldy air. He had been accustomed to unclean smells and been comfortable in his own grimy skin. But the inescapable, stifling filth now filled him with angst until he almost believed a mere brushing of the hairs on his arm at the wrong moment might ignite him like gunpowder.

When had he grown so weak, he asked himself, that he couldn't endure a little cold and dirt? And yet it seemed to him that this workhouse was far colder, far dirtier, far more vermin- and disease-ridden than any place he had ever been before.

He could not but compare the difference between his dreams of learning to read so he could attend university and become somebody worthwhile—dreams which had once seemed actually within reach—to his present reality of perpetual slime and toil. He was to have been something more than a hollow-eyed slave to his belly, but now all he looked forward to during the day was mealtime: the few bites of potato or grain that quelled the ache of his stomach.

How foolish of him. How foolish to expect that he could ever climb out of that filthy cellar where he'd been born. Better to have stayed there and rotted than try to change the bad things that were destroying his life.

He'd gone to school and made an enemy of the schoolmaster. He'd tried to save his sister and been imprisoned by the woodmaster. He'd gone to church and been scorned. Tried to learn to read and been mocked. Tried to defend himself and been punished.

How foolish of him to keep fighting his fate. He was not destined to climb from the slimy pit of beggary any more than he had been destined to save his sister's life. He ought to stop fighting before his circumstances became any worse.

But his real misfortunes began the evening he knocked a bucket of milk to the floor, and the cook, who had already suffered many instances of Tor's clumsiness and inattention, boxed his ear.

"I didn't spill it on purpose!" Tor snarled, coddling the bloody ear. He was agitated from weeks of sweaty work and shrill threats, and from many nights in his stifling quarters full of foul human smells and hacking coughs.

And now, this piercing pain of the cook's box on his ear. He would have roared if he had not feared it would aggravate his pain. Instead, he savagely kicked the spilled bucket across the stone floor. It clattered and scraped and dented horrendously against the sturdy leg of a table.

At this opportune moment, the overseer of the workhouse appeared in the doorway.

"I cannot bear this urchin in the kitchen another moment," screamed the cook. "Take it away!"

The overseer looked at Tor, weary frustration in his eyes.

"What is the trouble, boy?"

"The milk spilled, and she boxed me," said Tor, sourly. He felt his hand trembling against his ear. His frequent shakiness never used to trouble him much, but he suddenly recalled that since living with the woodmaster his body had grown increasingly strong and steady. Now his recurring weakness frightened him.

Pitiful, he thought.

"Come," said the overseer, "you must learn to get along."

"*Nej,*" Tor snapped. "Despite my humble gratitude for your generous help in giving me work, I want to get out of this stinking building. Find me work somewhere else if you don't want your kitchen set fire."

He knew full well the stupidity of his own attitude. The overseer was a fair and well-intentioned man, and to treat him with disrespect would only lose Tor a possible ally. But Tor was too distraught and angry to care about that.

The overseer looked at him, and Tor could see his gaze turning icy, and, as often happened, the drunkard's boy regretted his speech.

"Very well, boy," said the overseer. "I will arrange for you to work outside, starting tonight. Meanwhile, mop up this spill."

Tor had obeyed, desiring to appease the overseer by good behavior because he sensed he had trodden upon perilous ground.

But his change of heart came too late. That night, the overseer summoned him from the dormitory and escorted him to a cart that had pulled up outside the workhouse.

"Here is your new worker," he said to the bedraggled man who drove the cart. "Keep an eye on him." The man in the cart chuckled unpleasantly and leered at Tor in the flickering lantern light, and the overseer reentered the workhouse without glancing back.

"Do as you're told, boy," said the man in the cart, "and I'll give you no cause to cry." He chuckled again and straightened to snap the reins.

"Drive on!"

The cart reeked, and Tor and the other workhouse denizens assigned to the cart did not board but rather walked beside it. They didn't walk far before pulling off to the side of the dark, filthy street. Then Tor's companions silently took shovels and pails from the cart and entered the alleyways on either side.

"Move, boy! Clean out that night soil, or I'll rub it in your face!" called the supervisor, carrying a lantern high and herding Tor down the alley.

Tor took the last pail and shovel and entered one of the alleys.

The "night soil" was the excrement that residents of the city piled into alleyways. The drunkard's boy soon discovered that this labor assignment was a triple-edged strategy on the overseer's part. First, the work was punitively disgusting; second, it was not easy for Tor to make mistakes with; and third, the supervisor had a heavy hand and little patience, quite the sort of man, as the overseer no doubt believed, to lesson Tor's insolent tongue.

Not merely the smell—though this was enough to make one retch—but the sight of dung mixed with festering food scraps and swarming, shadowy vermin was nauseating. By the end of his first night as a worker of "night soil," Tor wondered how he could exist waking up each day to face constant nausea.

His supervisor carried the lantern along the alleys all night, scolding them into haste for their never-ending chore. He loved to make lewd and shocking threats that would jolt his workers out of their desolate lethargy, and for the time being Tor was his primary target, as he was freshest to the work and most easily disturbed.

It was at this time that Tor quite earnestly considered returning to the woodmaster. Nights of exhausting, revolting labor had sapped the memories of the woodmaster's injustice of much of their bitterness, leaving the drunkard's boy with nothing but regret.

He would return and apologize and beg the man on his knees to let him come back and slave away in his workshop. He would be more attentive. He would aptly learn whatever the woodmaster chose to teach. The man was rough. He had a temper and was violent at times. But he was not cruel. He would not kick Tor away like a dog, would he?

Then the drunkard's boy would consider that the woodmaster had no reason to take him back. He remembered how the woodmaster had often said he was free to leave if he could but escape. He recalled the woodmaster's annoyance at his frequent mistakes in the shop and the man's frustration at his absurd learning handicap. He remembered that the woodmaster hated him for stealing his Nativity.

He would imagine himself upon his knees before the woodmaster, only to be pushed away and shut coldly out of the man's house.

And where, now that he needed it most, was his righteous anger against the woodmaster's indignities?

❄   ❄   ❄

At the end of the third night, the "night soil" supervisor came and jostled Tor in the dark, causing him to step ankle deep in a pile of excrement.

Then Tor, shaking and despairing and furious, had cursed the man and run at him, aiming his shoulder for the man's stomach in an attempt to hurl him to the ground. The man was all too ready, grabbing the boy and twisting him face down into filth.

The man pulled his head up by the hair.

"You'll apologize to me, boy," he said, "or I'll push you back in."

Tor gasped in air wildly, writhing and ridiculously hysterical.

"I'm sorry!" he screamed. "Forgive me."

The supervisor chuckled, pushed him back down anyway, and held him to the ground for several moments longer.

"See that you mind me, boy, from now on," he said, smiling.

After that incident, Tor was wild to escape. Starvation and the coming winter were no longer even considerations to him. To get away from this nightmare and to do it without being caught was all he could think of. That, and the woodmaster's house, of course.

There were some, Tor knew, like that scamp Nils, who were easy-going and optimistic despite their filthy drudgery. Nils got on well with everyone, and he seemed to make the time pass quickly for himself and some of the others by teasing and joking. But Tor was hopelessly crushed. He wished he had Nils' buoyant spirit. He wondered what was wrong with him that the labor suddenly seemed so much more unendurable to him than to others.

He waited for a time when the supervisor was distracted, and at the first opportunity he simply ran. He had no provisions and no plan, but, worse than this, he was unfamiliar with the streets.

He ran blindly around every corner he came to, and as he ran he became acutely aware of the palpitations of his heart and the feebleness of his legs, and he wondered how he, the young devil that everyone had labeled audacious and insolent, had come to be so cowardly.

The shout of the supervisor reached his ears—an unintelligible threat, but a threat, no doubt, of how he would deal with Tor if he did not return. But it was too late now for repentance. Tor knew full well that the supervisor would abuse him just as badly if he returned as he would if Tor were caught. Indeed, the drunkard's boy was almost certain that surrendering would be the more torturous ordeal.

His calves now felt limp and tremulous as pork fat.

What, he asked himself in a frantic attempt to moderate his disproportionate fear, what was the worst that could happen to him?

Then he turned another corner and the supervisor bolted at him from the side, his outstretched arm just grazing Tor's sleeve. The leer on his face revealed to Tor in a flash that he had been anticipating this moment for weeks: he had wanted Tor to run away for the pleasure of running him down and punishing him.

Tor, to his infinite shame, yelped from fright. He veered away, his body jolting with a frantic energy that seemed only to weaken him more as he ran.

And the supervisor's footsteps drew closer and closer until Tor stumbled.

Then he discovered the worst that could happen.

CHAPTER FIFTEEN

November, 1853

The hollow-eyed drunkard's boy paused in the twilight of an early November morning to rummage deftly through a pile of frosted food scraps with his bony blue fingers. It was the well-to-do part of town, and he had learned to move with an energy he did not possess to beat the rats, dogs, and other workers to possible treats amid the garbage of this sector.

Today, to his good fortune, there was a roasted goose wing that had been only partially dissected and orange peels that were not yet stale. Till coming to the city, Tor had never tasted any part of an orange, and the peels had become a treat to him. He liked how they made his mouth feel fresh.

He lifted the picked over goose wing to his mouth and was about to taste a bite when a rough hand grasped the front of his neck, forcing his head back. Tor cringed and squirmed away, huddling close to the ground to escape the reach of the supervisor's hand. He held up the goose wing without looking up, hoping to pacify his tormentor. The supervisor snatched the meat away.

"You're here to work, not snack, boy," he said, even as he lifted the wing to his own lips.

Tor nodded and crept away to begin filling his bucket with

night soil. For months now, the will to resist the supervisor had been quenched.

That evening, as he had lain on his bed, stealing the last few precious moments of rest before dragging forth into the icy, stinking alleys, he had almost wished that cholera would take him as it had taken so many of the men around him this month. His loss would be a gain to the troubled world when he became one less mouth to feed. He had sincerely wished for sickness as he stared at the grimy, mottled slats of the bed above him. He wished for anything to end his present way of living.

But he trudged on through the alleys with his bucket, because, for some reason unknown to himself, he needed to live. Even his misery could not seem to throttle that desire out of him. At the end of his long shift he ate his miserable breakfast and went to bed, and when night came again, he rose silently to return to the streets.

But that night, Tor noticed a lapse in the supervisor's constant inspections. Instead of swaggering up and down the alleys to bully the workers, he sat sluggishly in the wagon, strangely quiet, flushed, and glassy-eyed. Still, he continued to drive the work forward obstinately, despite Nils' hints that he return to the workhouse.

In the end, the man fainted in the cart, and they drove him back to the workhouse.

To Tor's mind, the supervisor's debilitation was a great relief.

The drunkard's boy was watched as closely as ever by Inger, who took the supervisor's place, but he was not bullied and was left to shovel dung in peace. He spent the entirety of the morning feeding on the hope that the supervisor would die.

But soon he became aware of an increased trembling and flushes of hot and cold through his own body. By early evening, he could scarcely stay afoot. Then Nils, turning from dumping a load in the cart, glanced at Tor's face in the dim light and called to Inger, "Tor is sick."

The drunkard's boy was taken to the workhouse and laid in the quarantine room. In the very bed next to the supervisor's he was laid.

But the man did not notice him. He remained oblivious with his eyes shut, wracked with shivering and guttural moans that prevented Tor from sleeping for a long while.

When at last Tor began to doze, the supervisor jolted upright in his bed, crying, "*Nej!* I swear I'll fix it, I swear! Please, *nej*, Father!"

And then he huddled back down on the bed with his arms over his face, weeping and jolting from head to toe with deep spasms that made Tor's blood cold to watch. He covered his own head with a pillow, but the man repeatedly burst out in shouts of terror so that during the night Tor felt he did not sleep at all, despite his sickness and exhaustion.

Yet the next morning, he knew he must have slept, for he was jolted to sudden consciousness by sounds from the bed next to him. Chattering with cold under his paper thin blanket, he rolled over to see two men lifting the supervisor off the bed. The man's hands and face were grey and rigid. His countenance was now frozen in perpetual terror.

Tor slept then, but not peacefully. It was his turn for delirium. Figures appeared and vanished in his dreams, sometimes arriving to pry his mouth open and pour bitter liquids down his throat, sometimes appearing to laugh at him with red blotched faces, bugging eyes, and great pink and white tongues, and sometimes smearing his face and chest with handfuls of muck. Almost always, he saw the schoolmaster in the background, twirling about the room with the vicar's daughter to strange, dissonant music.

Every so often, he would see the woodmaster. The man would be always sitting by the fire, impassively watching Tor storm and stamp furiously about the little back room, threatening to run away if the woodmaster married the pretty girl with the heart-shaped face. The woodmaster would simply toss his head to one side and stare at him, making Tor so angry that he would finally turn and run. The back room would then become a long, dark alley of sickbeds and manure, with Tor running for the grey light at the end. When he looked over his shoulder he would see the woodmaster turn smilingly towards the pretty girl, who suddenly appeared by his side to shut a door that locked Tor out of the woodmaster's house forever.

Tor dreamt this—he knew not how many times—till the end of his sickness.

Then, at last, he came to himself, opened his eyes in the squalid makeshift infirmary, and sickened to remember what his life was. Yet he found himself too divested of strength to even mentally rebel. Every time a person approached him with a bowl or a cup he felt close to tears, but he never resisted them; instead, he meekly accepted the will of those who poured gruel and certain throat scouring liquids in his mouth.

After a time, he could sit upright, propped with a pillow, and watch the workers come in and out, administering medicines and carrying away the dead.

And then one night directly after supper, a large man came and pulled back Tor's blanket.

"Come," he said, "It's time you were up."

Tor looked at him in frightened shock.

"Up?" he repeated. "Do I have to clean the streets again? Do I have to go now? Can I not stay longer?"

"*Nej*," said the man. "I don't know what you'll be doing, but this bed is needed. Come." And he lifted Tor bodily from the bed and set him on his unsteady bare feet.

No sooner had Tor vacated the bed than two men entered with the arms of another man over their shoulders, whom they slung carefully upon the bed.

Staring at the new body that had so quickly replaced his, Tor felt like the refuse that was daily cast into the alley for him to clean. He was placeless and painfully cold. They'd thrust him out of his bed as if he no longer mattered. How cruel of them to pretend they cared for him, to feed him and nurse him, only to push him into the cold again, quite alone and weak.

"Please, can't I stay?" he asked, staring at the bed, silent tears streaming, sudden and irrepressible, down his face.

"*Nej,*" said the man, pushing him from the room. "You're recovered. Go to your own bed."

"I don't know where it is," pleaded Tor.

"Well, no more do I," snapped the man. "Come boy, move off. There are many sick. Have a thought for others besides yourself."

Tor picked up his shoes and stumbled down the hall blindly, searching for his sleeping quarters. The chipped grey walls seemed to tilt, sometimes together, sometimes away from each other. He heard faint scratches and skitterings just beyond the loud ring in his ears, sounds he vaguely recognized as mice and large roaches. He hugged his cold shoulders and tried to stop his tears with the thought of soon lying to rest in his bed under a little blanket—if he could find it.

But, faltering on with his hand against the wall and turning corners blindly, he felt repeated stabs of fear that he would wander here forever, never stopping for sleep at any small grey cot or pausing to huddle over any bowl of thin, steaming porridge.

He seemed to wander for a day—though it might have been but minutes—before he saw a pair of familiar brown doors, and he realized with an almost painful thrill that he was just inside the entrance of the workhouse. If he followed the corridor to the right it would lead him to the wing where the men slept. It would take him to his own cold cot.

He pursued his way almost with eagerness, gaining comfort in the familiarity of the mouldering doors whose sight had nauseated him so many times before.

At last he arrived at his cot. And he found a man sleeping there in his place.

Tor stared, staggered by this second slap of rejection. He truly was placeless. Where could he go now? The one spot in the world where he was supposed to be, where he belonged, had been given to someone else.

He remembered one of Isak Ahlberg's stories. A description of being lost at sea, drifting helplessly in endless waters, thrashing about in frantic search for ships only to see small grey sails announcing the presence of sharks lurking just under the surface, ready to bite off a leg. That was he, floating helplessly in a titanic world. He was at the mercy of almost anyone, and they would feed off of his body, sapping his energy till he died. People like the supervisor, who had wanted to feed on Tor's fear for his own pleasure, perhaps hoping to dull the pain which had tortured himself.

Emotions ravaged Tor's mind one after another as he stared at the man sleeping in his bed. The drunkard's boy had never been so helpless. He had always had control of his mind, always had confidence in his ability to repress his fears with a mask of bravado that often fooled even himself.

Yet now, as he tried to convince himself that his frightful imaginings were a product of sickness, reason could not check his wild fears.

Unable to bear the strain, he collapsed to his knees, muffling sobs that seemed to shred his throat. With nowhere else to go, he crawled under the bed on the cold, pitted stone floor, pressed his forehead to the corroding wall, hugged his knees, and shivered himself to sleep.

❄ ❄ ❄

He did not hear the workers grumbling and stumbling out of the room in the darkness of the next morning. He woke hours later when the door opened and two black shadows entered, one carrying a golden lantern.

"I can't think he would have been foolish enough to go out in the snow," one voice was saying.

"He's foolish enough for anything," the other man replied.

The voices paused and the men poked around the room. Their tones seemed thin and distant, but as they neared him the shuffles of their feet over the uneven floor grew loud and shrill. He whined and pressed tighter against the wall.

The walking stilled.

"I heard something."

"*Ja.*"

"Over there. Isn't that someone under the bed?"

The shrieking feet approached like grey fins swimming closer above the water. Only the water was on top. Why was everything upside down? Tor began to thrash.

"Sharks!" he cried. "Go away! Go away!"

Strong hands pulled his writhing body from under the bed.

"*Nej!* Don't!" Tor pleaded, shielding his eyes from the light and resisting the shark that held him in its grip. "Please go away! Have mercy! Sharks! Sharks!"

Long, five-fingered fins lifted him to sit upon an empty cot, but he continued to shout and push ineffectually at the creature holding him.

"He's overwrought from the sickness," said the other shadow.

"Is he well enough to travel, do you think?" asked the one

holding Tor. His voice was clearer now, and the drunkard's boy suddenly stilled at the sound.

"T'would be better for him than to stay in this cesspit," replied the other with a shrug.

"Well then," said the shark quietly, taking the golden lantern from the other figure and looking into Tor's now wide-open eyes, "I suppose we'll risk it."

They stared at each for a moment till the man looked away. He returned the lantern to his companion and shrugged off his brown coat to put over the shoulders of the drunkard's boy. As the man adjusted the coat collar at Tor's neck and wound the scarf close against his chin, the boy continued to stare, still trying to discern between dream and reality.

"Come, boy," the man said. "Can you stand?" He slipped his hands under Tor's elbows and lifted him to his feet.

At his gentle prodding, Tor made an attempt to walk, keeping his eyes fixed on the ground before him and clutching the man's sleeve tightly with one hand.

When they approached the steps that led from the workhouse door to the street, the man suddenly leaned down, lifted Tor into his arms, and carried him through the snow into a coach.

After placing him inside, the man paused to instruct the driver before swinging in and seating himself beside Tor.

The drunkard's boy stared up at his face.

"Well, do you recognize me now, boy?" said the man gruffly,

looking out the window.

Tor only shivered deeply and began to cough.

With firm, almost rough hands, the woodmaster leaned in, pulled Tor close against his warm side, and pushed the boy's head to rest against his chest.

CHAPTER SIXTEEN

A saffron dawn came again, and when it once more lit the brown walls of the woodmaster's back room Tor opened his eyes to see familiar rafters strung with *knäckebröd* and a fresh supply of smoked fish.

His head throbbed, and he took care to move it tenderly when he sat up.

The blanket fell off his shoulders, exposing him to cold winter air. He shivered, but a warm hand touched his back. Glancing to the side, he glimpsed the woodmaster's familiar build, clothed in the usual threadbare greys and browns.

Tor leaned forward. He folded his legs inward, settled his elbows on his thighs, and lifted his hands to cradle his head.

"Do you feel pain?" the woodmaster asked, not moving his hand from Tor's nightshirt.

Tor swallowed with difficulty against the roughness in his throat and tried to properly focus his eyes on the familiar blanket before him. Could it be possible that he was here again? In the woodmaster's clean, dry, stark back room, lying between thick woolen blankets and blinking in the light of a blazing fire?

How often had he dreamed of this? And how often in his waking hours had he driven the thought from his mind, telling himself the woodmaster would never accept him back though he crawled to him on his knees.

"I thought," he said, speaking slowly and hoarsely, for he felt he must say something, "you said good riddance if I escaped."

"And I thought you said you would not escape if I taught you to read," said the woodmaster.

The words gave Tor pause, and he stared at his woolen blanket for a moment.

"I forgot." He spoke dully, though the realization surprised him.

"Did you?" The woodmaster's words were dry but not accusatory.

"You tied me to the bench all night. How could I think of anything?" Tor replied, rubbing his forehead, his tone also lacking its usual challenge.

"You ought to have returned when you remembered then."

"I didn't remember," Tor mumbled. "I was only angry . . . trying to be angry."

"You are a fool," said the woodmaster, finally moving his hand away. "I ought to whip you."

Tor could not reply. He *was* a fool. But he was by no means frightened by the woodmaster's words. After what he had been through, the threat of a whipping seemed laughable and even, in a way, welcome.

"Why did you come?" he asked, looking at the woodmaster's grey blouse because he felt shy of looking at his eyes.

The woodmaster silently busied himself with crumbling bread into a bowl of buttermilk he had set on the floor and said nothing.

Tor felt suddenly peevish at the man's silence. His head throbbed, and he was hot and achy all over, and he was desperate to know the man's mind. Why had he brought Tor back? Did he want him? Would he keep him here despite the wrongs Tor had done him? Or did he keep Tor because he had a punishment in store?

What stupid fears.

Tor didn't think the woodmaster wanted to torment him, but he needed to hear him say it. Needed to hear it badly. Needed to hear it as much as he needed to breathe. Perhaps more.

"Why did you come?" he asked again.

"Because," said the woodmaster, "you still owe me labor." He set the bowl on Tor's lap and stood to walk away.

Tor took no satisfaction in such an obvious evasion of his question.

"How did you find me?" he pleaded.

The man turned to look at him with dark and rather sullen eyes.

"I happened to hear of you."

"How?"

"I sent letters." His voice now carried the defensive tone of a man who wished to prove to the world that he had every right and motivation to act as he had done.

Tor mused in silence for several moments, and the woodmaster busily engaged in small work about the room. Why on earth would this man who held such disdain and ill-will for the drunkard's boy, why on earth would this man search for him?

"I'm no use to you," Tor finally said. "You know I will never advance your trade, don't you?"

The woodmaster made a sort of snorting, spitting noise that clearly conveyed ridicule, but he said nothing.

"Why do you think that keeping me here with you is a punishment? If you wish revenge, leaving me to shovel dung from the streets would have done the job."

"*Ja*, I heard of that," said the woodmaster, dryly.

"I suppose the overseer spoke to you of me." Tor studied the texture of his blanket more closely.

"*Nej*, boy. You told me yourself, in the carriage."

The drunkard's boy stared at his hands apprehensively. What else had the man heard from him in his half-conscious state?

"Then you know it was very bad. Why did you bring me back?"

"There was a time when you said you'd rather go to work for the devil than for me. Can it be possible you have changed your mind?"

Tor, throbbing with an ache in his head and every one of his muscles, felt a childish frustration with the woodmaster's elusions. He lay back down and rolled over away from the man.

But the forgotten bowl of mush between his legs also rolled over, spilling its contents across the blankets and hitting the side wall of the bed with an ugly thud.

The woodmaster whirled, but he said nothing as he strode over and angrily picked up the bowl. Tor cringed back, struck with a sudden returning fear of the woodmaster's rejection. He forgot his headache and aggravation.

"I am sorry," he said, sitting up quickly. "I forgot it was there. I didn't spill the mush on purpose."

The woodmaster glanced at him suspiciously as he rustled among the blankets.

"If you would not have become upset for no cause," he finally replied, scraping up the mush with the bowl and spoon, "you would not have spilled it."

"I'm sorry. I don't know why I became upset," said Tor. Then he closed his mouth and stared at the blanket clenched in his fists, silenced by the beginnings of a strange epiphany.

The woodmaster said nothing but pulled up the soiled blankets and tossed them on the floor. He then stepped around the trundle and grabbed up the blankets that dressed his own bed. He laid these over Tor and then, retrieving the ones from the floor, thrust the soiled parts in a kettle of water that sat on the hearth before walking to the wood-shop door.

"You need more sleep," he growled before the door shut firmly behind him.

But Tor could not sleep. He lay on his back and stared at the rafters, listening to the woodmaster's husky saw and the sluggish pulse in his own head. He had realized in that moment of the woodmaster's anger that he didn't care why the woodmaster insisted on imprisoning him here. Perhaps for revenge, perhaps because the man needed help, or perhaps for more scrupulous reasons. It did not matter anymore. He no longer wanted to leave the woodmaster.

If it was vengeance the man wanted, then Tor preferred that revenge to the tender mercies of the workhouse and the idle entertainment of its supervisors.

He remained awake, thinking through the woodmaster's most egregious acts, the deepest humiliations. Not one had been unprovoked, whether by deeds or insults, unlike the torments visited upon him by his former work supervisor. The drunkard's boy wondered, if he behaved well, would the woodmaster stop humiliating him?

But then he thought of the times when others blamed him for fights he had not caused, for broken items he had not thrown, for lost things he had not stolen. What would the woodmaster do when such accusations came again? Would he ever see Tor as anything but "the drunkard's boy?"

Wearied by insoluble questions, Tor rose from the bed and looked for something to do. He scrubbed off the soiled sheets that were soaking in the pot and hung them up to dry. Then he swept the floor and put up any little object he found out of place. Then, shivering with cold, he wrapped himself well in a blanket and huddled by the hearth.

❄   ❄   ❄

He came halfway to consciousness when he heard the sound of sloshing water. The woodmaster was preparing a bath, dumping buckets of snow into a steaming tub. Tor continued to doze, sleepy and uncomprehending as the woodmaster moved about the room, a hulking shadow in the dim light. His presence was strangely comfortable.

Soon, the man knelt beside Tor and began to pull off his blanket.

"I'm cold," whispered Tor.

"The bath is warm," said the woodmaster.

Tor realized then that the bath was for himself. The woodmaster helped him into the tub and washed him until Tor humbly said he thought he could bathe himself. Then the woodmaster seemed to dismiss Tor from his mind as he turned to the fire to prepare supper.

They ate quietly. The woodmaster was usually quiet, but now he seemed determined, to a degree that he had never been before, to ignore the drunkard's boy.

Tor's mind was busily engaged during that silence. He was thinking about the workhouse and the night soil, contrasting it with the prison of the woodmaster's back room and his dusty carpentry work. He would be a good worker now. He would not be distracted and slipshod. He would show the woodmaster he had no cause to regret his decision to rescue him from the workhouse.

Everything would be better. The woodmaster would never have cause to complain of him again.

CHAPTER SEVENTEEN

It was not a week before Tor realized the work was just as tedious as he used to think it was. It was very difficult for him to concentrate upon it, but still, he hourly reminded himself, it was far less irksome when compared with his work with the night soil. All things considered, planing boards in a dry wood-shop was a much better job than he had a right to expect. He was determined to show himself useful.

Yet despite his struggles to be a good worker and show a willingness to help however he could, it seemed that with every passing day the woodmaster received his help more coolly and kept his focus more exclusively on his own work.

The man made no mention of spelling and reading. Tor accepted that this opportunity was lost—he, after all, had broken the bargain—and he made no mention of it. Education was no longer his chief desire. Becoming important and showing everyone that he was better than they were and revenging himself on those he disliked now seemed less essential than staying alive, clean, and well-fed.

Furthermore, Tor was becoming more aware of an intense desire to gain the woodmaster's good opinion. It was like hunger. And it frightened Tor because he well knew how vulnerable it made him to painful rejection.

On Sunday, the town was aghast to see the drunkard's boy once more at the woodcarver's side.

"What could possess the carpenter," the cobbler's wife whispered to her neighbor as they slogged together through the snow, lagging behind their husbands and children and unaware how closely the woodmaster and Tor walked behind them, "after all the trouble that boy has caused? He nearly broke my poor Albin's back by pushing him against the table on Midsummer's Eve."

"I hear," said Noomi Hansson, "that he sent a letter with a drawing of the boy's face to every jail and workhouse in the province."

"My husband says the man spent three days searching Stockholm himself," said the goodwife.

"Yet *some* say," replied Noomi Hansson, lowering her voice with irresistible mystery, "that the boy never left the town at all, but that the carpenter kept him chained to one spot, whipping him and feeding him on bread and water till the brat promised good behavior."

"And if he did, who can blame him," said her companion stoutly.

There was a momentary pause. Then, Noomi Hansson spoke in a very grave voice and with an air of profound reluctance.

"You must know, my dear, I would never dream of slandering any man of good character, but it truly seems to me that that man's attachment to the drunkard's boy is bordering on unnatural for someone so wholly unrelated to him. The boy plagues him like a demon from hell, yet he won't hear of letting the boy out of his sight!

"You know what they say of the man's past, how he won't speak of it to anyone. Why, one is almost forced to conclude that he had immoral dealings with the boy's mother, and that is the source of his unnatural attachment to the boy!"

The cobbler's wife lifted her hand feebly to her lips.

"*Nej!*" she whispered. "The woodcarver is such a pillar of the community! Every week he sings in choir, and all the menfolk respect him—even my husband, though he cannot like him ever since the boy attacked poor Albin."

Noomi Hansson allowed a moment of silence, then cocked her head towards her neighbor and raised her eyebrows.

"Not all who fold their hands are praying," she observed profoundly.

The woodmaster cleared his throat loudly, and both women started, casting back glances of chaste horror, and hurried forward at a quicker pace.

Even more distressed than these two pious women was Vicar

Arnman. In truth, the presence of the drunkard's boy offended him so deeply he was shaken.

He had prepared a most elevating sermon which he had envisioned himself reading with great dramatic expression. But that morning, after he had solemnly mounted to his pulpit, turned his closed eyes to the rafters and drawn his preliminary deep, inspiring breath through the nose, he looked out upon the humble sheep who had eagerly gathered to his pasture for sustenance and encountered the steady, dark-rimmed eyes of Tor Neeson. The boy was studying him with his usual twisted expression of scorn, studying him as if as he were a freak show at a circus.

The vicar realized in that moment as he never had before how detestable was this boy with his sly insinuations and hypocritical judgments. The vicar fought away a frown. For months he had endured those insufferable, ironic eyes staring at him from the woodmaster's pew. This boy who spewed profanities on the steps of the church—what right had he to question or accuse God's appointed leader? Faugh! The boy himself was a worse pestilence than cholera ever could be.

The vicar looked at his sermon and tried to collect his thoughts, deeply irritated that the boy should cause such discomfort in him. He focused upon the first words and then shut his eyes and took another deep breath to clear his head. At last, feeling with righteous triumph that he had beaten the thought of the drunkard's boy back into the properly insignificant recesses of his mind, he opened his mouth to speak.

At that very moment, in the sacred pre-sermon silence when every soul in that congregation ought to have been preparing themselves to accept the vicar's divine words, a rapturous, slightly slurred little voice rang out clearly through the church, crying, "It's Tor! Look, Klara, it's Tor!"

Vicar Arnman glared fiercely at the little idiot child, who was on her knees in her seat, leaning over the back of her pew to point out the drunkard's boy. The child's mother yanked her about by the skirt so that the girl sat with a hard thump in her pew. She began to cry, and the sound of her whimpers appeased the vicar somewhat.

He breathed in deeply yet again and prepared to speak as the clubfoot girl carried the idiot child out of the church. Then, his eyes caught the expression of his daughter in the front pew. She was staring right at him with an unmistakable smirk upon her lips. A blaze of fury—certainly something like the righteous indignation of Phinehas—flamed up in his heart.

What irked him most, he remembered, about this drunkard's boy, this…reprobate, was that his daughter was so infatuated with him. It was clear to the vicar that it was because of this wretch that she began to question the very precepts of the church. *Why* couldn't she do as she liked on Sunday? *Why* couldn't girls smoke as men did? *Why* was she prohibited from speaking certain words? *Why* did she have to say prayers every night when God said nothing to *her*? If God told the rich man in the Bible to sell all his goods and follow him then *why* didn't the vicar sell his luxurious house and carriage and give his money to the poor as well? Wouldn't this be more helpful than sitting about piously doing nothing all Sunday? The vicar remembered that particularly unacceptable gleam of malice which had been in her eye when she spoke of giving away their wealth to feed the poor.

She knew such an idea was ludicrous. She no more wanted to part with fine things than he did, but she had had the gall to suggest the thing merely from spite—just like that sly drunkard's boy when he'd called after him in the market last summer to ask him if the new house he was building was intended to be a hospital for the cholera epidemic.

The vicar's lips hardened. He had been far too patient, far too yielding and benevolent. In that moment he decided he would rid the town of this disease of a drunkard's boy by whatever means necessary. His own daughter shamed him with her disrespect and impropriety, and it was all this boy's fault. He had brought up his daughter to be pious. Certainly there was no possibility that she would have ever indulged in such heretical thoughts if not for her fascination with that wicked boy.

Fierce resolve rose in his heart and steadied him, and he began to read the text which he had chosen for his sermon with profound *gravitas*, rolling his 'r's longer and more richly than he had ever managed to do before. The sound of his own sonorous voice soothed him, and he became so exultant in his fluent tones that he felt transported. And so smoothly, so lucidly did the words run from the page to his tongue that he found he did not even need to process them with his mind.

The first to greet Tor at the conclusion of the service was Thea Ahlberg, who sat just two pews behind the woodmaster, and she arose with such a rustle of skirts and bumping of wood almost before the "Amen" was pronounced that the entire congregation had turned to gaze at her. She flew upon Tor, who helplessly watched her noisy approach with an inner conflict of horror and gratification.

He received her caress with the same awkward kindness he always showed her, and he nodded uncertainly at her insistent gestures. He had forgotten most of the signs she had taught him, but she, determined to be understood, made the woodmaster communicate her particular invitation to Tor to come to supper that evening.

Tor nodded and smiled and patted her sleeve, and then she, with her usual abruptness, departed in a flurry of gestures and colorful embroidery to plan for some delicacy that evening.

The woodmaster and Tor squeezed through the black or

curious looks of their fellow parishioners out into the dark northern daylight.

Then, a voice from behind stopped them.

"Good day, *Herr* woodcarver. Good day, Tor."

Tor looked around to see the vicar's daughter studying him with her mocking blue eyes.

"You look ill," she said, before he could stutter out a word of greeting.

"I have been ill," he managed to reply.

She frowned, pettishly.

"You were foolish to run away. You ought to focus your energies on some goal worthy of you. You could be so much more than what you are, you know."

The words surprised, stung, and inspired Tor all at once. He looked at the ground just beyond the vicar's daughter, flushing, trying not to notice how the woodmaster raised his eyebrows.

Suddenly, the vicar's daughter lurched forward most ungracefully, and would have fallen to the snow had not Tor caught her arms. His stomach seemed to cartwheel as he held her. She was so close that he could feel the softness of her hair and catch the sharp but delicate scent of lemon and pine soap.

But his moment of elation was rudely broken as he felt his knees ensnared in a warm if violently jerky embrace and heard a little girl's voice crying, "Tor! Tor! Tor!" Marta was clinging to his legs, jumping up and down and bellowing his name with the vigor of a hound dog on the scent.

The vicar's daughter pulled away from them and looked rather sardonically at the little girl, who seemed not to notice her at all.

Tor glanced about in some desperation, fearing the child's parents were close at hand, but all he saw was her older sister standing nearby, staring at the snow she was kicking up with her clubfoot, her hands stuffed in the pockets of her cloak.

Tor knelt before Marta and took her by the shoulders to still her wild jumping before she slipped on the icy stone path.

"Hello, Marta," he said.

"Hello, Tor, Tor, Tor!" she replied, still trying to jump up and down.

"Be still before you fall." Tor smiled despite himself and felt a startling urge to kiss her round red cheeks.

Suddenly he became aware of the voice of the vicar's daughter.

"Perhaps if the Karlssons had not had the misfortune to also have a clubfoot for a daughter, their little idiot child would be better managed."

Tor looked at the vicar's daughter, shocked by her cold, strident tone. He glanced at Marta's older sister.

The girl flushed but gave her persecutor a rather feral glare with her yellow-brown eyes.

"I apologize," she said, distinctly. She approached—Tor noted that she tried to conceal her limp—and laid a hand on Marta's shoulder. As she did so, her gaze flitted to Tor's, and he caught then the all too familiar marks of shame, hurt, and accusation in her eyes. She quickly looked away and attempted to lead Marta off, but the little girl was not to be deterred.

"I thought the woodcarver killed you!" she shouted, still laughing.

Tor winced at the loudness of her tone and noticed that the woodmaster looked startled.

"*Nej,* of course not," said the drunkard's boy hastily.

"But," Marta said, giggling irresistibly, "he was so angry. And then you never came out again to play."

"Shh, hush." Tor pulled her close rather roughly and hugged her head to his chest against his better judgment. He felt joy at her enthusiastic greeting, but he was also irritated by her ill-timed interruption as well as her loud and inappropriate declarations, which caused passing parishioners to stare.

"Can we play tonight?" cried Marta, ignoring his admonishment.

"*Nej,* silly girl, it is too cold and dark and snowy to play tonight."

Marta laughed and began to ridicule her own absurdity.

"How silly! Too much snow!" she said, spreading her arms wide. And immediately she took up a different subject.

"Christmas is coming and St. Lucia day! Tor! Tor! Tor! St.

Lucia Day is coming soon!" And she began to jump again.

Tor glanced up at the vicar's daughter. Those brilliant blue eyes seemed to have frosted over; they looked paler and cooler, a bit like the schoolmaster's. It almost made him cringe.

"Come, Marta," the clubfoot girl suddenly snapped, taking Marta more firmly by the shoulders. "It's time to go home."

"Tor, Tor, Tor!" shouted the little girl, suddenly beginning to cry.

She went off in tow of the limping clubfoot, wailing "Tor!" all the way down the path.

Tor stood and wiped the snow from his knees, trying to ignore the pointed stare of the woodmaster, as well as of the other villagers. He believed some apology was due to the vicar's daughter, but he was not certain why he thought so except that he knew the girl's expression was perfectly glacial as she looked at him.

"I'm sorry for the interruption," he said, his eyes flickering shyly between the girl's eyes and her muff.

Suddenly, she looked away from him, biting her lip a bit.

"I suppose a girl would forgive anything of you with a look like that, Tor Neeson," she said, and the frost melted from her eyes to reveal the usual deep blue.

The woodmaster raised his eyebrows further and looked on with obvious interest, but Tor could say and do nothing so long as the girl looked at him like this.

"Daughter!" Vicar Arnman called loudly from behind them. "Come away at once." He strode past with a flutter of grim black capes.

"Behave yourself, Tor Neeson," the vicar's daughter said, and then she turned away.

As she departed, the vicar spoke in quite audible tones.

"I do not wish you to have anything to do with that reprobate, daughter. Already he has poisoned you with rebellion and backsliding."

The vicar's daughter glanced back at Tor with an expression unrepentant and highly unflattering to her father.

As the vicar's voice faded away, Noomi Hansson's voice drifted clearly across the snow from behind them.

"How disgraceful. It's no wonder the vicar wishes to be rid of him."

The woodmaster turned on his heel and moved down the path with quick, stiff strides. Tor followed silently.

Though they continued in silence all that afternoon, Tor now had fresh thoughts to sustain him in the woodmaster's brooding atmosphere.

For a long time, he thought of the vicar's daughter. She was lovely and seemed to truly like him.

I suppose a girl would forgive anything of you with a look like that, Tor Neeson, she had said to him. Did he make her heart beat as she made his do? he wondered.

Then there was her father. Did the vicar want to be rid of Tor all because his daughter liked the drunkard's boy, or was it because God truly did want the drunkard's boy to be expelled from this community?

Tor did not like the vicar. The man was a wordy, pretentious hypocrite. He acted like a kind and sympathetic man. He took care to see that his clerk ran the almshouse smoothly, but he himself turned a blind eye to the real needs of the poorest people in the town. He pretended sympathy, but Tor could see past his empty words to a heart that wished nothing more than to distance itself from contaminates like the drunkard's boy.

Therefore, it had been much against Tor's will to listen and to show interest in the man's words that Sunday. But in truth he had been unable to keep himself from being drawn in by the reading of St. Luke's description of the prodigal son how the boy had treated his father with careless ingratitude and had run off to go his own way in the world; how his hopes of finding pleasure had deluded him into frittering away the very means of his existence. In the end he was gladly eating pig slops.

And then the son had "come to himself." These words found purchase in Tor's mind. He remembered exactly when he had come to himself—his face had been buried in ordure.

Yes, those had been precisely the words to describe Tor as he knelt, suffocating in muck. In that moment had come the desperate longing to return to the woodmaster. But unlike the prodigal, the drunkard's boy had had nothing like the right of a son to approach the woodmaster. He was already less than a hired servant, for he had no wages but food and shelter. Indeed, hadn't his crime delivered him into a sort of slavery to the man?

But now Tor believed, as he considered further, that he was not the only person with a counterpart in the parable. It was the woodmaster, who, in his own cool, rough way, had been like the father, had sought Tor out from "a great way off" and restored him to his own protection. Tor almost shivered as he remembered the warmth of the woodmaster's arm when he pulled Tor against him in the carriage.

He ached for that touch again.

That afternoon, when the woodmaster stretched on the ground to blink at the fire, Tor was still meditatively nibbling at his lunch.

Before long he was startled by the man's terse voice asking what he was staring at. Only then did Tor realize he was staring at the woodmaster. Had been doing so for some time.

"I'm sorry," Tor said.

"What's wrong?" sighed the woodmaster, eyes closed and sounding as if this query were a distasteful duty to him.

"I just was wondering why you came to look for me is all."

It was a question he had broached before, without success.

The woodmaster sighed.

"I haven't any idea," he said. "I don't know why I ever took you in at all. You've been naught but a thorn in my flesh."

Tor looked away, his face darkening until he remembered that the words were just. The woodmaster sat up suddenly and reached for the poker.

"I couldn't simply leave you in the cold. I knew you had no family." He stabbed at the fire, gashing red embers apart. "I could guess why you stole the Nativity."

He stopped speaking—he was not a man to say many words at one time—and the silence hung heavy between them for a moment before he continued.

"I certainly didn't want you in my sight, and yet it seemed that I was the only person interested in you at all, because I was the man you had robbed.

"And do not say," he snapped, turning to stare hard at Tor with cloudy grey eyes, "that you did not take the pieces, for I know you did, and your repeated denials drive me mad."

Tor looked down. There was nothing he could say.

The woodmaster continued.

"The vicar was all for sending you to prison or the workhouse." He paused to sneer at the fire as he attacked a charred log. "You had done nothing against him, but I, who had more cause than anyone to despise you, couldn't sleep after you ran away from the village in the middle of winter.

He looked back at Tor, his face hard—almost cruel.

"So, I suppose that is why I brought you back: to get sleep."

Tor looked down again, hurt and only half-heartedly trying to hide it. Last summer he would have tried to alleviate that pain with anger, but he was convinced now that he really had no right to be angry at the woodmaster about anything, and he was also afraid of where anger would lead him if he allowed it.

The woodmaster, however, seemed to grow more upset. He surged to his feet and began to pace the room.

"You took everything from me," he said. "All I had left of my family, you took.

"I began to carve that set at the beginning of my betrothal. My wife was my model for the Mary piece. I worked on the set over a period of five years before I took it away to show to my former master. He praised the pieces, saying they were exquisite and costly. I was excited to tell Kirsten.

"But I returned from my journey to find that our entire block of houses had been burnt to the ground in one night. Nothing was saved from our house. No one knew how the fire began, but my family was dead in the flames, and I had not even corpses to bury."

The man stopped pacing and leaned his forehead against the wall above the mantle, clenching the shelf with both hands.

"At night I see them blocked in by burning rafters, screaming, burn-" He choked and stopped speaking, his knuckles tightening to whiteness.

Then, once again, he turned to pace the floor.

"I used to pore over those figures. There were memories of my family in every cut. I could touch the lambs' wool and remember the taste of my little daughter's fingers feeding me berries while I worked. I could feel my wife's arm around my neck when I looked at the embroidered hem of the wiseman's robe. I remember how she looked when I saw Mary's face, or how my daughter looked when I saw the face of the little shepherdess. It was truly valuable. Many people came to examine it and try to buy it, but I already knew I would never sell it. Nothing was worth more than the memories of my family.

"And then," he said, pausing and staring at Tor, "you took it, and every day the memories fade a little more. And now, what I want to know is, how does your stealing of the Nativity make me responsible to take care of you?"

As he had spoken these words, the woodmaster had drawn closer and closer, leaning over the table till he was face to face with Tor.

"How?" he demanded once again, now shouting.

The drunkard's boy drew back. He had never felt more horrible, even when the supervisor had pushed his face in night soil. The woodmaster had spoken to him in this tone before, but never had Tor thought that the man's hostility was justified. Never had he believed that he was deserving of the woodmaster's hatred.

He remained seated where he was until the woodmaster abruptly went to his bed and lay down, facing the wall. Still, Tor sat miserably at the table.

Yes, the woodmaster's treatment of him was fully justified. He felt horrible guilt for his theft and for hiding the evidence of it away in the house of the very man he'd stolen from. The least he could do for this man who had sheltered him from cold and starvation was restore that single piece of his Nativity.

But Tor remained seated for hours, wondering if the return of the wooden piece would be his undoing. Perhaps it would distress the woodmaster, causing him to send Tor to prison. Which was worse? To bear the woodmaster's wrath or to look in the man's eyes every day and bear the guilt of the secret he'd hidden in the rafters?

At last he carried his bench to the wall and swung up on the rafters. He shifted down one rafter to the point where it met another diagonal beam, found the small parcel, and returned to the floor with it. He drew the bench back to its place and quietly laid the parcel upon the table. Then he crept out to the workshop, taking his boots, coat, and scarf with him.

Once again, he walked out the door of the woodmaster's cottage.

He trudged down the street, ignoring the eyes of the few

villagers hurrying to their warm homes.

He tried to think of what he should do. There was nowhere to go. He would freeze to death before he came to another village, and likely he would freeze to death before any of the upstanding residents of this town let him into their houses. Would they even feel sorrow when they found him frozen in the street tomorrow morning?

If he went to the almshouse they would no doubt turn him away because he was known to belong to the woodmaster. They would think Tor was running away and tell him to go back to the man.

But now he knew the woodmaster certainly did not want him. Tor had stolen the last scraps of his precious family. The man could not even remember what his wife and children looked like because of him.

Tor sat on a log and tried to remember what Nanny looked like; the indistinctness of the memory pained him.

Nej, the woodmaster could not truly forgive him. A man in pain did not think straight. A man in pain did desperate and hurtful things. He could steal others' greatest treasures without a second thought, or he could turn his enemies out into the cold, ignoring the possibility that they might freeze.

And Tor had seen a pain he recognized in the woodmaster's eyes, more pain than he would ever have thought possible for the man to feel.

After what seemed hours of staring at the white blur before him, the drunkard's boy looked at his fingers because he noticed they were turning from cold to numb, and this made him uneasy. The wind stung horribly at his nose and eyes. He felt like he had tiny lacerations across his face from the flecks of ice the storm dashed against his cheeks.

Sitting motionless as he had been, the weather had cooled him quickly, like a small fish in a large icebox.

Surely the woodmaster wouldn't let him freeze in this very village? Would his anger be so great?

Tor decided he must go back. He was afraid to die. He thought perhaps his toes were already lost to frostbite because his footsteps were less steady than before, and he hoped he would be able to stay on his feet long enough to reach the woodmaster's door.

As he neared the edge of town, scarcely able to see through the snow, his steps slowed, burdened with the weight of his heart and the pain of the cold. The woodmaster hated him, and Tor had no right to ask mercy of him. The best apology he could make was to never let the man see his face again.

He dropped to his knees, trying to think clearly, and leaned his stiff hands on his thighs. He shut his eyes and turned his cold, wet face to the sky, letting sharp crystals tear at his skin as a just punishment for the pain he had given the woodmaster.

At last he turned his face from the sky and opened his eyes.

To his astonishment, he saw a large figure approaching through the mist of the flakes. The woodmaster's shaggy cap and coat. The figure seemed to approach much faster than Tor could think, and soon a great arm dropped over his shoulder and forced him to move forward into the village. There was a blur of swirling snowflakes and a long, long struggle to keep moving his sluggish legs through the ever-thickening snow, and then they were in the woodmaster's house.

For some time, Tor had difficulty opening his eyes in the warmth, but between drowsy blinks he saw the woodmaster squatting before him, removing Tor's coat and boots and impatiently dragging a rough, snowy sleeve across his own strangely red eyes.

Tor was then wrapped in a blanket and settled before the fire, and the woodmaster sat down at the table to hover over something small in his hands.

The drunkard's boy understood after a while that it was the little burnished figure of the Christ Child which he had set in a parcel on the table. The woodmaster was crying over it silently.

"I'm sorry," Tor mumbled in a voice so slurred and low he was not even sure the woodmaster could understand it. "I wanted money for a doctor for Nanny."

The woodmaster sighed and again wiped a sleeve across his eyes again.

"*Ja,*" he said. He tucked the figure in his pocket and pushed himself up from the table. He poured sour milk into a pot and hung it over the fire.

"You must stop running away," he said gruffly, taking food from the cupboard. "Next time you will be punished very severely, do you understand?"

"*Ja.*"

"I will…"—the man seemed to search for words as he hacked a pickled herring to pieces—"I will tie you to the bench and leave you for two nights, do you hear me?"

"*Ja, Herr,*" said Tor, his choked voice hardly above a whisper.

"Good."

The man took cheese from the cupboard and set it on the hearth at Tor's elbow to warm.

"We'll not go to the Ahlberg's tonight. It is stormy and late."

"*Ja, Herr.*"

The woodmaster moved about in silence for some long minutes, making preparations for dinner. Then he spoke again, abruptly, and with exasperation.

"I would have given your sister help if you had come to me!"

"I didn't know," Tor said, humbly.

"*Nej!*" The woodmaster turned on him. "You do not know, do you, because you do not ask! You never ask for help—you are too proud and arrogant!"

"I asked the vicar," Tor replied, feeling at last a flush of familiar anger and trying to speak quickly despite his numb lips and tongue. "He only sent bread and told me to fetch Doctor Hansson, but Doctor Hansson had already told me she should see a specialist, and no one would give the money for such a thing. Not for a drunkard's family."

It was as he spoke the last words that the bitterness crept back into his voice.

"Some would," said the woodmaster, vehemently tearing bread to sop in the sour milk, "and, also, if you would not constantly remind the village where you come from, then it would forget that you are a drunkard's boy."

He pulled Tor up by the elbows and made him sit at the table before the bowl of hot milk porridge. Not until he had muttered the blessing and eaten several bites of the meal did he speak again, in a more moderate voice.

"You will remain here. You will be grateful and make the best of what displeases you. It is your own actions which have turned the village against you, and you must bear with the reputation you have made for yourself."

The words stung. They didn't make Tor feel guiltier— nothing, he was sure, could do that—but they did make him even more miserable.

"*Ja, Herr*," he said, subdued again, looking at the milk porridge in silent acceptance of the condemnation.

He took up a piece of cheese, but before he could open his mouth a faint knock was heard from the outer door. The woodmaster stood hastily and disappeared into the shop, but Tor sat still, eating tiny bites of food and trying to listen to the voices.

He could hardly hear the woodmaster's low tones, but presently there came a light, clear staccato voice that Tor could not mistake. It brought to mind the dream: running down the alley of hospital beds, running from the woodmaster and the woman who shut him out of the woodmaster's house.

She was saying in a pouting tone, ". . . and then I go for two full weeks scarcely seeing my betrothed? You never come to see me, Wilhelm. Ever since you brought the boy back he takes all your attention. You hardly care for me anymore."

Fear seized Tor. He ought to have known: the dream had of course been a premonition. He had run from the woodmaster once too often, and now when he found that the thing he wanted most in the world was the woodmaster's regard, she, the pretty girl with her heart-shaped face, would shut him out.

Still groggy from the cold, he leaned his head in his hands.

Why couldn't the woodmaster see what sort of person she was? He had been married before. Didn't he understand women? Didn't he know how shallow they could be? What angelic parts they could play when they manipulated men? The woodmaster was clever and analytical of people. Why couldn't he see through her pretty little game? And were they truly betrothed?

He finally caught some of the woodmaster's words, for the man's typically cool, flat voice had risen with a hint of urgency.

"Please come in and spend the evening with us. I think he will behave well toward you now if you try him with kindness. I wish the two of you might get along."

"*Nej*," said the pretty girl, "I don't believe I wish to spend the evening with that unruly devil. It is as the schoolmaster said: he has a foul mouth and a foul mind, and he is not fit to be in the company of a lady.

"I hope," she said, her voice growing more audible, though her firm footsteps indicated that she was moving toward the door, "that you will take this into serious consideration before our marriage."

Tor nearly choked with the sudden churn of his stomach. Even if the woodmaster chose not to expel him before his marriage, the pretty little woman would make life miserable for both him and the woodmaster till Tor was gone from *her* house. He knew full well that she was capable of it.

Tor thought of all the battles he had engaged in. Trying to read. Trying to protect Nanny and give her the life she dreamed of, then trying to just keep her alive. Trying to sell the Nativity. Trying to get away from this town, from the woodmaster and the vicar and the wretched schoolmaster and the pink-faced school boys. Trying to rise above his lot as a drunkard's boy, prove to himself that he was as good as they were. Even just trying to get a job that would keep himself out of the workhouse.

He had lost every battle. He had always had bad luck.

Dismally, he hoped that this battle with the pretty girl would be his last, that he would die in a workhouse this time rather than be revived to hope for an impossible future.

The woodmaster returned to the room. To almost anyone else, he would have appeared to be his usual cool, imperturbable self, but Tor saw deeper. Now keenly attuned to the woodmaster's moods, he saw how the slumped shoulders and tense features conveyed the worry which plagued the woodmaster's soul. He too, Tor suddenly realized, felt uncertain and vulnerable.

Tor had wanted to ask questions such as, When would the woodmaster get married? Did the woodmaster intend to attempt the impossible feat of keeping the drunkard's boy and the pretty girl in the same small house? Could the woodmaster . . . *would* the woodmaster think of any other place for Tor to go where he need not be starved by day and frozen by night? Did the woodmaster care for Tor at all, or was Tor simply the woodmaster's unwelcome duty?

But he did not ask these questions, first, because he was not brave enough, second, because he realized that his fears and sorrows were not the only ones in this room.

"Freja Lindqvist and I are engaged to be married," the woodmaster said, reseating himself at the table across from Tor. His tone betrayed no hint of distress.

Tor glanced at him, wondering if he had gauged the man's feelings correctly, then he quickly looked down, nodded, and nibbled at his *knäckebröd.*

"I must have you behave yourself when she comes to live with us, Tor Neeson. You must give her no reason to wish you gone, *ja?*"

"*Ja, Herr.*"

The woodmaster leaned back, massaged the base of his neck deeply, and looked with evident longing at the shop door. Tor knew the man's penchant for meticulous or exhausting work when he was troubled. But today was Sunday.

Tor next followed the woodmaster's eyes to his rumpled bed. He doubted the man would go there; tossing in bed would only exacerbate his worries, whatever they might be.

Then the woodmaster looked at the door.

"I will take a walk," he said, wearily. "Finish your supper and go to bed."

Tor did as he was told, but he remained wakeful till long after the woodmaster returned.

When at last the drunkard's boy fell to sleep he slept hard and woke only when the rays of the late winter dawn touched the panels of the workshop door.

The woodmaster, who had left him to sleep, was loudly sawing away in the next room. Tor rose, took some cheese and oatcake to eat as he dressed, and then went to the workshop to help the woodmaster.

The man looked up at Tor and studied him with weary eyes,

and Tor's heart sank. He recognized a hint of calculation in those eyes, and he understood that the woodmaster was trying to assess whether Tor was worth the coming struggle.

Nevertheless, he simply ducked his head and slunk further into the room. He was done running. He wasn't going to give the man any more trouble than he already had. It was the woodmaster's decision now. Tor would do whatever the man thought best. He wanted it that way.

"What should I do?" he asked.

The woodmaster crossed the room, picked up a board, laid it over the work table, and set the planer atop it, wordlessly.

CHAPTER EIGHTEEN

The week passed in silent monotony, as had the days before, and even Tor, as the week's end drew close, could never have claimed that he had behaved as a model apprentice. The work was so tedious and the atmosphere so strained that, battle himself as he might, he could not refrain showing hints of exasperation or even surliness a few times when the woodmaster grew impatient with his ever-faulty work.

On Thursday, Thea Ahlberg unexpectedly appeared with a basket of *pepparkakor*, quite to the relief of both Tor and the woodmaster.

She demanded of the woodmaster why he had not come on Sunday and seemed little pleased with his excuse of the bad weather. She said that she had made a special treat for Tor on that day and insisted they come without fail the next Sunday evening. Then she took Tor's face in both hands, kissed his dark hair, and departed with her purposeful stride.

For the first time since Tor's return, he detected amusement in the woodmaster's eyes as he watched the mute woman disappear into the dim street.

"It seems we have our orders," the man said, his lips slightly curved as he shut the door to the wind and its sparse powdering of snow.

And so, once again, there came Sunday. Though Tor often yearned for a respite from the tedium of the wood shop during the week, he hated when that day of rest arrived.

There was the gauntlet of shame to be walked through the town to the church door, then the inevitably tedious and often infuriating sermon to be endured, then the second gauntlet of shame back to town.

That Sunday the villagers seemed unusually stone-faced, and Albin, Jan, and Olaf appeared to have a peculiar flavor of spite in their sneering mouths as they repeatedly walked by Tor, lagged behind, and walked by again.

It seemed they had some insult on their minds that each boy wished very badly for the others to speak, for they kept nudging and poking each other as they walked.

Once, Albin and Olaf even shoved Jan almost into the path of the woodmaster, hissing, "Go on!"

But Jan had scrambled out of the way with a fearful glance at the woodmaster's impassive face. He'd glared at his friends and snapped, "You say it, cowards!" Then he had run off to walk with his family.

They arrived at the church, and Tor listened to the text in faint hopes that he might hear something that interested him as much as last Sunday's text. The text was Psalm 1:1. The sermon was entitled: The Path of the Holy.

After the text was read, Tor would have paid no more attention if he had not noticed a gradual stiffening of the woodmaster's body next to him, and then the pointed glances of certain goodwives who twisted their necks to look at the woodmaster.

"…only think of the depths to which great men have fallen—yea, even men such as the great king David—by allowing themselves to partake of impure company. The twenty-third Proverb saith, 'My son, give me thine heart, and let thine eyes observe my ways. For a whore is a deep ditch; and a strange woman is a narrow pit. She also lieth in wait as for a prey, and increaseth the transgressors among men.'"

Here Tor observed the woodmaster tilt his head just slightly back and to the side, his expression utterly flat.

"'But,' you ask me," the vicar continued, "'what of he who by some wretched misstep hath slipped once upon the steeps of sin and in doing so hath entangled himself inextricably in the company of evil persons?' He may think to himself, 'I am now burdened with the company of sinners in recompense for my error.'

"Such, no doubt, were King David's thoughts regarding his son Absolom, who plagued him even unto death. David would have spared his prince and received him back, but it was only after the vile traitor was executed that David was restored. I say to thee, cut thyself loose, even if it be from thy dearest loved one, for God will not hold him guiltless who would not forsake the company of a perverse sinner—though it be *his own child*—who standeth between him and his Maker."

Tor saw the muscles in the woodmaster's upper arm jump just slightly at these last words, and Noomi Hansson, who had turned to eye him, seemed to light up with fierce triumph.

Then Tor remembered what she had said of the woodmaster having improper relations with his mother.

The vicar continued.

"I say to you, as the mouthpiece of God: 'have no fellowship with the unfruitful works of darkness!' None! 'But rather reprove them.'

"We see that this text plainly says that we are to have no dealings with the works of darkness or with the people of darkness. As the our text says, 'Blessed is the man that walketh not in the counsel of the ungodly, nor standeth in the way of sinners, nor sitteth in the seat of the scornful.' And again, St. Paul quoth, 'evil communications corrupt good manners.' Think too of the wicked Amnon who defiled his sister. What doth the Scripture say? 'But Amnon had a friend…'

"Some piously pretend that they can restore these reprobates. These perverse miscreants who, because of the feckless leniency of their elders, return again and again to their sordid ways. But what doth the Apostle say in I Corinthians? 'Deliver such an one unto Satan for the destruction of the flesh, that the spirit may be saved in the day of the Lord Jesus.' Cast away the sinner for the good of his soul!

"This pretense of cosseting such a hardened creature into righteousness is but a weak and lazy excuse. I see those who shrink in a false and cowardly tenderness from delivering the sinner to the desserts of his sins, and I say to thee in the words of God: 'He who is not with me is against me!'"

Tor fully understood the purpose of the message now. He was the perverse sinner, and he was to be delivered over "for the destruction of the flesh" for his thievery and rebellion.

He glanced at the woodcarver, who stared fixedly at the vicar. Was this, Tor wondered, his stomach almost writhing with sick fear, the excuse the woodmaster needed to be rid of him before his bride arrived?

Suddenly, Tor became aware of a great scuffling behind him. He turned without thinking to see Thea Ahlberg on her feet, gesturing violently at the vicar. Fisherman Ahlberg, habitually acquiescent to his wife, stood beside her, feebly attempting to soothe her, catch her hands, and draw her towards the door, but she would not be subdued. Vexed by his interference and her inability to be heard, she opened her mouth vainly to formless words and grunts. She pointed repeatedly at Tor, and Tor understood that she, helpless, but enraged to a point she felt beyond endurance, was trying to defend him.

Around her, some of the villagers raised their eyebrows at each other. Some appeared to be trying not to laugh. The kindest looked down at their hands. Thea Ahlberg appeared to be almost crying with anger and frustration as she looked at her neighbors and realized that she was a laughingstock.

Suddenly, she ceased gesturing and marched from her pew straight towards Tor and the woodmaster. She stood at the end of their pew and held out her hand, motioning peremptorily for Tor to come to her. Tor straightened from his embarrassed slump and looked wildly at the woodmaster, who looked back at him and said nothing. Thea Ahlberg gestured again, more imperatively than before.

Slowly Tor unfolded himself from the pew and slunk past the woodmaster. Thea Ahlberg nodded, snatched his arm, and led him forcibly out of the church.

Tor felt withered with shame. But what else could he do?

Outside, the fisherman tried, without looking at Tor, to lead his wife away, but she shook his arms off and continued to gesture to him and to the woodmaster, who had come after Tor and was standing with his hands in his pockets, his head tilted to one side and his fathomless grey eyes fixed on Thea Ahlberg.

Tor understood nothing of what she said, but she seemed to be giving the two men a tongue lashing with her hands. Fisherman Ahlberg nodded repeatedly but continued to glance over his shoulder at the door of the church where *Herr* Lagerlöf stood with his brawny arms folded over his chest and his mutton chops bristling. The woodmaster did not move but continued to stare expressionlessly at Thea Ahlberg.

Finally, when she seemed to have had her say, she paused before Tor to tenderly pat his cheeks and kiss his head before stalking down the path with the somewhat dazed fisherman.

The woodmaster watched them leave, oblivious to the stare *Herr* Lagerlöf was busily drilling through his back. Tor, on the contrary, was all too conscious of the stare and tried to angle away and make his face as stoic as the woodmaster's. He failed and resorted instead to kicking the snow and wondering if the woodmaster had ever felt embarrassed in his life.

Finally, the man tossed his head, flicking his shaggy mane from his eyes.

"Let's go home," he said.

Tor followed him down the path, staring at the man's back. He had fully expected the woodmaster to turn around and walk right back into the church again, for the man was possessed of perfect equanimity.

All that could be heard for some time was the squeaking of the snow beneath their boots, but Tor at last screwed up the courage to speak.

"What made her so angry?"

The woodmaster glanced back at him.

"What do you think?" he said, speaking a question, not a challenge.

Tor kicked a snow clod.

"I think the vicar was speaking of me," he replied, looking up at the back of the woodmaster's head.

"Oh? Is there some evil companion you believe you must put away from you?"

"I mean, he was speaking of me as the evil companion. Your evil companion."

Tor knew not where he found the courage to say this. He had said many rash things in his lifetime, but that was before he had known what it was to be a slip of driftwood in an angry ocean. Since he'd returned to the woodmaster he'd become deathly afraid of alienating himself further from him.

But just now the unbearable agitation of not knowing, of having to blindly trust his fate to this unpredictable and rather unfriendly man was driving him beyond the voice of wisdom.

"Do you think so?" asked the woodmaster, his voice drifting back over his shoulder with his frosty breath.

Tor looked over the village as they descended the wide, gently sloping hill upon which the church sat. Frustration rose in his heart.

"The village thinks so," he said.

"Do you think so?" repeated the woodmaster.

"Since so many good people say so, I doubt my opinion

matters. I know nothing about holiness and religion. I've never respected the church. I'm the drunkard's boy. I curse and steal and lie. Why do you ask me?" His tone was bitter now, and he did not care.

"Does Thea Ahlberg's opinion matter? Or do you not think she is good?"

"I do not happen to know what Thea Ahlberg thinks," snapped Tor.

"I believe you do."

"I suppose *you* think I am an evil companion," Tor muttered after a moment. His heart beat rapidly; one never knew what to expect of the woodmaster.

"Do you think so?"

Tor remained silent and kicked another snow clod, only to find it was a frozen stump. He hopped on his other foot for a moment, grimacing.

"Have you ever been told you have a very bad temper?" asked the woodmaster, glancing down dryly at the injured foot.

Again, Tor said nothing.

"Very well," said the woodmaster, "Since it seems you want to know my opinion so badly I will tell you. You are an evil companion in that you are evil, and you are my companion." The man had slowed down to keep pace alongside Tor and was looking at him ironically.

Tor quickened his own pace. He was being laughed at. It

made him at once angry, relieved, and confused.

"But then," said the woodmaster, keeping stride with Tor easily, "I too do evil, and I am your companion."

"I do not understand what you're talking about," the drunkard's boy snapped, giving his nose a savage swipe with the back of his sleeve and hoping the woodmaster would not notice.

"The vicar seems to define an evil companion as a companion who does evil, *ja?*"

Tor said nothing. What was the man talking about? Of course he did. What a ridiculous question.

"*Ja?*" prodded the woodmaster.

Tor scrubbed his nose again and tossed his head irritably.

"As you say."

"Is there someone you know, Tor, who has never done evil?"

The drunkard's boy shook his head no. His patience was being stretched taut, and he felt he'd like to throw a rock at something.

"So then we should all give each other over to the devil?"

"You know very well," said Tor, nearly shouting, "that there is a difference between me and the rest of you. You don't swear and steal things."

"I have stolen. I have heard the cobbler swear. I have heard Noomi Hansson lie. I have even," the woodmaster paused, and Tor detected a smile in his next words, "seen Thea Ahlberg throw a fit of temper—quite recently I believe.

"I will tell you plainly, Tor," he continued, "that the evil companions mentioned in those verses refer to those who sin repeatedly even when they know it is wrong, who feel no guilt but show enjoyment in their sin, and who give no indication of present or future repentance."

Tor considered these words a moment, tension sapping slowly from his body as he did so.

"But how do you know?" Tor pressed. "That's not what the vicar thinks. Not what any of the other villagers think."

"Oh, it is what many of them think. Some are too embarrassed and confused to contradict the vicar, and others who blame you would be only too glad to argue from my point of view if they were defending someone they cared for."

Tor tensed again, wanting to ask the woodmaster if he were defending someone he "cared for."

But he could not bring himself to do so. Instead he asked a different question.

"Do you think I am repentant?"

"Are you?"

Tor hesitated.

"*Ja*," he said. Then after a moment added, "for some things."

The woodmaster barked a short laugh.

"Let me make a guess: you're not repentant about striking Albin?"

"I—*nej*, not really."

The woodmaster watched him long.

"It will come," he said at last.

Tor looked up at him, surprised at his forbearance, but wondering how he could ever be sorry for punching Albin and wondering why the woodmaster thought he ever would be.

They walked on in silence till they reached the woodmaster's door. He opened it and stepped aside to let Tor enter.

"They want to be rid of me," Tor finally mumbled as he removed his boots by the back door.

"Likely," said the woodmaster.

"Your betrothed wants to be rid of me."

Then the woodmaster turned a dangerous eye on Tor.

"I've said all there is to say concerning that subject. You will behave well toward her."

"*Ja, Herr.*"

CHAPTER NINETEEN

That evening, there were only one or two other rather nervous guests at the Ahlberg's cottage. The woodmaster, Tor noticed, glanced about the room in search of someone. Seeming disgruntled that he did not find that someone, he immediately requisitioned a dark corner where he brooded for the rest of the evening. The other guests said very little but sipped coffee and avoided looking at Tor and the woodmaster. Even the fisherman had little to say.

Thea Ahlberg had Tor into the kitchen as usual, but she seemed harried as she worked. They could discuss very little of what had happened at the church, but Thea Ahlberg clearly conveyed that she thought Tor very much to be pitied and that she was still smarting for him from his insult. She kept returning to him every few minutes to pat his shoulder or kiss his head.

It was the first time Tor had visited the Ahlberg's household since his return from the workhouse. Just as he had forgotten how wretched were the conditions of a workhouse before he had returned to it, so had he forgotten what a rich kaleidoscope of sound, color, smell, texture, and taste was Thea Ahlberg's kitchen. He had forgotten how sheltered and unassailable one could feel in this small other-world, like a bear, bundled warmly up in his dreamy winter den.

Gradually the merry, crackling, scintillating kitchen soothed Thea Ahlberg's nerves, and she began to knead the little potato dumplings with a deft rhythm. The fish soup seemed to sizzle with delight at the addition of each new dumpling.

A bleak memory of stinking gruel and small, wormy potatoes flashed to Tor's mind, making his heart constrict. He remembered years even before the workhouse when he had slunk shamefully about the fishermen's huts, furtively snatching up discarded fish heads to boil into a sort of chowder for Nanny.

Why, he suddenly asked himself, his eyes fixed upon the sweet dough that Thea Ahlberg coaxed with a light, floury touch, why was it that he, of all the people in that workhouse, of all the drunkard's boys in the world, should be seated in this bright little kitchen? What had he done to deserve this?

Thea Ahlberg met his eyes and smiled warmly, as if she knew what he was thinking and as if she had been thinking the same of herself. It was pleasant sharing the same wonder-full thought, he stirring the soup over the robust fire, and she, rocking back and forth on her toes, kneading and plopping, kneading and plopping the little dumplings.

"I have never met anyone like Thea Ahlberg," Tor said to the woodmaster as they walked home.

"Why do you say so?" asked the woodmaster, as if grudging his words. He was still in a sullen temper.

"She is so…she has such a strong personality."

"You have a rather strong personality yourself."

"Nothing like. She's not afraid of anything."

"She is. She fears society. Their scorn. That she cannot communicate her dearest values to them makes her anxious and upset."

"She doesn't *seem* afraid of them," said Tor. But after a moment's pause he added meditatively, "though I can see the other women seem to shun her."

Yes, that could make anyone afraid, even if they didn't show it, thought Tor.

The woodmaster tossed his head to one side.

"She makes them uncomfortable. They cannot talk with her, and her behavior is too forceful for their taste."

"You learned her sign language to help her?"

"I learned sign language for my daughter."

"Oh."

Tor fiddled with his coat cuffs, wondering how many more secrets the woodmaster might astonish him with.

"Was she like Thea Ahlberg?"

"Sometimes. But she was of a quieter nature." He paused and glanced Tor over. "She would have made a slave of you."

"A slave?" Tor asked, uncertainly.

"*Ja.*"

"What do you mean by that?"

The woodmaster shrugged.

"You can't say no to little girls."

Tor knew not what to say and so kept quiet.

Soon enough, the woodmaster spoke again.

"We will stop to see Freja Lindqvist on our way home."

Tor's stomach tightened as he remembered the pretty girl with the heart-shaped face and how she was going to drive him out of the woodmaster's house. He wished the woodmaster's first wife had lived. But then the woodmaster would never have moved to Tor's town. He would not have hunted Tor down for the stolen Nativity. It would have been better not to have known the man than to have known and disappointed him.

Freja answered the door, looking very fetching in a red skirt and dark blue vest.

"Hello," she said. Her voice was bright, but she eyed Tor coolly as she stepped outside into the dark, sparkling air and shut the door behind her.

The woodmaster looked at the closed door in some confusion.

"I stopped to wish you a good evening. We missed you at the Ahlbergs."

"Who missed me more," she asked brightly, "you or the drunkard's boy?" She smiled at Tor with a good will that did not reach her eyes.

The woodmaster said nothing but looked at her with rare uncertainty.

"Well, good evening," she said, turning to go back inside.

"Wait, Freja!" said the woodmaster, clearly distressed by her frostiness.

She turned.

"You said we had not been seeing enough of each other."

"*Ja*," she said, her sharp staccato very sharp indeed, "I did say that."

And she went inside and shut the door.

The woodmaster stared at the door blankly for a moment, then he turned away and strode so quickly down the street that Tor was hard-pressed to keep pace with him.

When they arrived home the woodmaster shut the door behind them and brusquely set about preparing for bed and the next day's work without noticing Tor.

The drunkard's boy pulled on his nightshirt and looked at his trundle with its little walls and the grey and brown blankets. He remembered the workhouse and the damp, moldy beds and the foul air and the cold, chipped walls.

He remembered having night soil pressed to his face, remembered the supervisor holding him by the hair and leering at him. He looked at the woodmaster as the man climbed into his own bed, and he noted how the man's thin nightshirt showed the raw power of his big shoulders. The drunkard's boy, of all people knew how strong the woodmaster was. Those arms were like iron. The woodmaster had full enough power to make his life quite as miserable as ever the supervisor had.

What was more, he probably had every right to do so: Tor had robbed him of his past and was now robbing him of his future.

The drunkard's boy went to his bed, sat down slowly, and stared at his fingers.

"*Herr*," he said at last, speaking, in a sudden burst of courage, a bit more loudly than he had intended.

The woodmaster, lying in his bed with his back to Tor, took a long moment before answering.

"*Ja*," he said.

"*Tack* for bringing me here."

The woodmaster waited another, longer moment, not moving.

"*Ja*," he said again.

Tor looked back at his hands, fully understanding the meaning behind the woodmaster's dry tone. Suddenly cold, he shivered and the familiar dart of dread that seemed to come with every recollection of the dark workhouse returned.

The woodmaster was sorry he had taken him in. He had been humiliated by the pretty girl before the very boy who had caused all his troubles.

Tor had wondered only that morning if it were possible for the woodmaster to be embarrassed. Now, he had his answer. The woodmaster was humiliated, hurt, and angry, and it was because of him. This, Tor knew, was the beginning of his ultimate defeat at the hands of the pretty girl with her sweet, heart-shaped face.

Too restless to go to bed, he stood and pulled his boots back on.

"Tor," came the woodmaster's voice, exasperated and threatening."

"I'm not running away," Tor said quickly. "I promise."

He went outside, where he could sit and think clearly in the darkness.

He had sat only a few moments when he heard a pounding and crackling coming from Marta's yard. As his eyes adjusted to the darkness he espied Marta's older sister jerking a wooden sled forward by a stout rope and intermittently pounding along the sides of it with a heavy ice pick, trying to break the sled free from the snow. Her efforts were remarkably futile.

Tor stole closer.

"What are you doing?" he called in a puff of frosty breath.

The girl paused to glare at him for a moment. Then she looked down and began tugging again, deigning no reply.

Tor went forward. He circled the girl and her obstinate sled, surveying the project as she continued to jerk with increased annoyance. He took the pick from the girl's hand and dealt a few well-placed blows. Then, taking the sled by its upright poles, he yanked it first to one side, then to another, breaking away much of the ice until the sled was free.

Yet even as he stood kicking the snow from the top of the sled the girl seized the rope and limped forward, nearly tripping Tor's kicking foot with the hindermost poles of the sled.

"Where are you going?" Tor asked, eyeing the set in the girl's jaw as she backed away from him, tugging the sled.

"To get wood," she said.

"At this time of night? In these drifts?"

"*Ja.*"

"On Sunday?"

"*Ja.*"

Tor stood still for a moment, watching her struggle through the deep snow on her bent foot.

"Let me help you," he said.

"Oh, please do not trouble yourself," she replied, turning to trudge forward. "A cripple is not worth your notice."

Tor recognized this tone very well. It sounded angry, but he knew it masked pain. He jogged forward.

"Then don't let me help," he said, snatching the rope from her hands.

He saw her wince before she turned her dark, yellow-eyed stare upon him, and only then did he realize that she wore no gloves. The hempen rope had likely burnt her hand when he jerked it away.

"Why don't you wear gloves?"

He said this out of irritation with himself for hurting her, and so he spoke without thinking. Instantly perceiving his fault by the angry gleam of her feral eyes, he paused and pulled off his own gloves.

"Take mine," he said, shortly.

She turned away.

"I don't need your gloves."

"I know," he said, stepping in front of her and pressing the gloves against her hand.

She stared at him, immovable.

"Take them or I'll wrestle them onto you. And if you think I won't you don't know me very well."

She continued to stare, but now she seemed to look through him.

"Don't be stubborn," he said. "It does not help. I should know."

He was surprised when she took them and pulled them on.

"And what is the cause of your sudden good manners?" she asked sarcastically, walking on.

"Perhaps you bring out the best in me," he replied, his tone equally sarcastic.

"What would your precious sweetheart say to you helping a clubfoot?"

This irritated Tor.

"And what makes you such an angel," he snapped, "that you hit your sister?"

He could see plainly that the words stung her.

"I do not hit her."

"I've seen the marks on her face and heard you threaten to hit her myself."

The girl glared at him again.

"I don't hit her, and why would a nasty boy like you care about a little "idiot" girl?"

"Am I nasty?"

"*Ja*, you are. You say dirty words in front of the girls, and you pick fights with the other boys—I've seen the ones you've beaten up—and you stole the woodcarver's Nativity, who is about the best man in the town and has never hurt a fly."

Tor nearly laughed at that, but he was suddenly distracted by the girl's attitude. She was looking at him warily through her lashes and cringing slightly, almost as if afraid he would strike her. At the same time, her gaze was defiant, daring him to punish her.

He knew not what to say. He had always been aware he behaved badly, but he had always assumed his behavior was justified. He'd never quite thought of himself as *nasty*, and, strangely, he did not like that this shy but fierce clubfooted girl should think him nasty.

They trudged down the street silently for a while.

Suddenly, the girl stopped walking and turned on him.

"You have no knowledge," she said, "of how difficult it is to be constantly watching that little girl. Every time she makes mischief, I am at fault: I do not watch her closely enough, I do not manage her properly, I do not move quickly enough. Yes, perhaps I have threatened to hit her, but I have never done it.

"You are very short-sighted for such a clever boy. I would have thought you, of all people, would know better. Do you suppose you are the only one in this village treated unjustly? You always complain that people judge you wrongly, but you yourself judge others wrongly." Though her yellow-brown eyes gleamed at him steadily, the girl's words carried a slight, uncomfortable tremble. Tor looked at her, but before he had time to reply, someone else called out.

"Klara!"

The voice that echoed down the cold street made Tor flinch, but Klara turned, her face suddenly lighting with an expression like pleasure.

"*Herr* schoolmaster," she said, smiling, "how do you do?"

"Well enough, I suppose, Klara," said the schoolmaster, slowing his stride as he overtook them and speaking as if bored with the world. He came alongside Klara, swept Tor with one glance of disdain, and then turned his attention exclusively back to the girl.

"I suppose," he said in disinterested tones, "that you've

already finished the last book by now and are eager for more reading material?"

"*Ja*," replied the girl, so animated that her cheeks flushed with color in the lantern light and her yellow-brown eyes looked warm as well as bright. She pulled a small book from her pocket and offered it to him. "I hoped I would see you tonight. I stayed up most of last night to read it."

The schoolmaster smiled as if he intended to look condescending, though in fact—Tor loathed to admit it—he did not quite succeed.

"Probably no benefit to your health," said the schoolmaster to Klara. "But we must make allowances for the vanity of youth until you are disillusioned with 'the making of many books,' I suppose." He pulled a book from his own pocket and gave it into Klara's hands.

"*Tack, Herr*," Klara said, her eyes already glued to the book. The schoolmaster, with another smile balancing disparagement and goodwill, turned away from them and disappeared round a corner down the lane.

Tor looked back at Klara. The girl was running her hands over the leather binding, and, though it was impossible to decipher the words in the dim light, she opened the book and scanned the pages.

Tor jerked the rope again and strode down the street, saying nothing more until they came to Sven Nyvall's, where wood was sold. Here, he waited outside while the girl made payment, and then he helped her load the sled when she came back out. He thought it strange that Sven Nyvall did not come out and offer to help the cripple load her sled.

He stared ahead silently as they walked back to their street. Klara looked at her book, flipping page after page, though she still could read nothing in the dim light. Her page flipping irritated Tor. He was jealous, knew it was petty, and was angry at himself because of it.

"Who strikes Marta then?" he suddenly demanded.

"Why ask me?" said Klara, coldly, slipping the book into her pocket. "You seem to have great confidence in your own assumptions. And now I believe I can take the sled from here if you think my company beneath you."

Tor said nothing, but he continued to pull the sled.

The girl rubbed her mittened hands together and tilted her head back to watch the clouds of frost that she breathed against the white sky.

"Why does he keep you?" she asked, as if she had no grudge against him. "Everyone says he should send you to prison."

"I don't know," said Tor. "He is a close man."

"He frightens you?"

Tor looked at Klara a moment to perceive the motive of her question. Her manner appeared hesitant, even shy.

"Sometimes."

"Papa frightens me. Sometimes he drinks too much. Then Mama gets angry, and then I am frightened of them both," she said, studying the ground before her.

They entered her yard in silence, unloaded the wood, and then departed with only a simple "goodnight" between them.

As Tor approached the door, he remembered his last conversation with the woodmaster, how the tone of the man's voice had conveyed all the regret he now felt for taking Tor in. Perhaps the man would be disappointed to wake in the morning and see Tor under the covers of the trundle bed, looking like the lumpish, unwelcome burden that he was.

His habit had always been to sleep on his side with his back towards the woodmaster. But this night, he slept facing him, staring at the huge back and shoulders in the dim light of the red coals, wondering what the woodmaster would decide, wondering if this might be the last night he would spend in the woodmaster's house, wondering on and on, till sleep overcame his thoughts.

CHAPTER TWENTY

Tor made fewer mindless mistakes over the next two days. He thought often of shoveling night soil with stiff, bleeding, chilblained hands and these thoughts made the ash and pine dust seem sweeter.

The woodmaster, however, seemed too despondent to notice diligence, indeed, almost too despondent to point out the blunders Tor did make.

Some time before noon on Tuesday, heavy footsteps were heard entering the front shop. The woodmaster dropped his hammer on the table and ran his dusty hands down his apron as he walked toward the doorway of the front shop to greet his customers. But before he'd even crossed the room they appeared in the workshop: the vicar and the mutton-chopped *Herr* Lagerlöf. It appeared as if *Herr* Lagerlöf's red face would explode at any moment and his bristling mutton chops be dispersed to the four winds.

"*Herr* carpenter," cried he, in irrepressible wrath. "That…that boy—that *devil* of yours," he pointed to Tor, who moved to place the table between himself and the clerk, his grip tightening around the planer in his hand, "has stolen the church's silver candlesticks! Stolen them *right* from off the Lord's Table!

"We demand," he continued, striding forward and slamming

his fist upon the woodmaster's work table, "that he be given over to the authorities and sent to prison!"

Vicar Arnman stepped forward and laid a smooth white hand upon *Herr* Lagerlöf's huge shoulder.

"Be calm, my dear friend," he said quietly. He looked at the woodmaster. "What he says is true. We are here for the boy."

The woodmaster picked up a chisel and wiped both flats of the blade carefully across his thick apron. He did not look at his visitors but stepped back and tilted his head to survey his work from different angles.

"On what grounds do you accuse him?"

The vicar shrugged.

"The candlesticks are gone, and I saw the boy with my own eyes skulking in the churchyard last night, and who knows better than you, *Herr* carpenter, what a thief and reprobate the boy is?"

"Exactly what," said the woodmaster, sighing, "did you see of the boy last night?"

"I caught a glimpse of him outside the window in the dark churchyard, but when I rose and went to the window to investigate, he was gone."

"You are quite sure it was he?" The woodmaster leaned in to make a mark in the wood with his chisel.

"Of course he is certain," snapped the volatile *Herr* Lagerlöf. "Did you not hear him say so?"

The woodmaster barely glanced at the clerk before returning

his gaze to the table.

"I am certain," said the vicar.

"It was dark," said the woodmaster.

The vicar stepped close.

"Are you so certain of his guilt, *Herr* carpenter, that you must defend him before you even bother to cross-examine him?"

The woodmaster tossed his head to one side and stared at the vicar, then at the clerk; then, dropping his chisel on the table, he turned on his heel and approached Tor.

Tor took an involuntarily step back. He feared the woodmaster's rough touch, but more, he feared the disgust and disappointment he would see in the woodmaster's eyes.

The woodmaster took him by the shoulders, pulling him forward, and looked down at him, his own grey eyes quite neutral, like the flat, opaque sea before a storm.

"Did you go to the church last night?"

For a moment, Tor could not speak. He looked at the grey eyes, wondering how far he could trust the man behind them.

"*Ja*," he said, at last "To my sister's grave."

Herr Lagerlöf snorted in disgust.

"You see how he plays on your pity."

The woodmaster looked at the vicar.

"Is that where you saw him, Vicar? In the graveyard?"

The vicar hesitated a moment, then spoke calmly.

"I saw him walk past the window of the church, but whatever

the reason, the fact is established by his own mouth that he was at the church the night of the theft."

"Walking towards the graveyard?" asked the woodmaster.

"The fact," repeated the vicar, more slowly, "is establish by his own mouth that he was at the church the night the candlesticks were stolen."

"When did you last see the candlesticks?"

"Yesterday afternoon."

"Has anyone else been in the church?"

"No one," said the vicar, still more slowly and distinctly, "but *Frü* Lagerlöf, who cleans."

"Perhaps she took them to polish."

"*Nej*. She has been asked."

"Was she the last to see them?"

"*Ja.*"

"This discourse is a waste of time," snarled *Herr* Lagerlöf. "I suppose you will next want to accuse my wife of stealing the candlesticks in order to protect you precious thief."

"I of all people have most cause to dislike this boy," snapped the woodmaster, losing his composure for the first time. "If I can forgive his repeated offenses to me, why can you not forgive his offenses to you?"

"You admit then," said the vicar, stepping forward again, "that he is the thief."

The woodmaster turned on Tor, his usually calm face

scintillating with anger while Tor's remained pale and rigid, hiding deep dread as his eyes searched the woodmaster's for some hint of pity.

"Did you take the candlesticks?"

"*Nej*," said Tor, still looking up at him, trying, without much hope, to communicate a silent plea with the pressure of his stare. "I swear to you I didn't."

"Do you know where they are?"

"*Nej.*"

"Do you know what happened to them?"

"*Nej.*" Tor shut his eyes for just a moment and breathed, trying to clear his head enough to decide if this was a nightmare. Instead of clarity, he found horrible visions of what the prison and its occupants would be like.

The girl with the pretty face had won without having to lift a finger.

When he opened his eyes the woodmaster was staring at him, and he did not look away for several long moments.

"Then you have your answer," he said abruptly to the vicar, turning to take up his hammer.

"What do you mean?" cried *Herr* Lagerlöf.

"I mean he says he did not take the candlesticks, and you cannot prove that he did."

"You would take his word when you know he is a thief and a liar?"

"You cannot declare him guilty until he is proven so." The woodmaster pounded his chisel into the wood with his hammer.

"You did as much, *Herr* carpenter." The vicar drew close, giving an obvious effort to moderate his voice. "You took him and forced him to work for you."

"That is because nobody cared to interfere," said the woodmaster, coolly. "And you forget that the pawnbroker identified his face from my drawings."

"*Herr* carpenter. This village will no longer accept you if you continue to shield this young reprobate."

"What would you have me do?" asked the woodmaster, throwing down his hammer and chisel and looking at the vicar. "Condemn a boy to prison on suspicion? Do you know what life in prison is like? Do you care?"

He turned away and picked up a thick, solid board.

"I understand your frustration very well, but if you want the boy in prison, your time would be better spent searching for evidence than trying to persuade me."

Herr Lagerlöf looked at Tor as if he wished to roast him for dinner, but the woodmaster seized a particularly toothy saw, laid his thick board on the table so that it blocked Tor off from the clerk, and began to saw, savagely.

The men did leave at last, *Herr* Lagerlöf shouting loudly before he slammed the door.

"No fear, carpenter! We shall find proof!"

The woodmaster stared at the board before him and gave no acknowledgment of the men's departure.

Tor looked at him sawing, his features set like stone. How easy it would be for the man to rid himself of Tor now. How he must desire it. Tor couldn't bear the thought that the woodmaster detested him, saw him as an obstacle to his own happiness and peace of mind, yet somehow felt he must protect Tor out of duty.

Surely this sense of duty only gave him cause to resent Tor the more.

The drunkard's boy approached the table and began to plane his board again, and, once more, the only sounds heard in the dusty shop were the sounds of woodworking.

For the rest of the day, the woodmaster scarcely looked up, and he did not look Tor in the eye at all. His cold silence made Tor miserable. Finally, when they were together in the back room that evening, Tor dishing out soup and the woodmaster laying out cups, spoons, and bread, Tor spoke.

"*Herr*," he said, setting down the last bowl on the table, "I did not take the silver candlesticks. I promise you I did not take them."

"You have said so," said the man, shortly.

Tor picked up his spoon but did not sit down. Instead, he stood, fingering it nervously.

"I am sorry I stole the Nativity," he finally burst out, sitting down abruptly and clenching the spoon tightly with both hands.

"I am sorry for lying and for swearing and doing so many things wrong in the shop. I will do better, I promise, and...and..." he floundered, embarrassed and small and loathing himself for his display of vulnerability because he knew it laid him bare to the hurt of the woodmaster's scorn. "And I did not take the candlesticks," he finished doggedly.

The woodmaster, sitting on his bench, stirred his soup in silence.

Before he could answer, they heard a knock on the shop door. The woodmaster stood and went out to answer it, still not looking at Tor.

The moment the door was opened, Tor heard a clipped female staccato.

"Is it true what they say?" Freja Lindqvist demanded of the woodmaster.

"Who are they, and what are they saying, my love?" asked the woodmaster, wearily. There was neither wind nor storm outside. The house was quiet enough that even the woodmaster's low rumble could be distinguished.

"That the drunkard's boy has stolen the silver candlesticks from the Lord's Table."

"Who says so?"

"Everyone! It is all over the streets that the vicar and parish clerk visited you this afternoon to demand that the boy be given over to justice, and you refused! Is it true?"

"It is true that the vicar has accused the boy of stealing the candlesticks, but there is no proof."

"Proof! What more proof do you need than his guilty past? You know better than anyone, Wilhelm, that he is an unscrupulous thief. He stole your most prized possession, and now it is gone forever!"

Tor sat, frozen, listening to the clip and scrape of Freja Lindqvist's boots pacing across the wooden floor.

"Furthermore," continued the girl, her staccato syllables descending like a volley of arrows hitting their mark in swift succession, "you know that the vicar saw him—and only him—in the churchyard last night. I've heard even the drunkard's boy doesn't deny it."

"Stop calling him that," the woodmaster suddenly snapped.

There was a long moment of silence.

"Pardon me?" said the pretty girl, icily.

"I said, stop calling him 'drunkard's boy' as if he's an evil species. He is just a boy. His name is Tor."

"Oh, of course, my lord," she said, much too sweetly. "Well, I can see we shall have a very merry household. I see the sort of life I am to lead in your house. I am to be the cook and laundress and maid of all work. I am to watch over your drunkard's boy so that you can escape to your precious wood-working, but if ever I dare to correct him or call his behavior into question *I* am to be scolded. He can do no wrong, your precious brat."

"That is unjust," replied the woodmaster, his voice once again subdued. "You know I've promised many times that I will never allow the boy to disrespect or take advantage of you. I've told you he will be my concern, not yours."

In the next room, the drunkard's boy winced at the thought of the woodmaster pouring out his complaints of Tor in the pretty girl's ear. He winced again at the thought of the pretty girl petting the woodmaster and soothing those grievances caused by the drunkard's boy.

"You know what they are saying all across the town, do you not?" demanded the pretty girl, her voice strident as ever.

"Many things, certainly." The woodmaster's voice was despondent and dismissive.

"They are saying"—Tor could hear the pretty girl stepping closer to the woodmaster—"that you are the boy's father."

Tor held his breath and gripped his wooden spoon so tightly it fractured. Strangely, he felt hopeful.

But when the woodmaster scoffed, Tor looked down and reddened, though there was no one in the room to stare at him.

"And this only shows how desperate they are to be rid of him."

"Are you his father?" Freja challenged.

There was a long pause, and Tor moved closer to the door, vividly imagining the woodmaster turning away from the girl in reluctant mortification. But when the man spoke, Tor knew he had been staring evenly at Freja's eyes.

"*Nej*," said the woodmaster, firmly. "I am not Tor's father. I was but fourteen years of age living with my family in a village no one here has even heard of when the boy was conceived. You know this, Freja. You are only asking to try to shame me."

Tor's humiliation slowly dispersed as he realised why the woodmaster had scoffed. It was not disgust at the idea being related to Tor but disgust at the sheer absurdity of the slander being spread.

For some moments all was silent but for the sound of shifting and a few wandering footsteps.

"Wilhelm," the girl finally said in a greatly softened tone, "you disgrace yourself before the whole community with your stubborn protection of that wild boy. You only enable him to commit worse crimes when you so blindly defend him.

"Please, I love you, Wilhelm. Do not ruin your prospects for this hardened thief and liar. Do not allow his wickedness to fester and spoil in your house until you—until *we*—are both a stench to this town."

Tor heard the tap of a little boot. He imagined the girl stepping closer and sliding her arms around the woodmaster's neck. It was a moment before the man spoke.

"And so you would have me send him to prison?"

"He is a thief, Wilhelm. Cosseting him and treating him as though he has done nothing wrong will only make him worse."

"And if he never took the candlesticks?"

"He took your Nativity. That was even more precious than the candlesticks, both in monetary and sentimental value."

Again, silence.

Then the woodmaster gave an audible grunt in frustration.

"After all the struggle I have been through with this boy, I can't just send him to prison until I make sure he took the candlesticks."

"And who else do you think took them, Wilhelm? The vicar? *Herr* Lagerlöf? You would suspect them over this boy?"

"I only know I can't damn a boy to prison upon mere suspicion. Have you any idea what he would suffer? Exhaustion, starvation, and abuse of the worst kind—do you know what could happen to him?" The man's last words intensified almost to a whisper, as if burgeoning with secrets unfit to be told.

"Well then, Wilhelm Andersson," said the girl—and her voice was very sweet—"I suppose you have your choice before you. You can marry me, and we can start a family together here, and you can be—as you earlier told me you would be—happy for the first time in years, or you can keep the wretched drunkard's boy and saw away in your dusty workshop, starved of companionship, good will, and respect till you shrivel up into a lonely, wizened old man."

She had moved away from him again.

Tor's heart was beating with anxiety and also with anger at

the girl's cruelty in drawing the woodmaster close with sweet words and a soft touch, tantalizing him with the happiness he most wanted, only to draw it away abruptly with a description of his bleak alternative.

He heard the woodmaster speak again.

"Why do you hate him so?"

His voice was almost pleading.

The pretty girl seemed to sputter.

"Why? Because he is a sly, arrogant, foul-mouthed thief, and he is making a fool of you!"

"Did you know he stole the Nativity so he would have money for a doctor for his sister?"

"And from what altruistic motive did he steal the candlesticks? Or curse like a sailor on the steps of the church? Or beat those boys at the Midsummer's Feast? Or disrespect his schoolmaster?"

"He apologized to me for these things, just today, of his own accord."

"Of course he did, now that he thinks he is to be sent to prison! Oh, what a fool he is making of you!" Tor heard her little boot stamp on the floor as she began to pace again.

"Why," she pressed, her footsteps pausing once more, "don't you simply find someone in another village who needs an apprentice? He will never survive in this town. You must know that!"

"*Nej*, he would not last with anyone else. No one would understand him. He would get upset, they would beat him, and he would run away and die in the gutter somewhere as he almost did last month."

"And so you would rather have him than me?"

Tor had been waiting in dread for this question.

"*Nej*, Freja. I love you, and part of the reason why I love you is because I think you have the goodness and strength to take in a boy whom nobody cares for and give him a second chance." Again, the woodmaster's voice turned pleading. "He might come through if you did, Freja. Please."

Silence. Freja paced. Then, she spoke bitterly.

"And just how many second chances does this boy require? You have given him several dozen."

"No more than God would give him."

"And now you pretend to be religious," Freja sneered, "while you fly in the very face of the vicar's teachings and desires."

"Is the vicar God?" The woodmaster's dry tone returned.

"He speaks for God."

"He speaks contrary to Scripture."

"One could scarcely count the number of texts he quoted last Sunday!"

"Just so. And perhaps if he had merely chosen a few solid texts and taken the time to properly expound them in *context*, rather than picking out several dozen scraps of verses here and there, his theology might have been more sound."

"Answer me once and for all!" Freja snapped. "Is it he or I?"

"I'm all he has!" the woodmaster suddenly shouted.

There was a long, dreadful silence.

"Then take your ring," said Freja, acidly.

Tor heard it hit the ground as if she had thrown it across the room.

The door opened and slammed for the second time that day. After a while there was a shifting sound, as of cloth rubbing on wood, and then nothing could be heard in the shop except for the faintly ticking clocks.

Tor felt too shaken and weak to remain standing by the door, but for a very long while he did not to move because he did not want the woodmaster to hear him and realize how easily the drunkard's boy had overheard the conversation.

At last, however, as weariness overcame him, he went and huddled in the corner where he had slept on his first night in the woodmaster's house. It made him nearly wince to think of the shattered woodmaster coming in to find him comfortably curled up in his bed or by the fire. If the man was to find him sleeping, he should find him as uncomfortable as possible.

He wanted to think about the things the woodmaster had said and assure himself that he would not be turned out, that the woodmaster felt more kindly toward him than he had thought possible, but he could only recall all the reasons why the woodmaster should not keep him now, why the man should reconsider and run after the pretty girl who promised to give him back all that he had lost.

After all, what the girl had said was true: if Tor stayed with the woodmaster, the man would become a stench to the rest of the village. His reputation, his work, and, consequently, his life would be ruined.

Why should he stand by the drunkard's boy? The woodmaster owed him naught. Naught but bitterness and beatings.

Hours slipped by, and the woodmaster did not re-enter.

At last Tor crept outside, shamefully driven by his old enemy, the cold, to fetch more firewood. He once again considered running away and saving himself the pain of being cast out and saving the woodmaster the trouble of casting him out, but he remembered how wretched and futile had been his previous attempts. He wasn't strong enough to tear himself from his only hope of happiness—possibly of existence.

Miserably, he returned inside, mended the fire, and went back to the corner.

CHAPTER TWENTY-ONE

Early the next morning, Tor heard sounds of work in the wood-shop. The woodmaster's bed stood untouched. Tor rose guiltily, took a bit of bread and salt herring, and went out to join the woodmaster.

"Thea Ahlberg is coming for you," said the woodmaster the moment Tor opened the door. He did not look up even when Tor laid food beside him. "It seems she wants help with Christmas shopping and baking. You'd better get a good breakfast. I'm going out and won't be back till tonight."

Tor shut the door slowly and returned to the fire. He was not hungry. He had no excitement for Christmas baking. All he could think of was that the woodmaster did not want to be with him, did not want to look at him.

He waited on the hearth for some time till Thea Ahlberg arrived. Then he donned his boots, coat, hat, and scarf, and stepped wearily into the street after her. She began immediately to speak to him with signs, lifting an imaginary spoon to her lips and intermittently holding up one, two, three, four fingers. He had to ask many questions before he could guess her meaning. It was a good distraction from the dark glances of the passing villages, who gave them a wide berth on the street and a wide anchorage in the shops.

Everywhere Tor went, the cheerful bustle seemed to cool. Most simply averted their eyes and looked uncomfortable, but some were frankly antagonistic. It was good that he was with Thea Ahlberg, for though she was speechless she had the power and the will to make a scene if she lost her temper, and nobody, Tor knew, particularly wanted to arouse Thea Ahlberg's temper.

So they moved through the village undisturbed.

Still, Tor was plagued by his own thoughts as he realized yet again that he could never live happily in this village.

He proved to be of some use at the butchers, the mill, and the mercantile, however, for when Thea Ahlberg desired an obscure ingredient, she wrote it on a paper, and Tor would use his eyes and fingers to help him slowly sound out the word to the vendors who could not read—which was most of them.

The vendors showed plain dislike at having to converse with the thieving drunkard's boy, but apparently the tales of Thea Ahlberg's wealth were true, for they seemed to wish to encourage her patronage.

Only the baker was truly kind, smiling and slipping a fresh *lussekatter* into Tor's hand, saying he hoped Tor would be good for Christmas and reminding him to lay out *pepparkakor* for the *Jultomten*. Admittedly, this felt like something of an insult to Tor's age, but it was so far removed from the insults to which he was accustomed that he was inclined to give a half-hearted smile and try to enjoy the *lussekatter*.

It was just when the sun had reached its zenith, as the bustle in the streets was escalating, and while Thea Ahlberg was in the Gustavsson's barnyard, haggling for the price of a plump goose, that Tor heard, amidst the clucking, honking fowl and the cries of Christmas greetings, discordant voices coming from an alley behind the coop.

He left Thea Ahlberg's little barrow of groceries by the gate of the barnyard and jogged past the fence and the large, disheveled coop to investigate. In a crooked, narrow alleyway, he dimly discerned Klara, hugging something tightly in her arms. Clustered around her were Albin Ovarsson, Olaf, Jan, Lisbet Hansson, and the vicar's daughter, looking like a bright and sparkling snowflake in her white fur cape.

"Perhaps," she was saying, "you can ask the schoolmaster to give you lessons in posture and grace next. He's so eager to teach you anything you want to learn, you know. Or perhaps you hunch like that in order to get boys to feel sorry for you? Boys like Tor Neeson, perhaps? *Ja*, I see how you always glance at him. Believe me, he has no interest in you."

Tor was now close enough to see how Klara's yellow-brown eyes glinted in the lamp-light like those of a cornered fox. She hunched her shoulders and tried to move away.

Olaf stepped in front of her, and the vicar's daughter continued speaking, her usual bright mocking tone now so sharp that it slipped through the thin winter air like blades.

"What good," she said, "do you think all that learning will do a crippled little mouse like you, Klara? You can show off all you wish before the rest of us at school, but for all the schoolmaster's praise you'll be good for naught but to trail about after your idiot sister. Why don't you deny it?"

"She's too afraid," said Albin, who had a nose for fear, being a great coward himself.

"And she knows it's true," said the vicar's daughter. "You'll never be anything but a drudge, Klara."

"Just remember what you are the next time you'd like to try to humiliate one of your betters in school, clubfoot," added Olaf.

"Now, give me the book or we'll take it," said Albin.

Klara hugged the book tighter and pressed against the wall.

"Why don't we just leave her alone, Albin," Lisbet whimpered, edging away from the group.

They ignored her.

"You know you really have no choice, Klara," said Olaf. "You can't get away from us on that miserable stump you call a foot."

Jan pushed Klara.

Tor felt something like the fury he used to feel when his mother abused Nanny. He also felt a chilling and bitter disappointment toward the vicar's daughter. She was nothing more than a pretty girl with a heart-shaped face.

He stepped forward.

"You had better hope she does," he said to Olaf, "if you care anything for that miserable mess you call a face."

He sauntered coolly into the alley, his anger too sharp for open display. He held his hands in his pockets, but they were flat with the thumbs out, ready to slide out at a moment's notice.

"Tor!" said Lisbet Hansson, looking mortified. The vicar's pretty daughter merely stared at him, her rosy cheeks flushing even rosier than usual. His eyes lingered on her, for he had never seen her look flustered before.

"Oh, it's the drunkard's boy," said Albin with a sneer as he backed behind Olaf.

"Come, Klara," said Tor, staring at Albin.

"No, stay with us, Klara." Jan said nastily, pulling the girl back by the arm as he tried to snatch the book away. "You don't want to be seen with a drunkard's boy, do you?"

Tor stepped forward, dodging around Olaf, and pushed Jan away.

"Let her be, Jan."

Lisbet began to scream, but Olaf silenced her sharply.

Albin glared at Tor.

"Hold him down," he ordered Jan and Olaf.

"*Nej*, Albin," said the vicar's daughter. "I'll not have you beat him."

"Just because you're sweet on the drunkard's boy doesn't mean I have to like him," Albin snapped. "Get him, Jan! Put him down!"

Tor edged further into the alley, drawing the boys away from Klara, who watched him with her frightened feral eyes.

Run, Klara! he thought with frustration—before remembering that she could not run. Groaning inwardly, he edged deeper into the alley, allowing the three boys to fan out around him and cut off his escape.

He finally noticed Klara inching away, and he wondered if her book and her feelings were worth getting beaten for. He caught a glimpse of the vicar's daughter. Her face now looked ashy white and not pretty at all.

Then Olaf dove at him with Jan coming immediately after. Following a short scuffle, he was pinned to the ground and held to await the pleasure of Albin, who stood above him and cracked his knuckles.

For one strange moment, Tor felt the woodmaster was justified in being annoyed at him for his knuckle-cracking habit. It really was distasteful.

Then, Albin's fist hit him.

The cobbler's boy proved to have a wild and vicious energy in him. Perhaps he was recalling all of Tor's many insults, dealing a blow for each one, or perhaps he was remembering the many times his own father had tirelessly drawn welts with his belt. In any case, Tor soon felt quick trickles of blood down his nose and throat.

"Do you know, drunkard's boy," panted Albin, pausing to lean in close, "the beauty is that no one will care what your face looks like. We caught you in the alley trying to kiss Olga, and when she fought you you started cursing at her. You'll be packed off to prison before you can say 'carpenter.'"

"*Nej*," snapped the vicar's daughter. "You won't say that. I shall tell them the truth: that you bullied Tor viciously."

"I wouldn't, Olga," replied Albin, "unless you want to be reported as accepting the drunkard's boy's advances."

"What do I care!"

Albin shrugged.

"Then go on and fetch help for your *sweetheart*, the drunkard's boy."

Olga stood where she was, her face a picture of irresolution.

Albin turned back to Tor and hit him again.

Then, a hard, resonant voice echoed through the alley.

"Enough!"

Albin turned once again, starting at the sight of the new arrival.

"*Herr*," he said, hurriedly. "The drunkard's boy—he accosted Olga, and-"

"Get up," interrupted the voice in a tone of manifest disdain.

"*Ja, Herr*," Albin said, standing quickly, quite shaken.

Tor rolled to one side, trying to shield his face from the newcomer and stifle the groan that the pain of his movements wrung from him. He tried to rise, but paused on his hands and knees and staring down, violently dizzy. The blood stain growing on the white snow beneath him was entrancing.

"Roll on your back," ordered the new voice. "You must stop that bleeding." A cold, wet handkerchief was placed on his face, smearing off blood.

"As I said, *Herr* schoolmaster," Albin repeated nervously, "he tried to accost Olga, and when she wouldn't let him he began to spew profanities, and that's when we found him. We were so angry we perhaps lost control of ourselves."

Tor shut his blurred, already-swollen eyes. The schoolmaster. How dreadful.

It would be the last straw for the woodmaster: accosting a girl in an alleyway. And if Albin's tale wasn't convincing enough, the schoolmaster's certainly would be. Tor would go to prison, undoubtedly, but even that would not hurt so much as the look of revulsion he knew would be on the woodmaster's face.

Tor felt another presence then, one both forceful and gentle. The clucking sounds soon revealed her to be Thea Ahblerg.

The drunkard's boy was unsure how long he lay in the snow, but after a time they pulled him to his feet and helped him out of the alley.

"We had better take him to the woodcarver's, Thea Ahlberg," said the schoolmaster, presently, as if trying to dissuade the woman.

Thea Ahlberg made silent signs and wrote on her paper. Tor

heard the scribbling though he could not see it.

Finally, the schoolmaster shrugged beneath Tor's arm.

"Well, if he is gone, then I suppose we have no choice but to go to your house, as you say. I doubt anyone else would welcome him."

The journey would be a long one with Tor leaning on the strength of the schoolmaster, and so he began to pull away.

"I can walk," he said. He was surprised at the rasp of his own voice and wondered what Albin had done to it.

"Very well," said the schoolmaster, shrugging again and this time shrugging Tor off. "See that you don't fall on your nose and start to bleed again."

Tor ignored the snide comment and stumbled away beside Thea Ahlberg, who was pushing her own barrow.

"I can push it, Thea Ahlberg," he rasped, reaching for the handles.

She shook her head and pulled away.

"I came to help you with packages," said Tor impatiently, "so let me do it." He had recovered his wits, balance, and sight, though his head throbbed like a great church bell.

The woman released the barrow slowly into Tor's care and they turned their steps towards the gusty bay and then along the rocky coast to the Ahlberg's cottage, bright red against the gleaming grey boulders and sparkling snow.

Tor entered the kitchen and emptied his arms of their

packages. Already the warm cottage smelled of Christmas spices that seemed to be trying to press away unpleasant thoughts.

Exhausted, Tor sat down in a chair while Thea Ahlberg began to unpack the baskets and packages. She laid out fresh candles, tall and creamy-white; small but deeply scented bundles of cardamom pods, brown cloves, cinnamon sticks, and nutmegs; sacks of freshly milled brown rye and speckled wheat flours, sacks of dusty oats and hard brown sugar; good, plump potatoes; pungent pickled fish and fish eggs; jars of jelly and marmalade, sparkling like gems.

Thea Ahlberg divested herself of her embroidered marketing apron and donned another of rougher texture, stained with grease spots, but evidently freshly laundered. With her own hands, she tied another work apron onto Tor and patted his shoulders heartily as if to pronounce him ready.

Tor meticulously followed her instructions, despite his aching head and bleary eyes.

He liked cooking. It was diverse work, full of interesting possibilities. It engaged all of his senses, distracting him from his dark thoughts. He liked to smell of the sweet, scalded milk pudding when he stirred it, to taste traces of spiced relish when he licked a spoon, to hear the click of his knife as he cut slivers of almond for cake, to see the bubbling froth lifting up the lid of a pot of fish stew, and to feel stiff rye bread dough pushing back against his palms as he kneaded.

He stayed to dinner, for Thea Ahlberg made him understand the woodmaster expected him to. And when the fisherman came in and saw Tor's swollen, stained face, he suddenly overcame his recent scruples concerning the drunkard's boy and regaled Tor with rowdy tales of pirates and whale-hunting. Tor, to his own surprise, was not bitter against Isak Ahlberg for his recent aloofness. He was only grateful that the fisherman was friendly again, even if he did continue to call him a little fish.

As Tor stood at the threshold of the Ahlberg's red cottage that night, he remembered again the workhouse with its wretched food, dank air, and endless coughs and complaints, and he turned to politely thank Thea Ahlberg for asking him to help with Christmas and Isak Ahlberg for sharing his sea stories.

They both smiled and nodded and fussed to a point of great discomfort for the drunkard's boy, Isak Ahlberg tousling Tor's hair and Thea Ahlberg kissing it.

Then, it was back to the woodmaster's house, back to wondering what his reception would be when he arrived there, back to wondering what the woodmaster would do to him for "trying to kiss the vicar's daughter."

Perhaps the woodmaster would still be unwilling to send him to prison, but he would send him to some coarse, unreasonable miller or bricklayer as an apprentice.

It was very much as it had been months ago in the early spring when Tor had returned to the woodmaster after helping Thea

Ahlberg with her fence. He found his heart beating fast as he approached the door of the woodshop, but he saw that there were no lights inside, just as on that other night.

He remembered wishing that the Nativity were still in the window, wishing that the woodmaster had no cause to hate him, and he glanced again, without thinking, through the glass pane on his right. The display shelf there was unusually sparse, no more than a fleecy white lambskin—much like the one Tor had taken last Christmas—and one tiny wooden piece sitting in the center of it.

Tor walked closer to examine the piece. It was the little Christ Child he had returned to the woodmaster.

Two big hands suddenly landed on his shoulders from behind.

"Deciding whether to steal it again?"

Tor started to turn, but the woodmaster wrapped one strong arm over his shoulder and down across his chest and pulled the drunkard's boy forcibly back against him, holding him for a moment with his chin resting on the boy's shoulder.

Heat spread over Tor. His heart beat so wildly he felt certain the man must feel it as he pressed Tor against himself.

Then the woodmaster pushed him toward the door.

Utterly discomposed, the drunkard's boy stood still, not knowing what to do until the man walked around him, opened the door, and stepped aside to let him enter.

"I see the schoolmaster did not exaggerate," the carpenter said as he entered behind Tor. "Your face does look like raw beef."

Tor waited for him to shut the door and then meekly followed him into the back room. He yearned to ask what else the schoolmaster had said.

"You've had supper," said the woodmaster, going to stoke the fire.

"*Ja.*" Tor took off his coat, feeling no need to wait for the fire to warm up the room. He still felt hot all over. He sat on the bench on the side of the table opposite the fire and began to pull off his mittens.

The woodmaster poked at the flames for a very long time.

"Well, I have heard everyone's account but yours, Tor Neeson," he finally said. He gave the fire a few last pokes and then braced his hands on his legs to stand. Tor's head was bowed, but from the corner of his eye he nervously watched the woodmaster approach him, slowly circling the table till he stood over Tor.

"What is your explanation of this?" the man asked, tilting Tor's head up and touching the hot, swollen cheek with his thumb.

Tor pulled away and fumbled with his mittens as the woodmaster moved past him to take a milk can from where it sat by the back door. He did not want to review the painful events because nothing he said could make a difference to the woodmaster. The bare thought of what an exhausting struggle it would be to combat the charges of his many accusers made him weary. He had not even energy enough to contemplate the injustice of it all.

The woodmaster returned with heavy footsteps to seat himself sideways the other end of Tor's bench and pour himself a cup of buttermilk.

"Come," he said quietly. "This is not the Tor Neeson I know. No glares, no protestations, no arrogance?"

Tor laid his mittens on the table, trying to purchase time to think what to say.

The woodmaster shoved the tin of milk down the table in Tor's direction. "Have buttermilk." He reached from where he sat and took a cup from the side table.

"*Tack*," said Tor. He poured a cup and they drank in silence, the woodmaster staring at Tor, and Tor staring at his buttermilk.

"What happened, boy?"

Tor fidgeted with the cap he had laid on the table, tracing his finger round its edge.

"Some boys were bothering Klara. I wanted them to stop, and they beat me."

"Why were they bothering Klara?"

Tor sighed.

"Because she has a clubfoot and they are jealous of how well she does in school."

"These sound like poor reasons. Are you sure that is all?"

Tor took another swallow of buttermilk.

"Tell me everything, Tor. It will be better for you."

These ominous words only made Tor want to retreat further into himself.

"She had a book the schoolmaster lent her, and they were trying to get it away from her."

"Who was there?"

"Albin, Jan, Olaf."

"Only they?"

"Lisbet and Olga."

"And so you only tried to defend Klara? Nothing more? You didn't antagonize anyone, didn't throw anything, or swear, or hit someone?"

"*Nej,*" said Tor, beginning to feel prickles of irritation and wondering if the woodmaster would pronounce him guilty of the whole kafuffle if he admitted to even one of these things. Wouldn't their attack on Klara perhaps have merited some of this behavior even if their abuse of Tor did not?

"Jan says you pushed him."

"When he grabbed Klara and tried to take her book."

"Did you perhaps try to kiss someone?"

"*Nej!*"

Tor jerked his head up angrily, only to see the smirk on the woodmaster's face.

"Olga is very pretty."

"And very mean," snapped Tor.

"Albin, Jan and Olaf agree that you accosted her."

Tor wanted to ask what the girls said, but he didn't. He shut his mouth, set his shoulders, and faced forward, away from the woodmaster.

"Lisbet says she arrived too late to see or hear anything." The woodmaster paused and drank deeply of his buttermilk. "Olga went home, locked herself in her room, and refuses to say a word about it. It seems she has 'no desire to expose herself to the town as a subject of idle gossip.'"

Tor grimaced, not oblivious to the woodmaster's exaggerated imitation of Olga Arnman's haughty tone. The man seemed to be enjoying this interrogation. It stung that he could laugh when he knew there was no possibility that the town would not rise up as one to send Tor to prison, or, at best, back to the workhouse.

"What are you going to do to me?" he suddenly asked, weary of the suspense.

The woodmaster tossed his head and eyed Tor.

"I'm going to ask you what you did that made the schoolmaster so eager to defend you?"

Tor stared at the woodmaster.

"He defends me? Why?"

"I believe I just asked that question of you."

The woodmaster poured another cup of buttermilk.

"He says those three boys have always disliked you and

would say anything to your detriment. He says they are also jealous of Klara, as you mentioned earlier. He says Klara is too intelligent and too well-bred to fabricate such a story against the word of so many of her classmates only for your sake. He says a great many things."

"What does the village say?"

"Only the usual nonsense—the ones who cackle loudest, as is customary, having the least worth saying."

"And . . . and what do you say?" Tor asked, closely inspecting the handle of his cup.

The woodmaster looked at his own drink as he swished it in circles.

"I say what I have always said." He took another swallow and paused to savor the buttermilk, staring at Tor.

"I say you had better not run away from me again, or I'll beat you worse than ever Albin did."

It was a strange comfort, that crude threat, but it was a deeper comfort than Tor had ever known in his life. He stared at his buttermilk, curling both hands around the cold cup, and felt very warm, from the inside.

"Boy."

"*Ja.*"

"You remember the day you broke the china plate, and I struck you?" The woodmaster's words were strangely rushed.

"*Ja,*" Tor said, watching the him without lifting his head. He couldn't imagine what the man was leading up to.

"I was wrong. I lost my temper. I should never have hit you like that."

He stared straight at Tor, looking obstinate, as though he wanted to shift his gaze but refused to do so.

Tor had never been more stunned. He knew not how long he stared at the woodmaster, but at last, when embarrassment overcame surprise, he looked away and shrugged again.

"I'm used to being hit," he mumbled.

"Perhaps, but I'm not used to hitting little boys."

"I'm not a little boy."

Had any man but the woodmaster insulted him so, Tor would have reviled him back, but he knew by now that the woodmaster purposely said things he did not mean simply to irritate Tor.

"I shouldn't have beaten you," said the woodmaster again, stubbornly. "I also lost my temper on Midsummer's Eve. You did wrong, but you were also wronged, I know. You were antagonized. I should have listened to you." He seemed to be waiting for a reply, but Tor did not know what to say.

"I am sorry for my behavior," the woodmaster said, finally.

Deeply embarrassed, Tor looked everywhere but the man's face. He wondered if the woodmaster was waiting to be forgiven, but Tor felt it would be ludicrous to say he forgave the woodmaster when he himself had been such a monster. And in truth, he'd quite forgotten about the woodmaster striking him.

"It's no matter," he finally said.

"It is. It was very wrong."

"I—I don't . . ." Tor began, wondering why he felt so uncomfortable. "It's all right."

"I hope so."

Though he was not a merry man, the woodmaster seldom spoke in such a serious tone. There was generally a note of mockery present. Tor studied his fingers, wondering if his cheeks were as red as they felt. No one but Nanny had ever apologized to him that he could remember.

Suddenly, the man stood, clapping his empty cup on the table with uncharacteristic and obnoxious loudness.

"Bedtime," he said. "Best get ready."

CHAPTER TWENTY-TWO

Tor opened his eyes on Christmas Eve and stared at the rafters. In the larger bed beside him, the woodmaster shifted under his mound of blankets. Tor sat up. He didn't know why, but he was elated.

He leapt silently out of bed and ran across the cold floor in his heavily socked feet to mend the fire.

When the fire was cheerful again he huddled beside the flames, assembling a porridge of cold, cooked rice, milk, eggs, sugar, and spices while snacking on cheese, which he first toasted over the fire on a fork. He leaned over the bubbling porridge pot often to smell the Christmas fragrance of scalded milk and spices.

"You make yourself quite at home, I see," a groggy voice rumbled.

Tor turned to see the woodmaster sitting up in bed and glaring at him from beneath shaggy, tousled hair.

"Thea Ahlberg made me promise to make a rice pudding for a Christmas Eve breakfast. She gave me rice and sugar and spices on purpose."

"I can buy my own rice," said the woodmaster, rolling back into bed. "I am not a beggar."

He went back to sleep or perhaps merely nestled under his covers for another three-quarters of an hour until Tor began ladling the porridge into bowls. Then he dragged out of bed, still clutching his covers over his shoulders. Tor stood to put the bowls on the table, but the woodmaster waved him back.

"Leave them," he said. "It's too cold for a mortal to bear." And he huddled down across from Tor at the hearth.

Tor tried to hold back the little smile that threatened to crack his swollen lips. How often had the woodmaster swung out of bed on mornings more frigid than this to mend the fire and make breakfast himself without complaint or a sign of discomfort?

"Is there no coffee?" the man demanded.

"I forgot it."

"Well, make some, will you?"

Tor went to the cupboard, again amused at the woodmaster's churlishness. He prepared the coffee and set it over the fire to warm.

The woodmaster bowed his head for the blessing but did not mumble the usual terse prayer. Instead, he began to quote the Magnificat. His low, rough voice was very different from the vicar's lofty and pompous tones, and he rocked back and forth slowly like a child reciting a lesson.

"My soul doth magnify the Lord,
    and my spirit hath rejoiced in God my Saviour.
For He hath regarded the low estate of His handmaiden:
    for, behold, from henceforth all generations shall   call

me blessed.

> For He that is mighty hath done to me great things; and holy is His name.

> And His mercy is on them that fear Him from generation to generation.

> He hath shewed strength with His arm; He hath scattered the proud in the imagination of their hearts.

> He hath put down the mighty from their seats, and exalted them of low degree.

> He hath filled the hungry with good things, and the rich He hath sent empty away.

> He hath helped His servant Israel, in remembrance of His mercy,

> as He spake to our fathers, to Abraham, and to his seed forever.

> Amen."

Tor looked at the woodmaster as he ended his prayer and straightened to toss the shaggy hair from his eyes.

"Why don't you cut your hair?" Tor asked without thinking.

The woodmaster blew on a small spoonful of pudding and looked at him darkly.

"I allow you to live in my house, but that does not mean I will let you advise me on the cut of my hair," he said curtly. He ate the bite of pudding gingerly with his teeth and seemed to consider the taste, looking prepared to spit it back out if necessary.

Tor looked down at his own porridge.

"Why do you say that?" said the woodmaster after a moment of silence.

"I think it would look better cut short."

"You have little right to criticize my hair," said the woodmaster, waving his spoon at the dark nest that covered Tor's ears.

"I would cut it if I knew how."

"Don't suppose I will let you practice on mine. Do not slurp your porridge, Tor. I'll not have slurping in my house. There is nothing more irritating than a boy slurping porridge."

For some time, no sound was heard but the crackle of the fire and the tap of spoons. Then the coffee began to boil, and Tor poured it out.

The woodmaster took a mug, breathed on it, and had a long, slurping sip, staring at Tor over the brim of his mug. The drunkard's boy cast his eyes upward.

"Unless it's a man slurping coffee," he said.

"Don't be insolent, boy," said the woodmaster. "You have always had the look of a goblin, but it is impossible to tell you how ridiculous you appear when you make faces."

"Probably something like you."

"Insolent," muttered the woodmaster.

He finished his porridge and laid the bowl on the hearth.

"Do you want more?" asked Tor, raising his eyebrows and daring the man to a second bowl.

"I suppose I've already eaten enough to be poisoned as it is," said the woodmaster, grudgingly holding out his bowl.

Tor ladled out the porridge.

"Do you believe the prayer you said?" he suddenly asked. "Or is it only something you say?"

The woodmaster met Tor's eyes, his own sharpening.

"Why would I not believe it?"

"Who...is it talking about when it says the hungry are filled with good things?"

"The hungry," said the man, staring at him.

"Anyone who is hungry?"

"Why not?"

"Me?"

"Are you hungry?"

Tor paused.

"I used to be." He wasn't sure how to say that he was still hungry in a way. Hungry for something more than food.

"And are you filled with good things now?"

"I think so."

"Then, *ja*, it is talking about you."

Tor tried to laugh.

"I don't think God concerns himself with me."

"Why not?"

The drunkard's boy fiddled with his spoon.

"Because . . ." He knew what to say, but he didn't want to say it. The vicar had called him an evil seed, and Tor hated to repeat the man he so despised.

"Because I'm nasty," he finally blurted, choosing instead to use Klara's word, as he knew that she, at least, was no hypocrite.

The woodmaster did not speak for a moment, but tapped his wooden spoon gently on his bowl in a way that irritated Tor.

"Why do you think we celebrate Christmas?"

Tor moved impatiently.

"They say it's because of the coming of the Christ Child."

"*Ja,*" replied the woodmaster, still staring at Tor. "And who was the Christ sent for?"

"People, I suppose."

The woodmaster tossed his head to one side.

"But not a drunkard's boy."

"I don't know," said Tor doggedly. "The vicar doesn't think so. Or the parish clerk."

"You heard me ask Freja if the vicar was God, I think?"

"*Ja,*" Tor said, reluctantly.

"Well, this is what one calls a rhetorical question." The woodmaster leaned forward, took Tor's empty bowl and set it inside his own, saying dryly. "He is not."

He laid the bowls on the hearth and suddenly took Tor's head in both hands, lifting the boy's face to meet his own penetrating gaze.

"As Saint Mark says, 'Those who are well have no need of a physician, but those who are sick.' You understand?"

Tor hesitated. The air seemed thick and heady as the woodmaster held his face, surprisingly tender of the bruises.

"*Ja,*" he said, unsure what else to say.

"Good. Then go to the Christ for forgiveness and healing without fear."

The man stood.

"I am going for a walk," he said, tossing his blankets across the room to his bed.

"I thought it was too cold for a mortal to bear?"

"Insolent," said the woodmaster again. "Here," he added, opening a cupboard and taking out a jar of ointment to set on the table. "Perhaps this can help your face, though I would be surprised if anything could." Then he pulled on boots, coat, and scarf and walked out the door.

When Wilhelm Andersson returned, Tor was asleep, still huddled by the fire, still in his nightshirt. He awoke to sounds of crushing coals and crackling flames as the woodmaster added logs to the fire and stirred the embers. With his head pillowed in the crook of his arm, Tor watched the man for a few moments.

He had dreamt that the pretty girl had returned, and the woodmaster had fallen to her feet in abject apology. She had told him if he would have her forgiveness he must lock the drunkard's boy out of his house. He had just shut the door in Tor's face when Tor woke to see the man before him, calmly—if somewhat despondently—feeding logs to the fire.

Tor deliberated for several moments, afraid to speak his thoughts, afraid to risk his future by asking what he needed to know.

"What is it, boy?" the woodmaster asked wearily without even glancing in his direction.

"What will you do if the town wants to send me to prison?"

"I will address the matter when the time comes."

"Will you agree?" pressed Tor, thinking with dread that there was no way for the woodmaster to stand against everyone.

The woodmaster began to jerk off his scarf.

"What do I need to do," he said, "to convince you that I am not your enemy?"

"I didn't think that," said Tor quickly and nervously, wondering if he lied. "Only..."—he sat up, fiddling with his blanket—"only if not for me, Freja would not have broken the betrothal."

The woodmaster rolled his eyes unsympathetically and

hacked at a burning log with the poker.

"*Nej*, if not for *me*, Freja would not have broken the betrothal. She does not like the kind of man I am. She does not value what I value. She has proven to be very different from what I thought she was, and it is best for us both that the betrothal is broken off." He spoke the words so adamantly that Tor understood they belied his heart.

The defenseless log now ravaged, the woodmaster leaned the poker against the wall and rose, dusting his hands.

"But I am not…what you want me to be either," persisted Tor, determined to have out the very worst of his thoughts. "Wouldn't you rather have her than me?"

The woodmaster looked at him witheringly.

"That is illogical. This is not simply a question of choosing between you."

Tor did not see how he was illogical, but he did not say so, only unwrapped himself from his blanket and began to fold it.

The woodmaster paced to the door to hang up his scarf.

"In the first place," he said, pulling off his coat, "a marriage contract is arranged by the consent of two equals. I would never treat a wife as I treat you."

Tor wondered—still keeping his attention fixed on the blanket in his hands—if the woodmaster thought he should be treated as an animal with no feelings.

"You have no right to this house," continued the woodmaster, seating himself on a bench to remove his boots, "except by my permission, and you have no say in how this household is run. Naturally, if I had a wife, she would have as much right to my goods as I have; also, I would respect and consider her advice. A wife must help me to do right rather than hinder me."

Having untied the laces of his boots, the woodmaster pulled them off one after the other and tossed them in the corner.

"A man does not give his half-grown son the kind of respect he gives his wife, and that—for the benefit of your dim-witted mind—" he said, "is only one reason why it would be a far more serious matter to take a wife with disparate values than to take in a rebellious boy."

Tor finally looked up at the woodmaster, who was now fishing in the cupboards for food, taking no notice of Tor's reactions to his speech. But Tor's mind had latched itself with eager tenacity to the word "son". His heart beat faster.

He stood and crossed the floor to his bed. After pulling up and tucking in the covers of his unmade trundle, he laid his extra blanket over the foot of the bed.

That word still seemed to echo loudly through the room.

"*Julotta* is early tomorrow morning," said the woodmaster, turning from the cupboards as he Tor apart a loaf of dark rye bread.

This observation roused Tor unpleasantly from his euphoria. It was on his tongue to ask if they really must attend the Christmas service, but he caught his complaint back. If the woodmaster would not shrink from church attendance for the sake of his own sensitivities, he certainly would not do so for Tor's.

They did little work that day and dozed by the fire in the late afternoon. The woodmaster, wearied from his long walk and no doubt by his irksome thoughts, lay on the floor, but Tor sat by the hearth and stared silently, first at the darkening window, then at the fluttering fire, then at the long brown floorboards until he too fell to sleep.

CHAPTER TWENTY-THREE

They woke hours before dawn to the clear tenor notes of a Christmas carol wafting by the woodmaster's house. It was the baker, Günter Nyvall, on his way early to the church, singing with gusto, oblivious to the thoughts or attitudes of his various auditors and bent only on pouring as much fervor into his carol as could be mustered from his substantial lungs.

Tor dared to hope that the woodmaster might sleep too late to attend the service, but the man rose, washed his face, combed his hair, and began to don his best clothes. Tor rose also, not wanting to be told. He had no desire to appear churlish when so much lay at stake before him. The woodmaster must not think that he intended to revert to his old ways.

Tor wondered if God cared to protect a miserable drunkard's boy such as himself from prison, when he had done nothing to deserve such protection. Then he remembered that he had not deserved the woodmaster's protection, and he took heart. If the woodmaster was good enough to stand by him, so might be God.

Just before going out the door, they took torches that the woodmaster had prepared, and each also slipped one taper of golden wax into his pocket before donning bulky mittens. Then they walked into the street amidst the stream of glowing lights that wound their way up the hill towards the church.

Some of the villagers were singing Christmas carols—though by no means as volubly as the baker had done—but they stopped when Tor and the woodmaster approached. The crowd seemed to thaw and break apart where they joined it, but the woodmaster strode forth as sturdily as ever, and Tor noticed a slight, obstinate jutting of his thick beard. It was the only indication that he noticed the coolness of his fellow townspeople and probably, Tor thought, it went undetected by them.

At first, no one within hearing of the woodmaster and the drunkard's boy spoke. But soon, murmurings began to reach their ears. None of the whispered communications could be fully heard, but there were many repetitions of the words, "vicar," "prison," "betrothal," and "drunkard's boy," and Tor felt the wind and chill damp sinking deeper and deeper to the core of his bones despite the warm river of little lanterns flowing around him.

He looked up and saw that a gale was blowing heavy clouds across the almost full moon, which seemed to be desperately trying to peep out at every opportunity in a fruitless effort to make itself seen. The chill in Tor's bones grew at the ominous sight of the smothered light.

When they arrived at the door of the church, they paused just inside the threshold to light their candles. Tor's heart gave an uncomfortable lurch as he looked at the common candlestick holders, no doubt borrowed from the clerk's household.

A sudden shiver trickled over him and he glanced furtively at the people surrounding him in the deep shadows of the church, their faces eerily lit by the candles they carried. Some met his gaze pointedly and stonily, others averted their eyes. Tor stiffened and glanced behind him at the door, but then the woodmaster's big hand clamped over his shoulder and drew him toward their regular pew.

As Tor moved further into the dark, glimmering church, filled with hollow voices and footsteps, he felt the beginnings of suffocation, a return of that old snarling, skulking fear he'd first felt in the woodmaster's captivity. He'd never realized he'd lost it till now—now, when it was returned.

For a moment, he thought he would break away from the woodmaster's strong grip and dart out of the church into the welcome arms of the clean and impartial winter night. He recognized the same desperate urgency he had felt when looking at the pane of glass that had seemed to separate him from Nanny's life. He realised that his heart was falsely starting again and again, just as it had done when he'd contemplated smashing the pane.

He knew he must get away from this crowd that was bent on sending him to prison. If he waited too long, he would be too late —just as with Nanny.

He couldn't be foolish enough to think that these people would allow him to live comfortably. They were angry at him. They hated him, and soon the woodmaster would as well. How could the man help but do so as time passed and the villagers turned their cold shoulders upon him, and he contemplated what he had lost in Freja? Dark thoughts, like a disease, would slowly turn him bitter against the drunkard's boy.

Tor huddled against the middle partition of the pew and slumped low. Casting a sideways glance, he saw that the woodmaster sat with his arms folded and his knees spread wide as he leaned against the back of the pew, seemingly aware of nothing but his own thoughts.

The church soon fell into a reverential hush as the congregation awaited its shepherd, who had no doubt paused in his inner chambers to allow the anticipation to build amongst his flock.

Most solemnly did he walk out into view of the people at the appointed time and, with majestic deliberation, pause to adjust his robes before ascending the pulpit.

He stood in the pulpit for several long moments and looked slowly around the congregation, sorrow etched in his face.

"My people," he finally said, and his sonorous tones rang pleasantly through the building. "My people, it is with heavy heart that upon this occasion of sweet celebration I must pause to address a distressing matter of flagrant rebellion amidst our own community.

"I ask you, how can we worship our Savior in purity of heart this Christmas Eve if we allow brazen wickedness to exist in our own congregation? There is in our midst a boy who has profaned this holy temple, who has taken our treasures, who has implanted in the hearts of our daughters a horrible fascination. And shall we be blameless if we stand idly by and watch him continue in his mischief?"

Tor's heart raced as the vicar pointed at him and continued.

"This boy has stolen the candlesticks from our very Lord's table. How much longer is he to be shielded from his just desserts by those too stubborn or weak-minded to do their hard duty? The time often comes when the righteous people of the Lord must stand against such profanity and expel hardened sinners from their midst, consigning them to darkness, as the apostle says.

"I will ask my clerk now to remove this blemish from our love feast that we may be free to worship God in purity. He shall be sent to prison as is just."

Tor sat frozen in his seat. In all his wildest nightmares he could not have conceived of a more horrible incident than what was unfolding before him. It was a painful irony: tonight of all nights. He had come to church with a hope for peace with God, but he had been lured to his ruin. He suddenly caught the large figure of *Herr* Lägerlof striding up the aisle with bristling mutton chops, and he braced himself.

But the woodmaster stood, his strapping frame casting Tor into a broad, dark shadow. He met *Herr* Lägerlof chin to chin.

"*Nej*," he said, his usually husky, low voice carrying the resonant edge that had so often thrilled the congregation as he sang. "This is wrong," he said. "You do not act in the spirit of the Christ but in the spirit of revenge and hypocrisy. The boy is a sinner, but he is not hardened." He tossed his head to one side and swept his eyes across the congregation. "You must know it is the duty of the church to lead sinners to Christ."

He turned to look up at the pulpit.

"And you are the blemish on this Christmas love feast, Vicar —you and those who espouse your views—when you twist the Holy Scriptures so."

An audible gasp arose from some of the women about them, most notably, Noomi Hansson.

"Stand down, carpenter," came the voice of the vicar in sudden thunder from the pulpit. "Do you think you are wiser than your vicar and all his congregation? Not one person condones your actions, except perhaps the simpleminded."

Suddenly, there was a great stirring two rows back as Fisherman Ahlberg lunged to his feet.

"I know not what you mean by simpleminded, Vicar," he said, "but I speak for both my wife *and* myself when I declare it an injustice to imprison this boy without proof."

"Well, well, then, Fisherman Ahlberg," said the vicar, quickly reverting to soothing tones again. "Leaving the candlesticks out of the question, what of the matter of the carpenter's Nativity, which, as the carpenter himself admits, is worth more than the silver candlesticks, and which he knows indubitably to have been stolen by the Neeson boy."

"*My* Nativity," said the woodmaster. "And my right to press charges or to refrain from pressing charges."

"What right then," challenged *Herr* Lägerlof, "have you to detain and beat him without conviction of guilt!"

"Lägerlof, he stays with me of his own volition." Catching a glimpse of the icy look the woodmaster gave the clerk, Tor believed that even his former self would have thought twice before contradicting that statement.

"Excuse me," said a silver-tongued voice emanating from the opposite corner of the church. "I also—like the good fisherman there—fail to understand the vicar's reference to the 'simpleminded,' but I should like to state my thoughts on this little matter."

The schoolmaster bowed charmingly, first to the vicar and then to the rest of the congregation.

"It is true, Vicar, that with enough men to testify, you could have this boy consigned to prison, yet I would just venture a word of caution, for if you testify without proof of guilt you do indeed perjure yourself, which, though few might be tempted to blame you, does cast you in rather an unsavory light, especially, perhaps, as an eminent clergyman. I should hate to see a stain upon your good name if ever such activity became common knowledge."

The schoolmaster bowed with a sneer and reseated himself.

After the vicar and his startled flock had recovered from their shock at the schoolmaster's unexpected defense of the drunkard's boy, the vicar returned the man's smile, somewhat wanly.

"As I said, I speak of the theft of the carpenter's Nativity, which, as I also stated, has been proven."

"Of course," said the schoolmaster, standing again, quickly, "and while the more astute might pause to question why you would allow a thief to live in your town for nearly a year without pressing charges—when you obviously deem him a threat—I suppose it is your prerogative to vacillate as you see fit. I would, however, like to take this opportunity to state before the town that if this is how the vicar intends to proceed, I do uphold *Herr* Andersson's right to prosecute his offender as he sees fit."

"All this," replied the vicar soothingly, "is irrelevant. We have been talking in circles, and naught has changed. As the wise will plainly see," he said, returning to the bulk of the congregation, "the boy has created a bone of contention between us. He is a disease of the devil, planted among us to bring discord to our town. There will always be his kind, trying to infiltrate and devour the flock of God, but it is the part of the faithful to exterminate this threat."

He turned to the small knot of men who now surrounded the woodmaster.

"Take the boy now, and we will continue our service."

The woodmaster stiffened.

"Do this," he said clearly, "and you bring damnation upon this entire town."

Even Tor, overwhelmed though he was with his own fears, started at the strength of the woodmaster's language.

"Step aside, carpenter," grunted *Herr* Lägerlof.

The woodmaster did not move. The clerk tried to push past him.

"You men there!" cried the vicar, "assist the *Herr* Lägerlof!"

"Stop!"

This was a new voice, neither a man's nor a woman's, but the shrill sound of a young girl nearly in tears.

"You must not take him!" cried Lisbet Hansson, nearly sobbing. "He did not take the candlesticks. I know where they are and who took them. They cannot take him to prison."

The girl dissolved into hysterical tears, and her mother turned upon her, shaking her shoulders and whispering harshly for her not to be a fool.

"Who took them?" demanded the woodmaster.

"I cannot tell," sobbed Lisbet.

"Did you take them?"

"She is infatuated with the boy," snapped Noomie Hansson. "She will say anything to protect him."

But Doctor Hansson stepped around his wife and addressed his daughter.

"Can you show them to us, daughter?"

For a moment she did not speak, only snuffled, but all of a

sudden, she wailed, "*J-ja!*"

"Then do it," ordered the woodmaster.

"They are under the steps of the church," said Lisbet, adding in a beseeching tone, "You see, they were not really taken from the church! It was all right!"

Not waiting for further explanation, the woodmaster strode down the aisle, pulling Tor with him. *Herr* Lägerlof, whose face had suddenly turned very white, was close upon his tail.

"Who put them there?" pressed Doctor Hansson, ignoring the buzz of voices and the rush to the church door.

"I cannot t-tell," Lisbet sniffed, burying her face in her father's coat.

The whole church hummed with whispered conversation as Tor and the woodmaster passed.

The man released Tor just inside the church entrance and ran down the front steps. *Herr* Lägerlof brushed by Tor to follow the him, but the boy remained still, staring into the night, clutching the door wide open. He suddenly realized that his chill body was covered in a soaking sweat.

Then the doorway seemed to explode with the returning figures of the woodmaster and *Herr* Lägerlof and the several men who had followed them out.

The woodmaster gripped a brown bundle in his hands, out of which peeked the gleaming cups of the silver candlesticks. The hum in the church increased as the woodmaster moved into the church, holding them aloft with almost a smirk of triumph.

Then, the vicar's voice cut through the chatter.

"This proves nothing!" he snapped, "except that the boy is so clever as to conceal his plunder in the last place anyone would look. The girl saw him do it, and she—infatuated, as her mother says, with the boy—confessed to its whereabouts in a desperate attempt to clear him of guilt. If only we were so naive," he said, his lips curved into a sneer.

"It w-wasn't Tor," sobbed Lisbet.

The woodmaster practically rolled his eyes.

"Then who was it?" he said. "You can't help Tor unless you tell who took the candlesticks."

"Was it Albin Ovarsson?" the schoolmaster asked, appearing silently and abruptly from out of the crowd like a prowling cat from the bushes.

Lisbet started and stared at him for several long moments.

Then, all at once, she seemed to break to pieces.

"*Ja*," she howled, burying her face in her father's chest again. "I'm sorry Albin, I'm sorry! I couldn't help it!"

"*Nej*," shouted Albin from across the room, "it's not true!" His usually ruddy face was pale.

"Tell us, my child," said the doctor, stroking his daughter's hair calmly.

The girl's broken reply could hardly be distinguished, but the townspeople hushed to hear her words.

"He said the vicar was right, and Tor was an evil s-seed, and God wanted us to drive him out, so he h-hid the candlesticks so everyone would think Tor had done it, and he said it wasn't at all stealing because he never took them from the church, and it was the w-will of God, and he would return them soon. It wasn't really stealing!" she again cried, pulling away from her father to look imploringly in his eyes. All this was said with an excessive snuffling and whining that Tor could plainly see grating on the woodmaster's nerves.

Once more, the vicar reclaimed the attention of his flock.

"And yet," he insisted, "we must prosecute this boy for his theft of the Nativity!"

His words were met with silence as the townspeople glanced at each other and at Lisbet and at Tor, anywhere but at the vicar.

Then *Herr* Lägerlof strode towards the front of the church.

"*Nej!*" he said. His face was still blazing scarlet, but his breath was ragged. He looked haggard.

"We have nearly convicted this boy for the fault of another. We never had proof, but we wanted rid of him because we disliked him. I do not want such a fault at the door of myself and my family. *Nej*. Let the woodcarver have the boy if he so chooses."

Tor sat astonished. *Herr* Lägerlof despised him. For that matter, the schoolmaster despised him. Why did they suddenly defend him now?

"But he *did* steal the Nativity!" bellowed the vicar, his fury now clearly visible.

"Leave it to the woodcarver," said the clerk. He had returned to the front pew of the church and was resuming his seat. His hands were trembling as he buried them in his thick, grey hair.

The vicar began to descend the steps, nearly tripping on his robes with a firm, stomping tread.

"I will *not*," he said, "continue to allow my daughter to be contaminated by this young devil! She is infatuated with him!"

"Perhaps then," said the woodmaster, standing still in the middle of the aisle and looking at the vicar, "the fault is not with the boy but with your daughter?"

The vicar slowed his walking to a dignified pace and advanced deliberately towards the woodmaster like a warrior upon his enemy. But despite his piercing glare, he choked upon his own words for a moment after coming to a halt before the woodmaster.

"I cannot," he finally said, "proceed with this service while my congregation is in such a state of rebellion. God is not pleased. How can you be so wicked?"

The woodmaster tilted his head to one side, tossing back the honey-colored hair and looked at him.

"Do you come only to call the righteous to repentance, Vicar?"

"This boy," said the vicar, through gritted teeth, "is not

repentant. You will see." And he swept past the woodmaster, his clerical capes fluttering violently behind him. In a moment his wife marched past the woodmaster as well, staring straight ahead and followed by the line of her children, who skulked after her hurriedly, seeming uncertain whether to appear haughty or embarrassed.

Except for Olga, who stared before her with flushed cheeks and bright, feverish eyes that angrily dared anyone to speak a word to her or of her.

All was silent. Then some parishioners stalked stiffly out the door in the wake of the vicar's family, Freja Lindqvist being among the first.

Yet most remained, and when the last villager had made his choice of whether to leave or stay, there was silence, and the people in the pews looked at each other, at the woodmaster, at *Herr* Lägerlof, even at the schoolmaster in search of some guidance.

The woodmaster had skulked back to his pew, having slumped into a sudden fit of awkwardness the moment Freja Lindqvist walked past him. The schoolmaster was leaning back in his seat, with his legs crossed and one arm stretched across the back of the pew, something like a sneer playing over his lips as he avoided the roving eyes of the congregation.

Herr Lägerlof was sitting in his pew, breathing laboriously, his head in his hands, but suddenly he stood and faced the congregation. His subdued face was now a strange patchwork of red and white blotches. His mutton-chops looked sadly wilted.

"I have been hasty," he said, looking down at the cap he twisted in his fingers. "As is so often the case, I have been hasty. I-I have often been consumed by too intense a desire for justice. My dear wife has often entreated me to temper my judgement with compassion.

"But I see now . . ." his voice trailed off, and he twisted the cap harder and looked at different parts of the wood floor, as if in search of words between the polished planks. "I have been hasty. I would have condemned a boy to prison for the fault of another and in doing so might have easily lost a boy forever.

"I shall . . . I shall certainly take great care in future before I so easily pass judgement. I would encourage all my brothers and sisters to do the same."

Then he suddenly sat down, and his head sank again into his hands. His good wife leaned close to lay her hand upon his shoulder.

Again there was silence, and the congregation looked one upon another in uncertainty.

Then Günter Nyvall began to sing a carol in his bright tenor, and the voices of the congregation rallied to his. By the end of the first verse, all but Tor had begun to sing. They sang so loudly that Tor thought they could certainly be heard by the departing vicar and parishioners.

At the end of the song, Günter Nyvall cried out, "*God jul!*" And he took his hat and strode cheerfully down the aisle.

Dozens of villagers echoed his words, and everyone rose, took their hats and muffs, and streamed out the door after him.

Tor remained frozen in his seat till everyone had gone. He watched as the woodmaster went up to the Lord's Table and placed the silver candlesticks in their customary spot. He smoothed down the cream-colored woven cloth and then drove his hands deep into his pockets.

For a little while, he remained slouched over the table, staring at the glinting platters, goblets, and candlesticks, then he snuffed the lit candles with his bare fingers and ambled down the side aisle towards Tor where the boy sat with his candle, glowing in one tiny pool of light amid shadows of the dark church. The woodmaster stopped at the edge of their pew and, in the darkness broken only by the small light of Tor's candle and the uncertain twilight from the window, fingered the design carved at the top of the curved pew edge.

"Are you coming along?" he finally asked Tor. "Or do you wish to go your own way?" he said, still seeming to study the design of the pew, but staring with sharp eyes at Tor from underneath his hair.

Tor shifted his fingers so that his left hand lay over his right on the candle.

"Do you want me to stay?" he asked.

"Should I?"

Tor had no answer for that. He reclasped his right hand over his left. Strange how the woodmaster fought for him only to others, saying words before Freja a few days ago and tonight before the whole congregation that he seemed incapable of saying to Tor alone.

"You would let me go?" Tor persisted, reluctantly, still not looking at the man.

"*Nej.*"

Tor's heart jumped, but he kept his eyes firmly fixed on his yellow wax candle.

"Why do you ask me, then?"

"Because I want to hear you speak your decision."

Tor stared down, hardly seeing his own thin fingers glowing in the small pool of candlelight before him. He thought about how impossible it would be to live in this village with people who hated him and would never see him as anything better than the drunkard's boy who cursed on the steps of the church. How many snubs and humiliations he would have to endure.

Could he live this way? His stout pride would be daily crushed by pretentious people who would never understand how grief and abandonment had cultivated what was worst in him. They saw him as so much worse than themselves. They could not understand how he could have allowed his heart to become so perverse and contrary, and since they could not understand, they could not forgive.

How could he tolerate their picking and pinching and pushing as they tried to root out his faults and squeeze him into a mold like some of Thea Ahlberg's *pepparkakor* dough? He would go mad and explode as he had done so many times before.

He stared at his fingers, thinking they looked grotesquely pale and bony in the candlelight.

The woodmaster shifted, and the drunkard's boy roused, recalling the man's presence, recalling that he awaited an answer.

Tor looked over at the man but could see hardly more than a shadow in the darkness. The same lean, strong body. The same intolerably commanding presence. The same inflexible will that forced Tor every day to do things he didn't want to do. There was no sign of friendliness or softness about him. He was a big, black, immovable shadow. For all Tor knew of his past, the woodmaster was still little more than a stranger to him. Could he truly, *fully* trust this man?

The woodmaster waited in silence, his thumb moving slowly, almost caressingly over the curve of the wooden pew. Tor stared at the hand. How the man loved the wood he cut and carved every day. How carefully and relentlessly he crafted every piece, never resting till it was a work of art.

Tor stood.

He'd experienced enough of life without the woodmaster. He'd felt like a human shell full of evil things and he'd hated his life and the way he was for as long as he could remember. He didn't care that this man told him what to do. The woodmaster had stood for him despite the persuasions and threats of his peers, despite the relationship it cost him, and, especially, despite Tor's own sins against him.

The man cared, and he could be trusted. Whatever the woodmaster chose to do with him, Tor was now persuaded it was for his good. He walked out of the pew past the man.

"I'm coming," he said. He moved down the aisle, listening to the woodmaster's boots treading the floor behind him with long, easy strides.

As he listened to that stride, the significance of his recent conclusions seeped deeper into his mind, nearly overwhelming him: the woodmaster was good, and he wanted Tor.

Distracted by his thoughts, Tor tripped on the corner of a pew at the back of the church and lost his balance, stumbling forward in the dark.

The woodmaster caught him, reaching from behind to catch him across the stomach with hard, digging fingers and clutching at the candle so that it did not fly into the red drapes before them.

The sudden grasping of his stomach muscles was painful, and the woodmaster's lean forearm felt bruising to his ribs. Tor's hands stung from a splash of hot wax and from scratches caused by the woodmaster's fingernails when he snatched at the candle.

The woodmaster, having steadied Tor on his feet, moved

carefully around him, holding the candle high, and led the way forward.

Tor followed, guided by the small light in the man's hand until the door was opened to reveal the luminous sun rising over the valley.

CHAPTER TWENTY-FOUR

That day they were expected at the Ahlbergs. With scarves covering their faces up to their noses and thick hats pulled low to shield their eyes, the woodmaster and his boy sallied down the street toward the rocky coast, each hugging a package under his arm.

At first, amid the soft whine of the wind and the brush of crystal snowflakes against the iced cottages, they did not hear the snuffles and whimpers emanating from the alley beside the cobbler's empty shop. But, as they came on top of the alley, the sounds became too insistent to ignore. Tor slowed his pace and glanced at the woodmaster.

The man stopped and looked into the alley at the source of the noise, though he did not move toward it. Following the man's gaze, Tor barely made out a figure huddled in a miserable bundle at the end of the alley, snorting and sobbing.

He looked back at the woodmaster, but the woodmaster did not look at him.

"Best see what's the matter," was all he said as he nodded at the figure and continued to avoid Tor's eye.

Tor walked slowly into the alley, approaching the figure with caution. Even when he was three-quarters into the alley, he could not think who the person was, though he was certain the woodmaster knew.

It was not till he at last stood over the figure that he recognized Albin, and he immediately took a step back, glancing behind him for the woodmaster.

But the woodmaster was not to be seen.

Tor looked back at Albin and saw that the other boy had become aware of him. The cobbler's boy was angrily scrubbing his face with a sleeve and rising to his feet, keeping his back against the wall behind him and using the flat of one palm to steady himself.

He was trying to look furious, but his eyes showed fear as he backed further down the wall in an attempt to distance himself from Tor.

"What do you want?" he demanded, eyes darting in apparent search for a way of escape.

"Nothing," said Tor. "I came to see..." He stopped talking. He had almost said, "I came to see who was crying," but he didn't. He knew well how humiliating such words would be, and for once, he didn't care to humiliate even Albin.

"Nothing," he finally repeated, after staring at Albin's hostile eyes for a few moments.

He turned to leave, but behind him, he heard Albin hack and spit.

"I despise you," the cobbler's boy snarled. "You're nothing but a gutter rat. And you're a criminal, but you get away with everything, don't you?"

"Thanks to you," said Tor, beginning to feel prickles of anger, "I was almost sent to prison for something I didn't do."

He moved away from Albin again, wondering why, knowing who was here, the woodmaster had sent him down this alley.

"And I was whipped, thanks to you! You *deserved* to go to prison, and I didn't steal the candlesticks, not really! And now my father hates me. Not that that's anything new. He's always hated me. But now he always will, and it's your fault!"

Albin choked and had to stop speaking.

Those last words, however, sounded familiar to Tor. He recognized the incoherent words of a wounded offender.

He stopped walking and considered a moment, recalling the stormy days when the woodmaster had bound him hand and foot and roughly pushed him about.

"He doesn't hate you," Tor said brusquely, not turning "and you're lucky to have a father who cares enough to feed you. Mine . . ."

Tor stopped. He didn't want to give Albin ammunition by telling him that his own father was a burglar who had scarcely spoken to or looked at his son, and had long since died in prison.

Albin did not ask what he was about to say, however. He only gave a sneer that sounded less cutting than he probably intended it to, as it was interrupted by an involuntary catch of his breath.

"*You* have your precious woodmaster," he said, venomously.

"You can do no wrong in his eyes. He treats you better than my father ever treated me."

Albin edged further away under his enemy's steady gaze, and Tor realized as he watched him move that the boy was in considerable pain from his whipping.

One lucid glimpse of the other boy's world flashed before him. He knew what it was to feel despised and, more than that, to despise one's self.

"Albin," he said, pulling his scarf from his mouth and speaking quickly lest he waver in his purpose. "Let's forget all this."

"Oh, you want me to forgive you and accept you despite all you've done, just like everyone else did? Shall we sing a carol and walk out of the alley arm in arm?" he jeered.

"*Ja*, forgive me, then," said Tor, smarting at the rebuff, but forcing out the words all the same, "and I forgive you."

Albin spat at his feet again.

"I've done nothing needing forgiveness," he said, and he glared at Tor, though still huddling in his corner and still with bright fear in his eyes.

Tor turned and stalked out of the alley. The woodmaster was lounging against a building just outside the alley, and Tor met his inquiring gaze with angry eyes.

The woodmaster said nothing, and they trudged down the street in the deep snow. Tor waited just till he was certain they were out of earshot of Albin before giving vent to his injured pride.

"I asked him to forget about everything," he said, ironically. "I even asked him to forgive me, and he threw insults in my face." Tor began to kick at chunks of snow in his path.

"He even refused to admit," he continued, "that he had done anything wrong. Said he had done nothing needing my forgiveness!"

"This all sounds strangely familiar," said the woodmaster, his dry voice muffled by his scarf.

Tor flushed and fell silent.

"It may be," said the woodmaster, "that though he is hard and hostile now, he will come round in time."

"I suppose anything is *possible*," mumbled Tor. He kicked at another lump of snow, which shattered with a soft, extremely pleasing sound. Then, feeling he couldn't help himself, he added, "But he has always been a bully."

"And you," said the woodmaster, "have always been a bad-tempered, conceited, and perversely stubborn liar."

Tor became utterly silent again and wanted to sink into the snow he had been so brutally smashing.

"Perhaps you and Albin have more in common than you supposed," continued the woodmaster mercilessly.

Tor hunched his shoulders, pulled his collar closer to his neck, and began to kick at the snow again. Yesterday, when he had asked God for forgiveness and healing, he had felt good, as if he would never be angry or spiteful again, and he resolved as much, but how quickly he had realized such a thing was easier to imagine than to execute.

He noticed the pernicious cold was irritating his mittened hands, and, after pulling his scarf up over his nose again, he chafed the rough mitten fabric over the back of one hand with the palm of the other. He hoped the activity would distract him from his pettish thoughts and would distract the woodmaster from his pettish behavior.

Then the woodmaster spoke again with words that sounded as though they were dragged painfully from his throat.

"As for myself," he said, "I would hope that any boy of *mine* would have the strength to use what he has learned of his failures for the benefit of others."

Rough though his voice was, it held sincerity.

Tor forgot his cold hands instantly. He could suddenly imagine nothing nicer than a cold Christmas morning walk to the Ahlberg's seacoast cottage where they would have cardamom rolls, meat dripping with rich broth, soft yellow potatoes, pickled fish, and *pepparkakor*.

He said nothing but tucked himself deeper into his coat and scarf and drew just a finger-width closer to the woodmaster.

EPILOGUE

Christmas, December, 1863

It was to be the first Christmas with the new vicar at the little village church up on the hill. Günter Nyvall was singing his way up the hill in a voice less resonant, but not less expressive than it had been ten years since.

A broad-shouldered, deep-chested man made his way through the snow some paces behind Günter Nyvall, joining snatches of the carol with his own rich base. A woman walked arm in arm with him, leading with her free hand a chubby little girl who had insisted that she was big enough to wade through the snow on her own legs.

On the other side of the broad-shouldered man strode a younger man of twenty-four or twenty-five, who sported an astonishing yield of curly hair that shifted in the lantern light between rich shades of dark blond and light brown. A young woman with yellow-brown eyes and a slight limp walked arm in arm with him.

The curly-haired man was absently slapping one hand on his thigh as he walked, entirely failing in his attempt to keep time to Günter's carol, and looking about at the snowy black landscape that was broken only by the river of Christmas candles. Abruptly, he turned to the broad-shouldered man and interrupted the hum of his deep base.

"It will be good to have the pulpit filled with a vicar of our own again finally," said he. "It's been nearly three years."

"*Ja,*" said the other man.

The young man slapped his mittened hand on his thigh for a few more moments.

"This will be your first time hearing him speak, *Herr* Andersson?"

The other man turned to look at him, tossing his head to one side to survey his companion, a habit he had formed years ago when his blond hair was long enough to reach his eyes.

"*Ja,*" he said, studying the curly-haired man. "And I trust that you will treat him more kindly at this service than you used to do ten years ago, Albin Ovarsson."

"Of course," said Albin, laughing, but looking down at his boots. Unlike his good friend, Tor Neeson, he had never lost his awe of this rough, taciturn man. Even to this day, though he had worked with Wilhelm Andersson in his shop for over eight years, Albin still felt childishly nervous when the man fixed those slate grey eyes on him with any particular pressure. Albin felt almost certain that the man knew this—and that it greatly amused him.

The woman with yellow-brown eyes laughed and squeezed Albin's arm, leaning around him to speak to the carpenter.

"Come, *Herr* Andersson, it's nice to smile when you tease people," she said.

"As you say, Klara," the woodmaster agreed with a smirk and an obvious lack of sincerity.

They ascended the steps into church, their progress delayed by the careful climbing of the little girl, and stepped across the threshold. The woodmaster's wife leaned closer to her husband as he paused to light his candle from the silver candlesticks in the foyer.

"Not feeling faint yet, dearest?" she asked lightly.

"I have much greater fortitude than I thought," muttered the woodmaster to her. "All I can say is that he is fortunate to know a woman like Thea Ahlberg. A scamp like him would certainly never have obtained such training and such a position if it hadn't been for the influence of her family."

And as he stepped into the sanctuary, the woodmaster nodded with a smile that belied his tone at the fisherman and his mute wife, whose wrinkled face beamed delightedly at him from her pew.

"Or without the support of such a stubborn man as the master craftsman, Wilhelm Andersson?" asked the woman in a mocking tone.

The woodmaster grimaced and made no reply.

Beside the fisherman's wife, a young woman with cornmeal-colored braids and slanted eyes waved exuberantly at them. Klara waved back, and she and Albin began to move in their direction.

"Mark my words," said the woodmaster's wife, her whisper

sharp with excitement as she stared at the retreating couple. "Albin will be a father by this summer! See if he won't!"

The woodmaster shot her an inscrutable glance and shook his head in weariness. His wife smiled saucily.

The family parted, the broad-shouldered man striding up to the choir behind Günter, and the mother and her child taking their seat decorously in a pew on the right side of the aisle towards the back of the church.

At the proper time, when all were in their places, the new vicar appeared from the side door, his dark head bowed as he walked in. When he approached the pulpit, he paused, staring at the Lord's Table. Sitting in the center of the table amid the polished silver candlesticks with their waxy yellow tapers, upon a beautifully woven runner of cream-colored cloth, was a single wooden figure of the Christ Child in the manger.

The vicar looked up from the small figure, smiling at the broad-shouldered man standing in the bass section of the choir as he ascended to the gleaming pinewood pulpit. Once behind the pulpit he slowly turned to face the congregation.

"Friends," he said, his smile widening and making his crooked nose look even more crooked, "Rejoice. For, in the words of St. Luke and the prophet Isaiah, 'behold I bring you good tidings of great joy, which shall be to all people,' 'for unto us a Child is born; unto us a Son is given.' Amen."

And as the congregation repeated, "Amen," he smiled again

the crooked smile to which they had grown quite accustomed over the years and turned his attention to the Bible lying open before him, flipping his hands quickly to crack his wrists before he turned the pages.

THE END

Made in United States
Troutdale, OR
12/10/2024

26227808R00227